I Love You Today

Book Two in the Trading Heartbeats Trilogy

Julie Navickas

I Love You Today
Book Two in the Trading Heartbeats Trilogy
Copyright © 2022 Julie Navickas
All rights reserved.

ISBN: (ebook) 978-1-958136-19-5
(print) 978-1-958136-20-1

Inkspell Publishing
207 Moonglow Circle #101
Murrells Inlet, SC 29576

Edited By Audrey Bobak
Cover art By Fantasia Frog Designs

DEDICATION

I Love You Today is dedicated to my children: Lillian, Colton, and Brady.

"Never let the fear of striking out, keep you from playing the game."
~Babe Ruth

May you three follow your hearts, dream big dreams, and always cheer for the Chicago Cubs. Mommy loves you more than anything.

JULIE NAVICKAS

CHAPTER ONE

Austin

"So long, Chicago." Austin dumped the last box in the moving truck. The kitchen glassware inside rattled, clanking together with the force of a tiny earthquake. *Who the hell packed this?* He scrunched his nose as his feet hammered down the ramp and returned to the city sidewalk.

Well, I guess that's it, Mavs...

His gaze lifted to the brick building beside him, searching for the third-story window. Mavis—the girl who stole his heart, and princess at the top of the tallest tower—was now the soon-to-be bride of his twin brother, Josh. From the day her feet fled Rosewood over ten years ago, she'd been his brother's missing puzzle piece. And for a decade, Austin had held her close and kept her safe in his heart for protection. But now, her edges snuggly fit beside Josh's with the ease of love, two halves meeting to form one whole. And Austin? The piece that got lumped into the wrong box and cast aside.

His stomach plummeted, the sinking feeling of defeat and heartache gripping his soul. *How the hell am I supposed to just let you go, Princess?* He slammed the back of the moving truck closed and maneuvered the lever to lock it in place.

And worse, watch you move on with my brother? He grumbled, the soft whine escaping his lips into the damp air.

"She's really leaving, isn't she?"

Austin turned, seeking the voice interrupting his pity party.

Casey's bouncy blonde curls hung in her face as her pink lips smashed together in a thin line. Her arms, laden with a giant pizza box, two plastic grocery bags, and a purse, lowered with a shrug.

A tingle along his spine shivered to his fingertips, complementing the gust of spring air chilling his skin. *Cinderella returned from the ball... er, pizza place.* "Umm yeah, back to California." He gestured to her full hands. "Can I help you with that?"

"Oh, yeah, thanks." She stepped forward and handed over the two grocery bags, the glass bottles inside clanking against each other.

Austin peeked inside and cracked a grin at the bottles of gin.

"Are you really out here moving her crap by yourself?"

He rolled his eyes as she started toward the building. "Yeah, umm, Josh said something about dropping off the last rent check to the landlord. They took off about half an hour ago. I figured I'd just finish the boxes for her."

Casey nodded as they approached the entrance. "Awfully nice of you, considering..." She set the pizza on the concrete stoop and sank to her knees to rummage in her bag.

"Considering?" He scrunched his nose.

"I'm sorry. It's none of my business." She shook her head as a blue lighter tumbled from her purse and onto the concrete near his toes.

"You're fine. You can say it." Austin bent down and retrieved it, resting it in Casey's outstretched palm. "Considering she picked Josh over me."

Her eyes widened. "Oh, ah... well..."

Austin sighed, swallowing hard. The pit in his stomach

deepened, the black hole in his heart filling with despair. The truth lived inside him, but speaking the words sliced new holes in his broken soul.

The glass bottles in the bags clinked together as he held a hand out to her. Squeezing his palm, Casey stood, her cheeks flushing pink. "Leave it to me to make things awkward." The right side of her mouth tugged upward in a smile as the sun poked out from behind a cloud. The light danced across her face as her gaze found his.

Warmth flooded his body as he adjusted the ball cap on his head, tugging it down to shadow his face. *What the hell is wrong with me?* "No, I think that one's on me, Casey." He grinned. "Oh, but hey… glad you turned up when you did." He pointed to the brick he'd used to keep the door ajar, cast off in a bed of weeds. "I couldn't get back in."

She sighed and rolled her eyes. "The people in this building are super weird." Ramming the key in the lock, she tugged on the door. "Like our new neighbor. He moved in about two weeks ago. Reeks like pot, and he's super loud and kinda creepy."

"Are you gonna stay living here?" Austin shuffled the grocery bags to free his right hand. He held the door open as she picked up the pizza and stepped inside.

Catching her foot on the lowermost step, she staggered. *Oh!*

"You okay?" he asked.

She giggled but started the climb to the third floor. "Oh, yeah. My dad always used to call me Klutzy Casey."

Grinning, Austin followed, his line of sight catching the wiggle of her butt as she moved upward.

"Are you staying for dinner?" she asked over her shoulder.

"Ah, I don't know. I'm not sure what the *happy couple* had planned. I really just came to help pack." Rolling his eyes, he sighed. "And maybe earn some points back with Josh."

Casey's hands grasped the doorknob of the apartment. She turned, pushing her back against the door before sliding inside. "Mavs told me he's pretty mad."

Austin nodded, following her with a snort. "You could say that."

"Well… he's not here, so you should stay and eat. Dimo's has the best pizza in the entire city." She tapped the box and inhaled, a smirk growing along her lips.

Placing the grocery bags on the kitchen counter, Austin surveyed the stark white walls of the little apartment as it blazed in the afternoon sunlight. It cast a hazy orange glow behind Casey as she shrugged out of her coat and dumped it on a chair.

Jarring the entire apartment, a door slammed in the hallway, followed by a burst of manic laughter.

"What the hell?" Poking his head out the door, Austin caught the tail end of a trench coat as it flew down the stairs. He frowned and ducked back inside. "You didn't answer me before. Are you going to be living here alone?"

Casey nodded. "I mean, until I can find a new roommate."

The tips of his fingers tingled with unease. "But that can't be that hard in a city like this, right? You'll find someone pretty quick."

Her gaze dropped to the floor as she freed her toes from the battered flip-flops on her feet. "Oh, umm, yeah, for sure." She pointed toward the bags on the table. "Want a drink?"

Austin snorted. "Always." His hand gripped the first bottle of gin as he pulled it from the plastic and set it on the counter, casting the disquiet sloshing in his stomach aside.

It's just a weird neighbor… no big deal.

Casey's bare feet pounded against the tile floor and into the kitchen as her head disappeared into a cabinet. She pulled two glasses from the shelf and yanked open the freezer. "Gin and tonic okay?" she asked as ice cubes tinkled into their cups.

Austin barked out a laugh. *Oh, the trouble that drink has caused me…*

"Something funny?" She pushed the freezer door closed with a wrinkled nose and uncapped the bottle.

"Hardly."

She poured, her gaze lifting to meet his. "Are you okay?"

"What makes you think I'm not?" *Am I that obvious?*

"Why are gin and tonics funny?" Snatching a spoon from across the counter, she stirred each drink.

Austin cringed. *Eww. That definitely wasn't clean.* "They're not. Er—they just tend to get me in a lot of trouble."

Casey smiled, stretching her glass outward to meet his. "Well… here's to trouble then. Cheers." She brought the cup to her lips and sipped.

"Cheers, Casey." The alcohol swirled in his mouth, the welcomed impending break from reality sliding down his throat. "That's good." He nodded. "You bartend with Mavis, right?"

"Used to. Before her knight in shining armor showed up." Smirking, she gestured toward the apartment door. "And I suppose I have you to thank for that." Casey tipped her glass in his direction.

With a roll of his eyes, Austin tugged an old, beat-up barstool from beneath the counter and eased onto the cracked leather seat. "Look, this whole thing didn't exactly play out the way I wanted it to either."

Casey plopped down beside him, propping her feet up on the tarnished metal rim of his chair.

"No, no, I'm sorry. I know it's not your fault." She swirled the ice in her glass, frowning into the drink. "I'm just being a grouch. I don't want her to leave."

The ping of a text message interrupted her admission as Casey's bag on the dining room table vibrated. She turned, leaning forward to tug at the strap. It caught the corner of the pizza box and Austin lunged to save dinner. "Oh, shit! Good catch!"

He pushed the pizza box back to the center of the table and smiled.

This girl is a walking accident…

"It's Mavis. She said they're stuck in traffic. A car wreck on Lake Shore and it's down to one lane. It may take them a while to get home." She typed a quick response and set her phone down on the counter. "Want some pizza before it gets cold?"

"Can't pass up Chicago's best now, can I?" Austin grinned, spinning in his seat to eye the pizza box.

It does smell good...

"You really can't. It's totally the best. You'll see, California boy." With a wink, Casey hopped from her seat and grabbed two paper plates and a roll of paper towels from the kitchen.

Austin followed her lead to the dining room table and opened the box. Big chunks of yellow fruit stared back, haphazardly spread across the greasy delicacy. He scrunched his nose. "Is that pineapple? On pizza?"

"Don't knock it 'til you try it." Her elbow jabbed him in the side as she pulled a slice from the box. "Come on. Be a big boy."

With a roll of his eyes, Austin snagged an extra cheesy piece. He followed Casey into the living room and watched as she plopped down into the sofa's corner. Dropping his fruit-covered pizza on the coffee table, he tugged his sweatshirt free from his body. "Figures that the best Chicago has to offer is a topping from California."

Casey shrugged. "Eh, these are probably from Florida."

He snorted, stepping back toward the kitchen. "Do you want your drink?"

"Yep! And don't be afraid to refill." She giggled, her bubble of light laughter soothing the bad mood accompanying him to the Midwest.

"You read my mind." Austin topped off their drinks and shuffled back into the living room as Casey shoved the last bite of her pizza slice in her mouth. He sank into the seat beside her, his knees greeting his face as his butt dropped into the dilapidated cushion.

"Sorry, shitty sofa." She smirked, her cheeks flushing

pink again. "Sit like this and you'll be more comfortable."

Austin pushed his shoes off and curled up with his feet tucked beneath him as instructed, mirroring Casey's position. He grabbed his pizza from the table and sniffed.

"Oh, my God, just try it." Casey rolled her eyes as his teeth sank into the first bite.

The sweetness of the pineapple exploded in his mouth, meeting the salt of the sauce and dough.

Oh!

"See. Delicious, right?" She tore off a piece of paper towel and tossed it in his lap.

"All right, it's not bad." He nodded, taking another bite.

Casey giggled. "Hey, are you a Cubs fan?" Leaning across his body, she swiped the remote control from the side table, knocking a magazine to the floor with her sudden movement.

His stomach dropped, her abrupt closeness warming his body. The sweet scent of lilacs infused with the pizza and gin as she settled back in her seat beside him.

Austin shook his head, ridding his body of the surprising warmth. "Umm no. Lifelong Dodgers fan," he choked out. He reached forward, gripping the magazine on the floor until *The Funny Part* met his gaze.

Ah, that's right. E. Banks…

"Figures." She scanned the channels, landing quickly on the Chicago Cubs. They led Cincinnati seven to five.

"So, Miss E. Banks… baseball then? That's your thing?"

"Guilty." She smiled and tugged the blanket from the corner of the couch around her shoulders. "My dad used to take me to Wrigley all the time as a kid. When you grow up here, you just kind of inherit the fandom."

Austin nodded. "My dad did the same, but mostly basketball games, I guess. Some baseball." He finished his pizza. "And you were right. This California boy is impressed." He tossed the empty paper plate to the coffee table with a wink.

"See. Stick with me, Austin Templeton. I'll teach you the

ways of the Midwest. And I'll even show you around the city if you want? There's more than just pineapple pizza." She giggled again, inciting a smile on his lips.

I think I might just have to take you up on that, Casey girl.

"Actually, it's funny you say that. The partners at the law firm I work for were considering opening a new branch here."

"Oh? That's right. Mavis told me you were a lawyer."

"You say it like it's a bad thing." His eyes met hers as he flashed a grin.

"No! I didn't mean it like that!" Another giggle bubbled over, tumbling from her pink lips. Her fingers squeezed his knee, triggering a shiver to zip along his spine.

Whoa.

As she tugged her hand away, her attention shifted to the eruption of cheers blaring through the TV. The Cubs increased their lead by two runs in the bottom of the eighth inning.

"Looks like a win for Chicago tonight."

"I'll drink to that!" Casey leaned forward and snagged her drink, bringing the glass to her lips as her eyes held steady on the TV. She sipped and coughed, wincing at the liquid. "You're a shit terrible bartender," she sputtered.

"Hey!" Austin jabbed his left foot in her direction with a laugh. "Not true."

"Holy hell, that's strong!" She sipped again but smiled, her cheeks flushing.

The door to the apartment opened, and Mavis and Josh walked in, gripping each other's hands as if the world would crumble if they separated.

Great…

"Ugh. I'm so sorry that took us so long," said Mavis, dropping her bag to the chair at the dining room table. "I'm sorry, Austin. I didn't mean for you to finish loading the truck alone."

Dropping his gaze to the floor, he shrugged. "No problem. You guys are all set." Widening his eyes, he brought his glass back to his lips.

I'm gonna need a lot more of these…

"Pizza on the table. Drinks on the counter. But don't let Austin make one for you!" Casey laughed as her elbow brushed his side.

His eyes met hers—two pools of beautiful sparkling blue.

"He does make strong drinks," muttered Mavis as she pulled a slice of pizza from the box.

Beside her, Josh frowned, the muscles in his forearms tensing.

Awkward…

"Fly that W!" Casey clapped as a chorus of "Go Cubs Go" streamed through the speakers.

Peeking at her smile, Austin grinned at the excitement of the win plastered across her lips. "We should celebrate, right?" *A perfect excuse to get out of this apartment.* He tipped his glass against hers. "Can I take you up on that offer to show me around?"

She nodded and drained her glass. "I'll show you how Chicagoans really have fun."

Lead the way, Cinderella. No promises about midnight.

JULIE NAVICKAS

CHAPTER TWO

Casey

Casey squeezed into a pair of black leggings and yanked a tight gold skirt over her hips, meeting her sheer black blouse at her midriff. Easing over to the full-length mirror, she frowned. A thick crack in the middle split her reflection in half and she shook her head.

What are you doing, Casey McDaniels? This isn't a date!

She tore the shirt from her body and pulled the skirt down in disgust, a flood of disappointment settling in her gut. "You're just his excuse to not have to sit and watch Mavis and Josh kiss all night," she whispered to herself. "It's not like he's actually interested in you."

Austin's sweet and sad grin tugged at her heartstrings, an instant connection of understanding resonating in her heart from the moment they'd met in the stairway—a sense of loss and defeat she recognized only too well. His eyes said it all, reaffirming the angst and turmoil consuming his being. Sadness... sorrow... *and now he has to watch his brother marry the girl he loves.*

Casey shook her head, a rush of determination radiating through her body. "Just show him a good time tonight. Help him take his mind off of it," she told her reflection. With an exhale, she tossed on a vintage Cubs jersey and slipped her feet into a pair of royal-blue flats; her big toe threatened to pop the seam.

Geez, I need new shoes.

After checking her teeth for leftover pizza in the mirror, she tugged the door open and stepped down the hall.

"Where are you going?" Mavis stuffed another piece of pizza in her mouth, her brow furrowing as she chewed.

Casey rammed a blue Cubs hat on her head and smashed her blonde curls. "Celebrating a Cubs victory, of course."

"Oh…" Mavis's gaze fell to the floor. "Okay…"

"Hope you don't mind." Austin yanked his sweatshirt back over his head and entered the kitchen. "Casey offered to show me more of the city while I'm here." He snaked his arm around her waist.

Oh!

Her skin sizzled at his gentle touch, an ignition of fire warming her body.

He's not interested. He's not interested. He's not interested.

"Sounds like a good idea," mumbled Josh as he rose from his seat at the dining room table. "Thanks for coming to help pack." His hand extended in Austin's direction.

Wrinkling her nose as the twins begrudgingly shook hands and avoided each other's gazes, Casey gulped.

No wonder he's dying to get out of here tonight. Talk about awkward…

"Umm, yeah… have fun, guys." Mavis drew Casey in for a hug. "Be safe, okay?" she whispered.

Casey nodded and pulled away, grabbing her purse and jacket from the table. "Don't leave without waking me in the morning."

Mavis smiled and stepped aside, leaving the path to the apartment door clear. "Wouldn't dream of it, roomie. But I know you like your sleep. We're planning to leave around nine, okay?"

Grief gripped her, the loss of her best friend weighing

heavy on her heart as each footstep carried her closer to the door and away from the last night they'd call each other roommates. Her gaze fell as her vision clouded. A gentle touch on her lower back urged her forward as a whispered, "You okay?" met her ear.

Casey nodded and stepped into the hallway. The door's latch clicked behind them, and she swiped away the sorrow filling her eyes. "This… this just sucks."

He nodded. "I know the feeling."

With an inhale, Casey blinked away the unwanted tears until Austin's face came into focus. His hat shadowed his eyes, but the light-blond stubble on his chin caught the light. Her heart fluttered as she peeked at him beneath the brim of the L.A. Dodgers logo. *Get a grip on yourself, Casey.* With a forced smile, she gestured toward the steps. "Sorry. I'm done with the tears, I promise."

He sighed and looped his arm around hers, escorting her down the staircase. "Let's go forget them both, huh?" A devilish grin consumed his face, his blue eyes blazing in the dim lighting.

"I know just the place for that."

The live music radiating from Old Crow pounded against their ears as they joined the shoulder-to-shoulder crowd on the ground floor. *Holy shit, it's packed in here tonight!* Casey tugged Austin behind her, leading him up the side staircase until they reached the rooftop beneath the light of the spring moon and neon bar signs. A small corner of a picnic table caught her eye, and she zigzagged through the maze toward it with Austin in tow.

"I like it here." He looked around, his gaze falling on the nightlife and illuminated skyscrapers. His head bumped against a low-hanging twinkle light above their table as he lowered himself to the wooden seat.

"What'll it be, you guys?" A blonde waitress rounded on their table faster than Casey could unzip her jacket.

"A pitcher of Old Style, please."

The waitress nodded and darted away.

"Old Style?" Austin raised a brow.

"If you want the full Chicago experience, you have to try it. Plus, it's dirt cheap." She giggled and pushed a sticky menu away. "Payday isn't until Friday."

"Tonight is on me, Casey." Austin's eyes widened as he heaved out a sigh. "You did me a huge favor. I really didn't want to sit there with them all night." His gaze dropped to his lap as a sad smile crept along his lips.

He's really hurting.

A surge of anger swelled in her gut, a bout of irate fury directed at the choices Mavis made and the consequences of her actions sitting before her. Casey huffed out a breath and exhaled the heartbreak.

Why do I feel so connected to you? I just met you!

"Thanks for taking me out tonight. This place is really cool." His gaze circled the space again as he pointed over her shoulder. "Wrigley Field?"

She grinned. "In all its glory."

The waitress returned with a foaming pitcher of golden liquid and two plastic cups. "You guys need anything else?"

"Just keep 'em comin'." Austin winked as she stepped away and pulled the plastic cups apart. He poured, tilting the cup like an expert. "Reminds me of college," he said with a stilted laugh.

"Where'd you go to school?" she asked, accepting the beer he held out.

"Harvard."

Playfully, she tapped her head in jest. "Oh, duh. Lawyer."

He flashed a smile. *And that's probably the first real one I've seen all night.* Her heart fluttered, skipping a beat. *You sure are something, Austin Templeton. Handsome. Successful. Charming. And hopelessly in love with another woman.*

Sipping his beer, he scrunched his nose as the cup left his lips. "This isn't bad."

Aren't lawyers supposed to be better at lying?

A belly laugh burst from her gut. "Old Style is terrible!" She giggled, shifting her butt on the wooden bench beneath her. "It's just what everyone drinks here. It's like a pastime!"

Austin snorted, a smirk growing on his lips as he downed the rest of the beer. Wiping his mouth with the back of his hand, he grimaced. "It tastes like shit!"

"Chicago's finest." Casey tilted her head, eyeing his hands as he refilled his plastic cup.

"You gonna keep up?" He nodded in her direction.

Oh! Challenge accepted!

Bringing the cup back to her lips, she gulped down the beer in full. Grinning, she handed the empty cup back to a wide-eyed Austin.

Oh, my God. I just grossed him out. Casey wiped her mouth with her sleeve. *Shit. Quick, change the subject!*

"So… umm, what kind of lawyer are you?"

He rolled his eyes and handed her back a full cup. "Divorce and estate planning."

"Cheerful. How'd you get into that?"

He shifted in his seat and yanked his hat from his head, resting his elbows on the table. The change in position brought his face closer, the new proximity speeding her heart rate. Above, the twinkle lights illuminated his face and lit up his eyes, accentuating the smattering of white lashes tucked in the corner.

How did I not notice that before?

Austin blinked and rubbed his fists against his eyes, breaking the trance of her fascinated gaze.

"Umm… I'm not really sure. It just kind of fell into my lap when I started at the firm. They needed someone to cover the clients in both areas, and then I just never stopped."

"Do you like it?"

He shrugged. "The estate planning isn't terrible, but the divorce part is depressing." He gulped another mouthful of beer. "But if it leads to being made partner someday, I'll keep doing it."

Casey nodded. Having never held on to a boyfriend for longer than six months, her knowledge of divorce proceedings lacked, and estate planning? Far from her wheelhouse of expertise.

Austin drained his cup as the twang of a country song drifted from the ground floor to meet their ears. "All right, your turn, Miss Twenty Questions. I know you mix a good drink and you like baseball. Tell me something else about you."

"What do you want to know?" She pulled the ball cap from her head and set it beside his on the table. With a practiced hand, her fingers threaded through her curls as his gaze followed each movement.

"Umm... anything." He swallowed. "How about school? Where'd you go?"

"Sorry, Mr. Harvard. You're looking at a community college drop-out."

"Oh, umm. I'm sorry. I didn't mean to..." He shook his head.

Frowning, she dropped her gaze to her lap, recalling the miscarriage that derailed the previous fall semester. "No, no, it's okay. It's my own fault," she admitted. "But I guess I was toying with adding a summer class to my schedule. You know, just to try and get back into the swing of things? I'm not *that* far from graduation."

He emptied the pitcher into her cup. "Oh, yeah? What class were you thinking?"

Casey pursed her lips, tapping her toes against the picnic table's legs. "Well, I think I need one last social science class for my associates. So, I don't know. Maybe political science or something?"

His back straightened as he leaned closer, his eyes widening with intrigue.

Of course, that would interest you.

"You'll love it! Political science was always my favorite in undergrad. And it has so much practicality for any career.

Law, politics, government, you name it."

"Good. You can help me. I don't know a thing about it!" She snorted and downed her beer.

"I'd be happy to." His eyes met hers as a soft smile danced along his lips.

From the main stage, the music turned slow and the lead male's voice dedicated the next song to a woman named Jillian. The lights dimmed, leaving the roof magically lit by twinkle lights—a forest enchanted by fireflies.

The change in lighting highlighted the magnificent cityscape, a view Casey had seen a hundred times before. But tonight, the beauty magnified in the spring evening. The sting of winter had finally gone.

"How about a dance, Case?" Austin extended his hand as he shifted to pull free from the picnic table.

Her stomach dropped, his offer stirring fear and anxiety to mix with the Old Style in her belly. *You've seen me walk. In what world do you think I can dance?* "Oh, umm… I mean, this isn't really a dancing kind of place."

The couple to their left stood and swayed away, their shadows twirling along the brick wall behind them to the guitar solo.

"Well, they're not playing chess." He pointed with a grin and circled the table to meet her.

He's still not into you. This means nothing. He's still not into you. This means nothing.

With an eye roll, she clasped his palm and stood, allowing him to steer her away from the safety of their table.

He led her toward the railing. Peeking over, Casey cast her gaze over the edge to peer at the mass of couples swaying to the slow song.

"Looks like a dancing place to me," he whispered, resting his hands on her waist and tugging her closer.

A butterfly burst free from its cocoon in her stomach at his warm touch, his closeness spurring her heart to pound beyond any recognizable pattern. Old Style clung to his breath, but his sweatshirt smelled of sandalwood, the mixture purely exhilarating.

Casey placed her hands on his shoulders, reminiscent of a junior high dance. *Why do I have to be so awkward?*

And as if she'd spoken the words aloud, a soft chuckle penetrated her ear as Austin lifted her hands to cup the back of his neck.

"It's just a dance," he whispered as his fingers tucked a curl behind her ear. He steered her body in slow circles, swaying in tune to the music with ease and rhythm.

Her feet left the floor as the song pulled her body from the earth. Confidence exuded from him as he twirled, and Casey breathed, her skin melting into his as she reveled in the unexpected source of comfort and safety his arms offered. His nose met her hair, and his warm breath tickled her neck. And as the music faded, she tripped, staggering over his shoe. "Oh! Shit, I'm sorry! Two left feet..." She grinned, embarrassment rising to color her cheeks pink once more.

He smiled and led her back to their table. "Thanks for the dance, Princess."

Princess?

Casey sank into her seat as her gaze fell to the full pitcher and fresh plastic cups on the table. Peeking at Austin, she eyed him as he rammed his hat back in place and reached for the beer.

You were pretending I was Mavis, weren't you?

Casey stirred. The aftereffects of cheap beer wracked her body as consciousness called. Swallowing, she built up the courage to open her eyes and experience the spinning room.

Why do I always drink too much?

The covers tugged to her left, and her eyes shot open. *What the hell?* Austin, shirtless and sleeping, rested directly beside her, his chest rising and falling with each peaceful inhale and exhale.

Oh, shit... What did we do?

Panic gripped her, unease squeezing her stomach like a sponge and wringing the memories of last night free. The Cubs game... Old Crow... dancing... and the beer. *So much beer.* Her mind whirled, blurred memories materializing before her as her gaze raked over his bare torso.

Cringing, she peeked under the covers. *Please let me be wearing clothes! Please let me be wearing clothes!* Beer-stained leggings, her jersey, and one royal-blue flat shoe still clothed her body as she lifted the blanket. Breathing out a sigh of sweet relief, Austin stirred and opened his eyes, confusion growing on his face as he awakened. His gaze settled on her before a wide grin stretched across his lips.

"Morning," he muttered, lifting his arms up and above his head.

Casey snorted and sat up, running her fingers through her hair. "I umm... don't remember how we got back here," she admitted, battling with a scratchy throat. Rubbing her eyes, she blinked the sleep away.

Austin dragged his hands along his cheeks and snickered. "All I remember is the beer."

"I definitely remember the beer." Groaning, she dropped her face into her palms, disguising the embarrassment flushing her cheeks. The light tickle of his fingers grazed her back, and her body jolted, sending shivers prickling along her skin.

"Whoa, sorry!" He leaned behind her, his torso disappearing over the side of the bed. "I just need my shirt." Austin pulled from the floor a wrinkled ball of cotton and tugged it over his head. Bringing his knees to his chest, he rested his back against the wall and sighed. "How do you feel?"

Casey rubbed beneath her eyes, clearing the remaining traces of melted eyeliner. She grinned. "Like death. You?"

"Same." He closed his eyes and let his head drop back.

Her stomach lurched as the taste of Old Style returned to her mouth. Swallowing, she fought the urge to upend her stomach in his lap. *Ugh, what the hell time is it?* Casey twisted and reached for her purse on the nightstand. Grasping her phone, the screen flashed 9:30 AM.

"Oh, shit! It's 9:30 already!" She swung her feet off the bed, and the sole surviving blue flat dropped from her toes to the floor.

Austin snickered. "Josh hates being late."

"Which means Mavis is going to kill me!" The hinges on her bedroom door creaked as she tiptoed outside, the scent of fresh coffee impaling her nostrils in the hallway.

"About damn time, girlfriend!" Mavis tossed a bite of bagel in her mouth and chewed. "I was just about to wake you. We've gotta hit the road."

"I'm so sorry!" Her fingers dragged along her cheeks. "I had no idea how late it was."

Josh poured a cup of coffee and pushed it in her direction across the counter.

"Thanks," she murmured, welcoming the cup of caffeine that would, with hope, cure the growing headache pounding in her brain.

"Did you guys have fun last night?" he asked.

The whine of the rusty hinges squeaked behind her as Austin opened the bedroom door and slid into the bathroom.

Josh snorted. "Never mind. I think that answers my question."

"Oh, Casey!" Mavis slammed her bagel down on the counter, poppy seeds scattering left and right. "Please tell me you didn't!"

"I didn't! *We* didn't! I swear!" Casey yanked at her leggings, pinching the fabric between her thumb and index finger. "I woke up completely clothed!"

The bathroom door opened, and Austin stepped down the hall with a grin. "I can't say the same though, can I?" He elbowed her in the gut.

"Oh, come on Austin. Are you fucking kidding me?" Mavis rested her hands on her hips. "Really? You can't keep your pants on around my best friend?" Her eyes narrowed, the green of her gaze X-raying them both.

Austin rolled his eyes and nodded toward his brother. "Lay off, Princess. You have no room to talk. I could say the exact same to you."

Ouch.

"All right, that's enough. Mavs—" Josh stood, his amused smile faltering fast.

"Uh-uh. Not yet. I need a moment alone with my beloved *roommate* first."

Sneering at Austin, Mavis gripped Casey's arm and pulled, tugging her into the privacy of her bedroom.

Casey's stomach sloshed, each footstep inviting vomit to rise in her throat. With a groan, she fell back into bed and stuffed her head beneath the pillow. As she inhaled, the scent of Austin's cologne settled in her nose.

"You don't know what you're doing, Case."

Mavis's butt sank to the bottom of the bed, her weight rocking the mattress and rattling the tiny number of still functioning brain cells powering through the hangover.

"What's wrong with Austin?" she murmured through the pillow.

"Nothing's *wrong* with him. I just need you to trust me on this. He's not a good idea."

Casey pulled her head free and squinted. "Look, you really don't have to worry about it, okay? He's not into me. You made sure of that."

Mavis squeezed Casey's foot and frowned. "What the hell is that supposed to mean?"

"It means that he's still hung up on you."

Gripping the charm on her necklace, Mavis tugged the heart along the length of the chain. "You know I never meant to hurt him," she whispered.

"Yeah, well you did anyway."

Her arms snaked around her body in a self-hug as her gaze fell to the floor. "You're awfully quick to pick sides there, Case."

What am I doing? Why am I fighting with you when you're about to leave?

Sighing, Casey swallowed the bile rising in her throat. Battling the bass drum in her brain, she shifted to rest her head in Mavis's lap. A curl fell on her face as her cheek met her best friend's sweatpants. "I'm sorry. The last thing I want to do is fight with you right now."

Mavis tugged the stray curl away, threading her fingers through her hair. "What am I gonna do without you?" Her voice quivered.

Pulling her head from her lap, Casey frowned. "You don't need me. You never did. The real question is what I'm going to do without *you*." The last eight years of her life stared back at her. Her roommate. Her best friend. Her surrogate big sister. Always there to support and push her forward, the best cheerleader the world had to offer. And with each passing second, her foot stepped further and further out the door, ready to begin a new chapter in her life. "I hate that you're leaving."

Mavis sighed. "I'm going to visit you all the time, probably more than you'll ever want!" She smiled, pulling Casey in for a hug. "And you always have a place to stay when you visit me in Rosewood," she whispered in her ear.

Casey nodded and swallowed, clinging to the person she loved most in the world.

"This isn't goodbye," murmured Mavis.

"I know. It's just a see you later." Pulling away, Casey closed her eyes and fought the dizzy spell descending on her body. She tugged Mavis from the mattress and opened the bedroom door, bracing herself for the imminent final farewell.

Silence met their ears as they entered the hall. Austin stood, hunched over the countertop with a cup of steaming coffee in his face. Josh scrolled through his phone in a seat at the dining room table. Neither Templeton twin acknowledged that the other existed.

"Ready?" Josh asked, pocketing his phone as he looked up.

Mavis nodded and stepped to his side, snuggling her body into his. "Yep, I think so." She brushed a tear from her cheek as she looked back. "See you this summer, right, Case? The wedding."

"Wouldn't miss it, Mavs." Casey dropped her gaze as they moved to the apartment door, scooping up their last bag and travel coffee mugs.

"See you back home," murmured Josh as he pulled the door closed, his gaze lingering on his brother. The latch clicked, and their footsteps faded down the staircase.

Sorrow squeezed her heart, puncturing it with a dull blade of distress. Tears burned the back of her eyes as she rammed them shut and buried her face in her palms. In her moment of weakness, of sadness, of grief, Austin's arms wrapped around her, circling her with sympathy and support.

"She's gone," she choked out into his chest, tears staining his wrinkled t-shirt.

"Yeah, she is."

JULIE NAVICKAS

CHAPTER THREE

Austin

The plane's wheels collided with the LAX tarmac with all the grace and skill of a pilot's inaugural flight. Austin rattled in his seat as the speed of the aircraft decreased. *Who the fuck is flying this thing?* He swallowed, fighting the growing desire to search for the air sickness bag in the seat pocket. A hangover was one thing, but a hangover on a four-hour flight sobered him of any alcohol-related plans in the near future.

He survived the baggage claim and called for a ride home. Within minutes, Austin strapped himself into the back seat of a silver Prius. The car pulled away from the terminal, and he breathed a sigh of relief to be back on the familiar highway and out of the air.

Chicago flashed through his mind. On his trip to the Windy City, he had just one intention—a small glimmer of hope to earn a spot back in his brother's good graces. But he'd left with something unexpected instead. Casey tripped into his brain, the charming, quirky girl with a love of Wrigley Field, lessening the sour mood of his soul.

"Cinderella…" he whispered.

"You say something?" The driver lifted his gaze to the rearview mirror.

"Oh, sorry, no." Austin shook his head as his pocket vibrated. Pulling out his phone, Casey's name lit up the screen. He tapped her message and smiled at her remarkable timing. *Hope you made it back to L.A. safely. I'm sorry for sobbing like a fool earlier, and I'm even sorrier for ordering us Old Style last night.*

Snorting, he replied. *Don't apologize. You can cry on my shoulder any time. But next time I get to order our drinks, okay?*

She sent back an emoji of a face blowing a heart kiss. Austin stifled a laugh, grinning at his lack of emoji knowledge. He tapped a few icons and surveyed the unfamiliar menu. With a snicker, he selected a winking face and clicked *send.*

Austin's chair squeaked as he swiveled, each circular rotation offering a different view of the Los Angeles skyline from his thirteenth-floor office at Boyd & Bernstein at Law. He stared at the mountains in the distance and frowned, the images of the magnificent Chicago skyscrapers settling in his mind. A week had passed since he returned to California, but even time couldn't shake the memory and pull of the Windy City.

With a sigh, he straightened the files on his desk and wrinkled his nose as the intercom broke the silence.

"Mr. Templeton?"

Tapping the button, he rolled his eyes. "What's up, Bernice?"

"You're wanted in conference room B."

"On my way, thanks." Snapping his laptop shut, he yanked the power cord from the outlet and stood. *Now what do they need?*

As he stepped toward the door, the vibration in his pocket tickled his leg. Casey's name returned to his phone screen, causing his stomach to dip and a welcomed grin to tug at his lips. Opening her text, Austin dropped back in his seat with a smile and read her latest note. *All right, California boy, POL 101 is on my summer schedule. You better not have been lying when you said you'd help me!* The same winking face emoji followed her words.

He snorted and tapped *reply*, the flutter of his heartbeat egging his response on.

"Mr. Templeton! Conference room B!" Bernice's voice bit into his flirtatious musings through the intercom.

"Oh! Shit," he stammered, pocketing his phone and snagging his laptop. His hand gripped the doorknob, and he bolted down the hallway, the silly grin on his face faltering at the door of conference room B. He peeked through the window, greeted by the intimidating gazes of both Steven Boyd and Rodger Bernstein. The pitter-patter of his heart waned as a wave of intimidation and nerves blanked his body.

What do they want with me… alone?

He gulped and knocked, sticking his head in through the ajar door.

"Templeton! There you are, kid! What kept you?" Steven Boyd, the senior-most partner at the firm, leaned back in his seat and plunked his thick feet on the conference room table. Rodger Bernstein eyed him as Austin sat and tucked his flyaway gray hair behind his ears while adjusting the pair of bifocals on his long nose.

"So sorry, Mr. Boyd, Mr. Bernstein. I umm, got distracted. My fault. It won't happen again."

Steven waved his apology off, tapping the arm of his chair with enthusiasm as Austin opened his laptop.

He pointed. "You can close that, Templeton. Pack your bags instead."

Austin gulped. A lump formed in his throat as the beat of his heart stilled in his chest. *Are they firing me?* "I'm sorry, sir, what?" He blinked, lifting his gaze to meet the dark-brown penetrating stare of Steven Boyd.

Rodger closed a blue folder and sent it flying across the

table.

With shaking fingers, Austin's palm flattened it to the surface as the air in his lungs escaped in a single breath.

"It's all there. Go ahead, take a look."

He opened the folder, and his eyes grazed over the numbers and graphs on the first page. *Profit per partner... client satisfaction ratings... case win percentage.* The words glared back from the page, and Austin forced his brain to process the information amidst the increasing panic in his heart.

"You're it, my boy. You've earned it." Steven smacked his thigh and grinned, a manic gleam in his eyes appearing.

"Earned it..." Austin repeated, still skimming the papers. The lump in his throat cleared with a swallow as slow understanding seeped into his brain. His name appeared at the top of every metric.

Steven snorted. "Let me break it down for you, Templeton. You're young. You're smart. And you're *promising as fuck.* Just look at that track record!" He pointed to the folder on the table. "There's no better man for this job."

"This job..." Austin repeated.

With a roll of his eyes, Rodger stretched his arms in the air and tilted his seat backward. "Steven, let's get Smith in here instead and offer it to her. I thought he was smarter than this." He toyed with his mustache, the hairs curling around his index finger.

Wait a minute...

"Sir, are you asking me to lead—"

"The new branch in Chicago!" Steven dropped his feet to the floor with a thud, replacing the same spot on the table with his elbows. "Weren't you just there, kid? Come on now, you're perfect for it!"

"And you've earned it, Templeton. It's all there, your record, your history here with us. It all speaks for itself." Rodger gestured to the folder again. "Like Steven said, no better man for the job."

Austin bit his bottom lip as understanding touched his

soul. *They're offering me the Chicago job.* The lights of the Magnificent Mile flashed through his brain as the iconic ivy of Wrigley Field snaked around his spine, tingling with anticipation and excitement. A breath escaped him as the opportunity warmed his heart. *And it's two thousand miles away from here... and her...*

Steven's voice boomed. "What do you say, kid?"

"You want me to lead the new branch in Chicago." His fingers tapped the blue folder, shockwaves radiating through his body as the opportunity sank into his psyche.

Rodger winked, and Austin nodded, his heart leaping forth from his chest. As he dragged his fingers through his hair, a wide grin overtook his lips. "Without a doubt, yes!" Austin stood, reaching his hand across the table to shake on the offer with both men. "Thank you," he choked out in stunned disbelief.

Steven's hand clapped against his back. "Get packing. We'll talk details soon, but start making your plans to relocate, at least for the foreseeable future. We'll see how it goes. Opportunity, and the Midwest awaits, partner."

Partner? Wait, are they saying...?

Austin pulled his Corvette into the garage. Snagging his briefcase from the passenger seat, he bounded up the small set of steps and entered his bachelor pad. Heading straight for the kitchen, Austin grinned from ear to ear, a celebratory beer calling his name.

With the clink of a bottle, Austin selected an IPA from the top shelf and headed to the living room, his butt sinking into his favorite chair.

His heart hammered in his chest, bouts of adrenaline coursing through his bloodstream, reminiscent of the day he received his acceptance letter from Harvard. *And now it's all finally paying off...*

"Who should I tell first?" he whispered.

Instinct took over, his fingers tapping his phone to find

his twin's name—his brother and his best friend. *Wait*. Austin swallowed, the recall of recent reality slicing into the euphoria. He sighed and bypassed Josh's and Mavis's names in his contact list. "They'll probably offer to pay for my flight out of here," he muttered, shaking his head as the excitement of the day lessened.

They'll be happy to see me leave.

With a sigh, his gaze fell to Mitch's and Lauren's names. He frowned. *Lauren will just cry. I'm not ready to tell her yet.*

"Mom and Dad?" he whispered. But scrunching his nose, he cast John and Susan Templeton aside too. "Eh, not right now. They'll make it about Josh somehow…"

Everyone kind of hates me at the moment, don't they?

Setting his phone on the side table with defeat, he turned the TV on instead, navigating automatically to the sports menu. His thumb tapped the usual sequence of buttons for a basketball game, but a foul ball collided with his brain mid-press.

"Casey."

With a grin, he snatched his phone back and opened her unanswered text. His eyes skimmed her message, rereading her words. *All right California boy, POL 101 is on my summer schedule. You better not have been lying when you said you'd help me!*

A twinge in his stomach invited a smile to his lips. He typed out, *Sounds like I better move to Chicago then. I can't go back on a promise.* With a snort he tapped *send*, reveling in the slowly returning state of excitement he'd come home with.

"Casey girl…" he whispered, picturing her response. The memory of her giggle broke the silence in his head. He stared at the screen, willing her to respond.

But nothing happened.

His gaze returned to the TV as he flipped to the baseball menu she inspired. At the top of the list sat the L.A. Dodgers, but two taps down offered the Chicago Cubs. Cringing, he scrolled past his hometown allegiance and selected Chicago. They led Milwaukee four to two.

Sipping his beer, Austin eyed the fans belting out "Take

Me Out to the Ballgame" in the seventh-inning stretch, not quite ready to buy into the fandom and betray his Dodgers just yet. *I better try to get used to this though.*

Beside him, his phone pinged, and Austin lunged, dribbling a sip of beer down his chin as his gaze raked the screen, seeking a response from Cinderella.

Ugh. It's Josh.

Disappointment flooded his body, his stomach sinking to the floor as he read his brother's words. *Are you home?*

"Ugh…"

Austin rolled his eyes and drained his beer. *Great… round thirty-seven commence.* He tapped out, *yeah, I am,* and hit *send,* sinking lower into the cushion as the air deflated from his lungs.

Good, I'm stopping by, flashed across the screen, and Austin scrunched his nose and pocketed his phone as angst settled in his heart.

The bat hit the ball as a resounding groan streamed through the speakers. Milwaukee brought in three runs with a homer and took the lead. Austin snorted as the front door opened and Josh appeared.

Were you in my driveway already?

"Hey," Austin murmured, smashing his face into the side of the chair.

Josh closed the door and kicked off his shoes, padding into the living room with a six-pack of beer. "You okay?" He pulled one from the carton and set it on the coffee table before plopping into the opposite sofa.

Austin straightened and snagged a bottle, twisting the top off with fervor. "Just surprised to see you over here, I guess."

Josh nodded, his gaze finding Austin's. With a slow exhale, he pulled his leg up and rested his ankle across his thigh. "I hate fighting with you," he admitted, sinking back into the couch.

"Same." Austin shrugged. "But Josh, I don't know what else to do except say I'm sorry *again*. I never should have acted on my feelings for Mavis. It was dumb. It was stupid. And… I just made a lot of mistakes…"

Josh brought the bottle to his lips and gulped, swallowing the liquid with a grimace as cheers erupted on TV. He furrowed his brow and squinted. "Why are you watching the Cubs?"

Warmth descended, tingling along his skin with the tiny pinpricks of a needle. He shrugged and sipped his beer. "Trying something new, I guess."

A *V* shape creased Josh's forehead. "You're not really even into baseball."

"Says who? I like the Dodgers."

When the Lakers aren't playing.

Josh shook his head. "All right, whatever… I didn't come over here to talk about baseball."

"Why're you here then?" Austin cringed, readying his body for another brotherly spat.

Josh straightened and dropped his feet to the floor. He propped his elbows on his knees and leaned forward. And for the first time in months, anger didn't radiate from his eyes and betrayal didn't exude from his heart.

What gives?

"Austin… I want you to be my best man when I marry Mavs."

The breath escaped him, his stomach plummeting to the floor.

You want what?

Austin gulped, choking on the air in his throat. An invisible force squeezed his heart, tugging at the frayed heartstrings—battered and ragged from the last few months of being dragged through the depths of hell and back.

Josh sighed and pulled his hands through his hair. "I know it's a big ask… and things kinda suck between us right now, but I just can't imagine anyone else but you standing beside me." He shook his head, honesty dripping from his lips.

Are you really asking me to stand beside you and watch you marry the woman I love?

Austin frowned and dropped his gaze to the carpet, his brother's request tearing him apart internally. "Josh, that's umm, kind of asking a lot right now. I mean, Mit—"

"I don't want Mitch." Josh snorted and flung the cap to his beer at Austin with a grin. "Look, I get it. I really do. But Austin, you are my best friend, and despite everything that's happened, that hasn't changed."

His soul softened, Josh's words repairing the beaten edges, slowly knitting back together after suffering months of what felt like irrefutable damage.

Austin dropped his face into his hands, dragging his palms along his cheeks. "But you know I still love her," he whispered.

Josh stiffened, a breath slowly escaping his lips. He nodded and set the empty bottle on the floor. "And I know you always will," he murmured. "I can't change that, but I can try to make peace with it. Because I understand why it happened now."

"What changed? You've been hell-bent on hating me!" Austin tossed his arms in the air, letting them fall to his lap with a thud. "I don't get it."

"You really want to know?" His head tilted.

"I mean, yeah?"

Josh bit his lower lip. "Two days in a shitty truck driving across the country... there's nothing more you can do but *talk.*

"Why didn't you just pay for a mover?"

Josh rolled his eyes. "It's Mavis. She insisted. The girl won't do anything the easy way."

Austin snorted. "True." With a deep breath, he exhaled. "So, what did you talk about then?"

"*You*, man!" He shrugged. "I lost her for ten years! Geez, I lost myself for ten years, but if it hadn't been for you, I never would have her back in my life today. I may not like how you brought us back together, but you did." Josh grinned and shook his head. "And let me tell you, that girl is going to defend you until the day she dies. She…" He gulped. "Loves you too."

The blade of his words pierced a hole through his heart, the new wound dripping with fresh blood.

She loves you too.

Austin stared at his brother. Josh's eyes radiated the forgiveness he'd desperately sought. His words spoke the desire of his heart, ready to return to the relationship they'd shared all their life. But the simple truth remained. Love existed in a place it shouldn't. And as long as their lives continued to intertwine, that love would only persist—or worse *grow*.

"Josh, I'm moving to Chicago." The words tumbled from his lips, spilling from the ache in his heart.

His brother snorted, his gaze sneaking a peek at the Cubs on the screen. He pointed and laughed. "What did you say?"

"Chicago. I'm gonna move for a little while." He stood, lifting his defeated body from the chair. His eyes sought the TV as the Cubs pulled ahead by a run. The crowd erupted with screams, cheers squelching the silence of the living room.

"Why?" Josh shook his head, his gaze resting on Austin's face.

"The law firm. They offered me the opportunity to start the new branch. I can't turn it down. And I can't shake the feeling that I need to get out of here for a little while… for all of us."

Josh hung his head. "I don't know what to say." He bent forward and tugged at his socks, picking at a piece of lint on the seam. "Except I guess it's my turn to apologize. I never meant to make you feel like you weren't wanted here. Because it's the exact opposite of that."

Austin swallowed, stuffing down the emotions rising in his throat. "It'll be good for all of us," he murmured. Mavis appeared in his mind, an image of her in a long white gown walking down the aisle. Breathtaking and radiant, her smile warmed his heart with each step forward. But when she reached the altar, her hand dropped into Josh's and not his own. Forever a fantasy, forever just a dream.

And I need to accept that.

Austin stepped toward the kitchen, collecting empty beer bottles on his way. "Josh, I'll be your best man." The words left his lips as the familiar heartache settled back into place, the excitement of the new job consumed beneath the fresh mountain of anguish burying him in guilt.

JULIE NAVICKAS

CHAPTER FOUR

Casey

For over an hour, the lure of the unread text message had plagued her mind. But Jim, the manager at The Broken Shaker, loomed, his rules forbidding cell phones while on the clock. Curiosity grew in her heart as her hands shook and poured another round of martinis for table two—anticipation creeping along her spine as the minutes ticked by. She tapped her foot, willing each second away until she could pull out her phone and see if it was Austin who had responded.

Mavis's replacement, Samantha, clocked in and wrapped an apron around her waist. And on the dot at 8:00 PM, she stepped to Casey's side and took over. Snagging her purse and jacket from beneath the bar, she bolted from the restaurant. A blast of icy wind lashed at her skin, whipping her hair into her face.

Isn't it supposed to be spring already?

Dipping her hand into her bag, she rummaged for her phone. A wide grin consumed her lips as Austin's name appeared. Her heart flip-flopped, his name sending a bout of nerves to swim in her belly as she turned the corner. The tips of her fingers—now numb from the cold air—tingled. Opening his text she read, *Sounds like I better move to Chicago then. I can't go back on a promise.*

Casey grinned, falling in love with the silly text banter they now shared. She tapped *reply* as her apartment came into view, the lack of light in the third-floor window an unwelcome reminder Mavis had indeed moved away.

She typed out, *You know… I do have a spare room. Chicago calls, California boy.* As she hit *send,* her aching feet carried her through the front door of the building. She trudged upward, each stair sucking the last remaining strength after a nearly nine-hour shift at the bar.

Casey's fingers clasped around her keys as the phone rang, Austin's name appearing on her screen. *You want to talk, not text?* Butterflies attacked her empty stomach as she tapped *accept* and unlocked the door.

Stepping inside, her foot grazed a stray winter boot in the entryway. She staggered forward, throwing her hands out to grip the dining room table chair before her face met the tile. "Oh! Shit!" Her purse dropped as the chair upended, her butt meeting the floor with no more grace than a toddler in ballet class.

"Casey?" Austin's voice called through the phone. "Are you okay?"

She rubbed her butt and brought the phone back to her ear. "That hurt." Tears burned behind her lids as she kicked the chair aside.

"What happened? Are you all right?"

"Oh, I'm fine… just tripped on a stupid boot."

"You're sure you're okay?"

"Ugh… just some wounded pride and a sore butt. Nothing new. I'll be fine." She wiped the tears from her eyes and snorted. *Way to make an impression, Casey.* Forcing her body to stand, she stumbled to the couch and plopped down. "Umm, what's up? Are you calling to interview for the political science tutoring position I have open?"

He laughed. "I don't know. How much does it pay?"

"Payments are fulfilled with pitchers of Old Style."

"Oh, hell no. I rescind my interest completely."

A laugh burst from her belly, the eruption of joy welcome after the long day on her feet.

"Damn it! I'll pull your application. And I had such high hopes for you too. Your qualifications were perfect."

He chuckled, each bubble of laughter lifting her spirits. With little effort, he'd quickly become the soother of her soul in small, yet meaningful ways.

"No joke, though. I'm really happy to hear you enrolled in a course for summer. You'll do great, Casey girl."

She smiled, the sweet and simple nickname warming her heart. "Umm well, yeah… don't hold your breath. I told you, school isn't really my thing."

"I don't believe that for a second. But hey, if you do need help, I really am here. I love that stuff."

"So, it's okay if I call you in tears at three in the morning to ask you how a bill becomes a law?"

He snickered. "You definitely can, but it might be more fun if you just walk next door and ask."

Huh?

Casey scrunched her nose. "Next door?"

"Do you remember when I told you that my law firm was considering opening a branch in Chicago?"

"Oh, my God! No way! Are you saying it's happening? You're moving here?"

"They asked me today if I'd lead the effort."

"No fucking way! Austin! Congratulations!" The excitement bubbling in her chest exploded like a jack-in-the-box bursting from its tin prison.

"Thanks!" He snickered. "I really can't believe it. They've been talking about it for months, but I never expected them to ask me."

"Well, I mean, you're umm, kind of impressive, sir." She giggled. *Did I just say that out loud?* "They made a good choice. And I can't wait to celebrate with you. Drinks on me, okay?"

"Oh, hell no. I get to choose next time, remember?"

She smiled, the recall of Old Style night replaying in her brain. Her skin tingled at the memory of his hands wrapped around her waist, swaying to the music… and waking up beside him in bed.

"Oh, my gosh, it wasn't that bad!" Her cheeks flushed, the grin on her lips widening.

"Not that bad? I had a hangover for like three days!"

"Oh, California boy, you'll have to learn how to hang like a Midwesterner now." She laughed again and reached for the remote, scanning the channels for the tail end of the Cubs game. "When are you coming?"

"Umm… next week sometime? I don't have any real plans yet."

The Cubs led Milwaukee by a run, and Casey smiled, a bad day officially reclaimed on many levels.

"Well, you're welcome to stay here. It's not much, but I'll be glad for the company until you want your own place." Her gaze jumped to the apartment door and the dead bolt she neglected to lock. Rising from her seat, she tiptoed to the door and twisted the metal. "I kinda hate living alone."

"Call it done, roomie. You really don't mind?"

She snickered, the word *roomie* ringing in her ear. The broken boy from California tugged at her heartstrings—his sweet grin and battered soul colliding with her own to smooth the edges.

"Definitely not, Austin. And hey, congratulations again. You can pick the pizza topping when you get here."

"Pineapple it is, Cinderella."

Sleep evaded her. Tossing and turning, Casey flung the blanket from her body.

I can't believe he's moving here…

She laughed and tumbled out of bed, giving up on a night of any true rest. Lifting the window open, she poked her head outside and lit a cigarette. The silence of the city streets echoed in the early morning hours, the rattle of public transit closed until dawn. The ash danced in the wind as it floated away in the spring air—a bad habit persisting since her father passed away. She drew in a puff of smoke, letting it fly from her lips in a single exhale.

The ping of a text message broke the stillness of the moment, her screen lighting up in the darkened bedroom. Casey smashed the cigarette into the windowsill and tugged the glass down as she lunged for the phone. Her heart surged with adrenaline as she tapped *open* on Austin's latest text. "You can't sleep either, can you?" she asked, eyeing his kissing face emoji.

She hit *reply* with a wild grin. *Is that you kissing up to me after turning down my job?*

Austin quickly replied. *LOL. No, that's for making this move a little less daunting. How will I ever thank you?*

Casey's mind jumped straight into the metaphorical gutter, running away with a few naughty ideas. Her cheeks warmed with embarrassment as she shook her head, ridding her body of the images flooding her brain. *Oh, I've got a few chores waiting for you, don't worry.*

Her phone buzzed a few seconds later with his reply. *Well, I am good at cleaning, but I also make a mean cheesy sandwich!*

Casey laughed and sent a chef's cap emoji with the words, *You're welcome in my kitchen anytime, Gordon Ramsey.*

He responded. *Those grilled cheeses fueled many late nights studying for the bar. They'll get you through a political science class too, Casey girl.*

She laughed and sent a cheese + apron = brain emoji.

A full two minutes passed with no response. Casey's heart sank into her mattress as she assumed their teasing had concluded. But a photo popped up and a squeal escaped her lips with a layer of pure elation. Her eyes grazed over Austin's sweet face and upper torso donning a Harvard apron. He included the message, *Don't knock it 'til you try it!*

"Using my own words against me, Austin Templeton…"

That's it. I'm a goner. Hopelessly falling for you and your cheesy

45

sandwiches.

CHAPTER FIVE

Lauren

"Shit!" The last egg rolled from the counter and hit the tile, a gunky yellow puddle oozing across the floor. "Damn it!" Lauren snagged the roll of paper towels and dropped to her knees, scooping the shells and yolk straight into the trash. "Sorry, Austin… I guess no banana bread this week."

"Why not?" Mitch breezed into the kitchen, his gaze intent on the coffee pot.

"Oh, I just dropped the last egg on the stupid floor." Lauren moved to the sink to wash her hands and flipped the faucet on. The water collided with a dirty pan, projecting the spray onto her pajama top. "Ugh! Fucking fabulous…" she mumbled, shutting the faucet off and peeling the wet shirt away from her skin. "Just fucking fabulous…"

Mitch snickered, pulling a spoon from the drawer. "I didn't know about the wet t-shirt contest." A smirk grew on his unshaven face. "But it's a guaranteed way to liven up Sunday brunch."

Lauren folded her arms across her damp chest as her cheeks flushed pink with embarrassment. Her gaze found her husband's as his smile grew. The beat of her heart thumped, increasing in speed as the coffee pot beeped. Mitch moved closer, his line of sight falling to her chest.

When's the last time you looked at me like that?

Adrenaline pulsed through her body as his hands unfolded her arms and pinned them to her sides. His forehead brushed against her own, a moan escaping his mouth as he backed her body into the counter.

Lauren closed her eyes, melting into him as his lips found hers, a surge of heat running rampant along her spine.

And when's the last time you kissed me like this?

Tugging her hands free from his grasp, she raked her fingers through his dark, unkempt hair, groaning with growing passion as his palms cupped her wet breasts.

"Mitch…" she whispered, pressing her body into his. "What's gotten into you?"

The coffee pot beeped again as he nipped her bottom lip with his teeth. "Let me take you upstairs, Peaches."

She giggled and pressed her lips to his neck. "I mean, it's not really the right time of the month to try."

His body froze, his back straightening as he pulled away, inching backward until his butt collided with the opposite counter.

"Mitch… no wait, please!" Lauren stretched her hand out, tugging at the thin fabric of his t-shirt. "I didn't mean it like that!"

His hand swatted hers away as he turned to open the sugar container, dumping a spoonful of white crystals into his mug of fresh coffee. "No, no, I know the rules in this house. I'll look at the calendar next time."

The air deflated from her lungs as a sob left her lips. "Mitch, I'm so sorry! I didn't—"

"That's just it, Lauren… *we both know you did.*" He snorted and stepped away, the scent of coffee trailing behind him as he left the kitchen.

Tears welled in her eyes as a chill erupted on her skin. She shivered. "Where are you going?"

"Low on eggs, aren't you?" he called over his shoulder.

Her feet stopped short as her breath caught in her throat.

Mitch paused at the foot of the staircase and released an exaggerated exhale. He turned. "The market…"

Lauren hung her head, the tears streaming down her cheeks.

That was low, even for you, Mitch.

Lauren laid a heaping bowl of fresh fruit on the table and straightened the pile of napkins. Stepping back, her eyes grazed over the picture-perfect brunch she'd prepared for the family. With one last adjustment of the teacups and saucers, she huffed out a breath and marched back into the kitchen.

That's as good as it's gonna get today.

She rubbed her eyes, mopping up the mascara staining her cheeks. "How did things get this bad between us?" she whispered, squeezing the muscles in her neck. Her elbows dropped to the counter, a groan tumbling from her lips as her upper body fell to the hard surface. With a sigh, she squeezed her eyes shut, willing the burn behind her lids to disappear.

The front door banged open, and Lauren snapped her body up, dragging her palms across her cheeks and her fingers below her eyes once more.

Come on! Pull yourself together.

"Anyone home?"

"In here!" she yelled, checking her blurred reflection in the microwave door.

Austin rounded the corner and dropped a white cardboard box on the counter. "Got there too late for any of the good donuts—had to settle for bear claws instead." His face fell as their eyes connected. "Whoa, what's wrong?"

Lauren shook her head and forced a smile on her lips. "Not a thing. Everything's fine." She popped the box open and surveyed the treats, inhaling the sugary scent.

"You don't look fine. What gives?" He turned, poking

his head out of the kitchen door. "Where's Mitch?"

"The market, I think." Her stomach dropped, recalling her husband's snide comment. The tears welled, pooling in the corners of her eyes. She dropped to her knees, burying her head in a corner cabinet until her hands landed on a ceramic platter. Lauren tugged, the clank of the dish muffling the sob escaping her lips. The pit in her stomach grew—the anger and resentment living in her heart heightening. She inhaled, pushing aside the guilt consuming her soul over a slowly crumbling marriage, fraught with the struggle of infertility.

"Where's the banana bread?" Austin called from the dining room, disappointment coating his question.

Of course. The fucking banana bread.

Laughter bubbled from her belly, the last shred of sanity leaving her gut. She sank backward until her butt met the tile.

I really can't win today, can I?

"What's so funny?" Austin peeked his face over the countertop with a furrowed brow.

Lauren hiccupped and pulled herself to her feet with the platter in hand. "You know, Austin, nothing has ever been less funny in my entire life." She dropped the ceramic plate to the counter, its vibrations echoing throughout the kitchen.

"I don't understand." He shook his head.

With a flip of the box top, Lauren transferred the bear claws to the platter, sniffling into her sleeve. "Can I ask you something?"

He nodded. "Always."

"Have you ever lost the person you love most in this world?" She flattened the box and tossed it aside.

Austin frowned, tapping an askew bear claw to align with the others. "You know I have," he whispered.

Dear Lord, why did I just ask you that?

"Shit, Austin. I'm so sorry. I don't know what I was thinking." She reached forward and squeezed his elbow.

God, that was a stupid thing to say!

He wrinkled his nose. "So, which Benson are we talking about here?"

She sighed and scooped up the platter, slouching from the kitchen and into the dining room with Austin on her heels.

"You know what, just forget I said anything. I'm being dramatic." She shook her head and rested the bear claws on the table beside the steaming breakfast casserole.

"Look, you can't just drop a bomb like that and expect me to forget it. What's going on?"

Her fingers smoothed the tablecloth, brushing away the non-existent crumbs until his hand covered hers. He squeezed, the warmth of his palm instilling comfort.

Lauren sighed. "It's just been a really rough morning. I'm sorry I said anything."

What have I gotten myself into here?

"Don't be sorry. You know you can always talk to me."

"I know. And I appreciate that." She sighed again. "But Austin, you've got your own stuff to deal with. You don't need my drama too."

He snorted. "Lauren, I lost Mavis, but I never really had her to begin with," he whispered, pulling his hand from hers. "You and Mitch are a completely different story though. Come on, what gives?"

She nodded and sank into a chair. With her sleeve, she blotted her eyes and dropped her face into her palms. "Really. Just ignore me. You've got enough to deal with... sitting here every Sunday for family brunch, watching wedding plans unfold. That can't be easy."

Austin tugged her hands away and freed her face. He smiled, his gaze falling to his lap as he sank into the seat opposite her. "Well, since you brought it up, I think this is actually going to be my last one for a little while."

Her heart faltered. A sob caught in her throat as the breath stilled in her lungs. "What's that supposed to mean?" she choked out.

He squinted. "Don't freak out, okay? It's nothing permanent."

She nodded.

"Boyd and Bernstein… They offered me the Chicago job." He grinned. "And I accepted it."

Lauren pressed her hands over her mouth, muffling the inhale of breath. "Oh, my God, Austin… that's fucking huge!"

"It is, yeah." He smiled.

"I can't believe it." *No, I can.* Her stomach rolled as her chest tightened. *You're probably dying to get out of here.* "I mean, that's real—"

"Big for his career." Josh rounded the corner, his fingers tapping the doorframe. His gaze landed on Austin. "Spreading the good news?"

"Good news?" Mavis followed, dropping into the seat beside Lauren. She scooped up a bear claw and grinned as Josh sat in the seat beside Austin.

"Someone got quite the promotion the other day." Josh clasped his hand on Austin's shoulder and squeezed. "Come on, don't be shy."

"Josh…" Lauren rolled her eyes. "Don't be a dick."

He snorted. "You think I'm being a dick?" Josh tugged a teacup in front of him and stretched across the table for the coffee carafe. "I'm not the one running away to Chicago."

"Chicago?" Mavis wrinkled her nose as she wiped sugar from her lips.

Austin slouched in his seat and rolled his eyes. "It's not a big deal. It's not permanent." He dragged a hand through his hair.

"It is a big deal though, Austin! Don't minimize an accomplishment like this!" Lauren scooted her chair in his direction and frowned at Josh.

"Wait, you're serious?" Mavis shook her head. "I move back here." Her finger tapped the table. "And then you move there?"

"Look, it was really unexpected. I never thought Boyd and Bernstein would offer me the job." His gaze fell to his lap again. "I just can't turn it down. They could make me a partner if I do this right."

"How long?" Josh stirred a spoon around his coffee.

"A year? Maybe? I don't know. I've never done anything like this before." He snorted. "I have no idea what I'm doing."

"You'll be great, Austin. There's no doubt." Lauren reached forward and squeezed his hand, a smile spreading along her lips.

And you do need to get out of here. These two are something else.

"Austin the Midwesterner…" Mavis giggled, bringing a teacup of coffee to her lips. "You'll need a warmer jacket," she said with a wink.

"Eh, Casey can help me."

She choked. Coffee spattered the tablecloth, coating the casserole, fruit, and bear claws. Mavis coughed, tears welling in her eyes as she inhaled. "Did you just say Casey?" Her eyes narrowed. "*My* Casey?"

Austin grinned. "I'm sorry, *your* Casey?"

"You still talk to her?"

Austin flashed a smile. "Why? Jealous, Mavs?"

Josh sent an elbow flying, jabbing his brother in the gut. "Knock it off."

"Oh, my God, you people are insane." Lauren rose from her seat, resting her hands against her hips.

Austin leaned around her. "You know, Princess, believe it or not, I'm not moving to Chicago to piss you off! It's a job opportunity." He huffed out a breath and rolled his eyes. "And Casey isn't yours, okay? She's just helping me move, giving me a place to stay for a little while until I can figure it all out."

"A place to stay?" Mavis dropped back in her seat, working her way around Lauren's body to glare. "Dear Lord, Austin! You can't be serious right now! My apartment? My old room?"

"So, what if I am?" He glowered, folding his arms across his chest.

A bubble of laughter fell from Mavis's lips as she stood and marched out of the room. "You're fucking unbelievable," she muttered under her breath.

Her sandals flip-flopped away down the hall as Mitch stuck his head around the corner, a carton of eggs in his hands.

"What'd I miss?" he asked.

Our last family brunch.

CHAPTER SIX

Austin

Austin's plane touched down at O'Hare International a week later. A wave of irritation descended as every passenger beside him stood, racing to collect their belongings from the overhead bins the second the plane reached the gate.

With a sigh, Austin rolled his eyes and rested his forehead against the tiny window, gazing out at the tarmac. The air traffic marshals in neon vests pocketed their orange glow sticks and moved to open the cargo hold. Below his feet, the thump and bump of luggage jarred the floor. He grinned, lifting his gaze to the gunmetal-gray sky.

That can't be snow, can it?

He pressed his nose to the window and cringed. *Eww! Why'd I just do that?* Rubbing his sleeve along his nose, he frowned as the small flecks of white wafted in the wind and collided with the side of the aircraft.

"First time in Chicago?"

Austin turned away from the smudged plastic and grinned at the flight attendant. A bag of trash crinkled in her hands.

"Umm, no. I was just here a few weeks ago. It was like sixty degrees!" He tapped the window. "What the hell happened?"

"Welcome to the Midwest, sweetie." She smiled and stepped sideways, scooping trash from the seat pockets in the adjacent row.

"Yeah. Welcome to the Midwest," he muttered, tugging his phone from his pocket. The device powered on, Lauren's name flashing before his eyes. He tapped the screen to reveal the first text that read she missed him, and another to ask if he'd landed safely yet.

Oh, Lauren…

He banged out a response and hit *send*, opening a new message to Casey with a smile. He tapped out, *Just landed!* And with a snort, he searched for a snowflake emoji. *What's this white stuff?*

The aisle started to clear as the line of passengers slowly deboarded. Snagging his backpack, Austin stood and stretched. His phone vibrated, and he glanced down to read, *Oh California boy, this is going to be an adjustment for you!* A winking face followed her words before she added, *Be there within an hour to pick you up. Text me when you're outside.*

He inhaled, and the stale air of the cabin circulated in his lungs. A ball of nerves bounced around in his belly as he followed the line and exited the plane, each step hammering in his new reality.

Sweet home Chicago.

He continued through the gate and out of the terminal. The greasy smell of French fries and the sugary sweetness of Cinnabon infused, infiltrating his nose as he followed the signs toward baggage claim. Austin breezed past the airport shops, momentarily getting sidetracked as his gaze scanned the racks of magazines until *The Funny Part* appeared. He swallowed, pushing down the unease gripping his soul as he hopped into an overcrowded elevator.

A burst of icy air tingled along his skin as he approached the conveyor belt moments later. It spun lazily, rotating a single brown bag with a red ribbon. Above him, the Chicago flag danced in the cold air each time the revolving doors of the terminal opened.

I hope I made the right choice moving here.

Two thousand miles away, he'd left his safe and familiar job. He'd left his family. He'd left his home. "And I left you there too, Mavs," he whispered as the bell rang and red lights flashed on the carousel.

Time and distance. We both need it.

His small duffle bag turned the corner, and Austin grabbed it, tapping his phone to open a new text.

Ready or not, Casey girl. Here I am.

They traveled down the slushy path of Lake Shore Drive in Mavis's former little blue Ford Fiesta. Casey switched lanes, weaving in and out of the stop-and-go traffic.

"Casey!" Austin slammed on the imaginary brake in the passenger seat for the eighth time.

"Oh, my God, Austin! Relax! I'm just switching lanes!" She rolled her eyes as the engine died. "God damn it! I hate this car!"

"Do you even know how to drive a manual?" Austin turned, peering through the rear window at the line of angry traffic behind them.

"I mean, kinda?" She rammed both feet against the clutch and brake. "Mavis taught me." The car resumed life as she inched forward in the line of traffic again with a grin. "See... no big deal!" Her fingers twisted the dial on the dashboard, turning down the heat blasting into the cabin. A sea of red taillights emerged again, and she slammed on the brakes, lurching the car forward.

The blood drained from his cheeks as his heartbeat tripled in rhythm. "So, umm... how far away are we again?" Austin clutched the seatbelt, tightening it across his chest.

The tiny snowflakes that freckled the sky on the plane had now morphed into heavy lumps of cold snow. Flakes fell in droves, coating the road in dirty slush.

"Well, like twenty minutes with this stupid traffic." Casey craned her neck to see beyond the car in front of her.

Austin sucked in a deep breath and turned the knob on the heat back up to full blast. Tugging his sweatshirt tighter around his body, he shivered and snuck a peek at Casey with a grin.

How are you not wearing a jacket?

"So, what's on your agenda for the rest of the day?" She snickered and aimed the middle vent in his direction as the engine hummed, working overtime.

"Oh, ah, just thought I'd hang out with you if you don't have any other plans. The Cubs play later, right? In Atlanta?"

She nodded, her smile alight in her eyes as she turned and tilted her head. "They do."

His heart fluttered. And for the first time since landing in Chicago, a natural warmth washed over him unaided by the questionable heating system of the Ford. Austin cranked the dial again, adjusting the heat to a lower temperature. His eyes grazed the rearview mirror as a stilted laugh escaped his lips.

"What the hell?" He tapped the mirror, running his finger over the duct tape holding it to the windshield.

"Oh! Don't touch it! You have no idea how long it took me to tape it at the right angle!" Casey slapped his hand away as the traffic inched forward.

"That can't be legal, Case." Austin shook his head as he leaned forward, examining the DIY job closer.

"Oh, it's fine. Put your badge away, officer." She flipped the turn signal on and exited the highway.

Austin exhaled, thankful that their time spent on Lake Shore Drive had ended. "I'm gonna get that fixed for you," he muttered.

Several turns and one clutch slip later, Casey pulled into the building's parking garage and squeezed into a tiny space on the fourth level.

Austin tugged at the handle and pushed the door open, gaining a mere twelve inches to squeeze his body out. "Everything in this city is really close together, isn't it?" He shuffled sideways, exhaling only when Casey popped the trunk.

"Did you really move across the country with just one bag?" She pointed at the single duffle bag in the trunk.

Gripping the straps, Austin slung the bag over his shoulder and grinned. "I've got everything I need right here until I can find a place to rent." He tapped the bag as her face fell. "You okay?"

"Oh! Yeah, sorry… just spaced for a second." Gripping his arm, she led him to the elevator.

Austin pushed the call button with a finger tucked beneath his sweatshirt sleeve.

"A tad pretentious, no?" She rolled her eyes and stepped inside.

Hardly! Who knows what germs are on that button!

"Josh is worse," he mumbled. His brother appeared in his mind, the slowly repairing relationship left two thousand miles behind.

She snorted and shook her head. Her blonde curls bounced, distilling the scent of lilacs. And what had just been a smelly urine-soaked parking garage elevator moments ago transformed into a field of fresh wildflowers. Austin closed his eyes, inhaling the sweet scent as a sense of calm radiated throughout his body.

A fresh blast of icy air stung his skin as the doors opened, the field of lilacs wilting as quickly as they had bloomed.

Casey stepped forward into the blizzard, each puff of white clinging to her hair as she giggled. "It's fucking April!" she screamed into the storm.

With quick steps, they made it to the building's front entrance, and Casey rammed her keys into the lock. Her foot caught on the first step as she started the climb with a snicker.

"This is where we first met, Cinderella."

Her feet halted on the second-floor landing as she turned to grin. "You need a wand and a blue robe, fairy godmother."

A laugh fell from his lips as he moved past her, continuing up the stairs. "Hard pass on the blue robe. But I'll take the wand."

She giggled, following his footsteps until they reached the third floor. Casey inserted her key in the lock and pushed the door open. "Welcome home, roomie!"

The bare white walls returned his gaze. Little had changed in the weeks since he'd left; even the tattered blanket on the couch still rested in the corner of the sofa. Austin stepped inside as his eyes caught sight of a pink flower-shaped balloon tied to a dining room table chair. It read *Congratulations!* along each petal.

With a grin, he gripped the ribbon of the balloon, running it through his fingers as Casey dropped her purse on the table beside him. "How'd you know pink was my favorite color?"

"Women's intuition."

He laughed and reached forward, inviting her into a hug. As she fell into his embrace, his arms encircled her, squeezing her small form—the chill of her clothing meeting his own. "Thanks, Case," he whispered, tightening his grasp. "You've made this move really easy on me."

She snorted. "I mean, it's just Midwestern nice."

His hand rested on the small of her back, cradling his sole friend in a new place, in a new space. Seemingly content to stay wrapped in his arms, she sighed and closed her eyes.

Don't move, Casey girl.

"You know, you really should wear a coat when it's this cold."

"So should you, California boy."

He giggled. "I definitely don't have one for this weather."

"Well then let's go shopping, roomie."

His mind raced. With a glance at the clock, the bright red numbers changed from 12:59 AM to 1:00 AM. Austin groaned and flipped the pillow, his eyes searching every corner of the new room.

She's still here.

Her essence—her soul—every piece of her still lived and breathed in the depths of the shadows. Austin inhaled, pressing his nose into the pillow. *Mavis's pillow.* He moaned. *Mavis's bed.* Rolling his body, he turned to face the wall. A smudge caught his eye, and he ran his fingers over it with a frown. "That's definitely not marker, Princess."

A knot formed in his stomach as he curled his legs into his body, recalling the moment he first saw the red smear. *FaceTime. Five months ago.* "So much has happened," he whispered to the darkness.

The back of his eyelids prickled and burned. Blinking hard, Austin swung his legs off the bed and dropped his feet to the cold floor. He dragged his hands across his cheeks and sighed. "This was a really bad idea," he muttered. His gut churned, bubbling over with the familiar sense of defeat and sorrow. He shook his head and let his hands fall back to the mattress. Gliding his fingers over the new jacket Casey had picked out for him, a small smile tugged at his lips. She was a single light in the darkness—an unanticipated new friendship.

He turned his head, dropping his gaze back to the pillow as Casey fell from his mind. The white linen sheets had wrinkled beneath the weight of his body as he tossed and turned. He ran a hand along the creases, each small mountain of material inviting Mavis back into his heart. He pictured her, snuggled beneath the blankets as every curve of her body rested atop the sheets, nestled into the warmth—*and me curling up beside you...*

Austin shivered, hurling the image from his mind. *Fuck this.* He bolted from the room, tiptoeing out the door and down the unfamiliar hallway to the living room. A stray pink shoe caught his big toe and he stumbled, catching himself on the kitchen counter. He scowled and kicked it away with a frown.

Sinking into the sofa, his knees greeted his face as he sighed and stuffed his feet beneath him. He snatched the remote control and powered on the TV, impatiently tapping each button until the room glowed in the tiny source of light. A rerun of a nineties sitcom ... an infomercial... a court show... "Total bullshit," he murmured until John Wayne looked back from the next channel.

Where's the Lord of the Rings *marathon when you need it?*

Pulling Casey's blanket from the corner of the couch, he draped it across his bare shoulders and snuggled in. A grin tugged at his lips as John Wayne bet his cat, General Sterling Price, in a game of poker. He snorted, some of the heavy weight from his heart lifting and floating back to the bedroom behind him.

Take a deep breath, Austin. Remember... time and distance can only help.

Padding back down the hallway to the kitchen, he opened two wrong cabinet doors before his gaze landed on Casey's mismatched set of glassware. Austin wrinkled his nose. *Which one would Mavis have had her lips on?* Cringing at the question, he snagged a small mason jar. *Definitely not this one.* He flipped on the faucet and filled the cup to the brim as Casey's door squeaked open.

"Austin? Everything okay?" Her bare feet tapped against the tile.

"Sorry, Case!" Water dribbled down his chin as he wiped it away. "Was I too loud?"

She shook her head. "Eh, I'm a light sleeper." She rubbed her eyes with two balled-up fists and joined him at the counter.

His heart flip-flopped in his chest as a shiver snaked down his spine. Heat radiated from her body as her elbow bumped into him. Austin grinned, taking in her gray tank top, neon-yellow pajama bottoms, dilapidated ponytail, and rosy cheeks.

"Sorry, I'm not used to living with anyone." He smiled, his gaze following her hands as they lifted above her head to stuff a stray curl into the hair tie.

Her belly button appeared, and something dark blue peeked out from the waistband of her shorts. Austin inhaled, intrigue flooding his system.

"Is that a tattoo?" He smirked and pointed to her stomach.

Her hands fell, yanking down the material. "Umm… maybe." She wrapped her arms around her body, the gesture utterly familiar as Mavis and her signature self-hug materialized before his eyes.

"What're you watching?" Casey staggered away, dropping onto the couch in the living room. She tugged the blanket around her shoulders and wrapped herself up like a mummy.

"*True Grit.*" Austin plopped into the seat beside her with a sigh. "So, what's it of?" He smiled, poking her in the rib.

"Wouldn't you like to know, Mr. Templeton." She giggled and tugged the blanket around her body tighter.

"Call me intrigued, Ms. McDaniels." His gaze turned back to the TV as John Wayne won in a shootout.

She smiled and squinted, raising her brow. "You like Westerns?"

"Not really. But there's not much on at 1 AM." He sighed and shifted his butt, snuggling into the corner.

"So, why are we awake then?"

"Couldn't sleep." Austin let his head fall backward on the couch as he closed his eyes. "You know… new room… new bed."

"You mean Mavis's old room… old bed…" She picked at an overgrown cuticle on her index finger.

You fucking see right through me.

Austin heaved out a breath and covered his eyes with his palms. "I think I… underestimated…"

The cushion shifted beside him as sudden heat collided against his skin. His eyes popped open as Casey snuggled into the crook of his arm, her breath light and warm against his chest. She tugged the blanket from her shoulders and draped it over their laps.

"Mavis is my best friend..." she whispered.

Instinctively, his arm fell to embrace her small body. His heart hammered as a bout of adrenaline surged through his bloodstream. He breathed, relishing in the moment of sudden connection.

"But she's fucking dumb." Her fingers squeezed his knee beneath the blanket.

Goosebumps erupted on his skin as her breath beat against his chest.

"Why?" he whispered, wrapping a silky blonde curl around his finger.

Casey sighed. "She never could see something good right in front of her."

He swallowed, inhaling the lilacs perfuming the air. Her soft lips pressed against his skin, sparking fire at the touch. And her kiss—innocent and sweet—built pressure around his heart, a spark fueling a flame amidst ash and rubble. A weight lifted as his soul breathed for the first time in months, warming his body as the air in his lungs caught at the back of his throat.

Austin's hand fell, his fingers gliding along her lower back. Her breath hitched as he pinched the skin at her waist. "And what do you see, Case?" he murmured. With a single finger, he coaxed her gaze upward with a tap of her chin.

Her eyes sparkled in the dimly lit room, bright and expectant. She ran her tongue along her bottom lip as her gaze settled on his mouth.

Time. Distance. And just maybe... someone to distract me?

Austin pressed his lips to hers, melding his mouth to her own until a roar filled his ears. The blood in his veins hammered through his system, raging with excitement and arousal as euphoria took control of his actions.

Her back arched as his palm caressed the length of her bare thigh beneath the blanket. She nibbled on his bottom lip and released a moan. "I see you," she answered before shifting to straddle his body. The blanket fell to the floor and the pressure and friction mounted—each prick of her fingernails against his skin granting permission to explore, to move on from the past, beyond forbidden love.

A pounding on the door stalled his heart.

"Who the fuck?" Casey tumbled from his lap, snatching the blanket from the floor. She wrapped the material around her shoulders and wiped her lips with the back of her hand. "It's one in the morning!"

And I'll fucking murder whoever it is…

Austin rose from his seat and stepped to the door, pressing his right eye to the peephole. "Oh, no fucking way!"

His fingers gripped the deadbolt, turning the lock to yank open the door. A hand snaked inside, gripping the door frame as the stale fumes of weed and alcohol billowed in.

"Damn! Did I get the wrong apartment?" His words slurred together as his fingers raked through a mop of greasy black hair. His unfocused eyes scanned the room until a wide smile crept along his lips at the sight of Casey. "Aww naw, there's blondie." He wagged his finger in her direction and leaned forward.

Austin's palm slammed into his chest. "What the fuck do you think you're doing?" He pushed him back into the hallway.

"Hey, hey, it's cool, bro!" The man stumbled and staggered across the hall, gripping his own apartment doorknob. "I didn't know she had a boyfriend."

"Yeah, well, she does! So, stay the fuck away from her!"

A manic burst of laughter filtered through the hallway as something fell and crashed inside his apartment. Austin stepped back inside and slammed the door, securing the deadbolt with fervor.

The desire that fueled his passion moments ago subsided, replaced only with a fierce sense of protection. Austin tapped his fist against the door and turned. Casey sat, perched on the couch, her small body buried beneath the tattered blanket.

"I told you he was weird." She shrugged, and the blanket fell.

Returning to the living room, Austin tugged Casey back to his body. He sighed and pressed his nose to her hair as she snuggled into his chest. "Case, that wasn't just weird. That was…" He shook his head, tightening his grip. "That could have been really bad if…"

If you were alone, what would he have tried to do to you?

Her gaze lifted, peering into his eyes.

"I don't think you should live here alone." Austin shook his head, wrinkling his nose.

"But my lease isn't up until the end of June."

Of course, it isn't.

He nodded, gazing around the apartment. His eyes landed on the sofa behind her, the memories of moments ago jump starting his heart.

"Well, how do you feel about a more permanent roommate then?"

"I mean, you did just tell him you were my boyfriend, so…" She snickered and pressed her lips to his chest.

"Boyfriend. Fairy godmother… same thing."

Call me what you want, Casey girl. I'm not leaving.

CHAPTER SEVEN

Casey

Casey opened her political science textbook as the first day of class loomed. As she stared at the course syllabus, her eyes glazed over reviewing the class description and demanding summer schedule.

"So, what the hell even *is* political science?" She frowned and tossed the syllabus aside, flipping the pages in the text to chapter one. A whine escaped her lips as she read the first paragraph—the core concepts and vocabulary instantly jumbling in her brain. "Austin, you're going to think I'm such an idiot…"

Casey dropped her hands to the cushion with defeat. Her palms raked over the material as the memory of her and Austin's first night as roommates reclaimed her mind. *I can't believe I did that.* She snorted, recalling her bold words and even bolder actions. *I can't believe you let me do that.*

For the last several days, Austin had kept his distance—happy to cuddle, happy to hold hands and continue their flirtatious banter, but he hadn't kissed her, or even brought up that first night together.

He's conflicted, still unsure of what or who he wants.

Casey huffed out a breath and tugged at the note she'd found from him on the kitchen counter, resting it atop her heart.

Case—
I didn't want to wake you. I forgot I had an appointment at nine to meet with a realtor. I need to start looking at locations for the firm. Keep the door locked until I get back, okay?
Austin

Her phone rang. Shoving the textbook from her lap, Casey tapped *accept* on Mavis's name.

"Casey!" Her former roommate's excitement reverberated in her eardrum.

"Hey, Mavs!" Casey grinned, putting her best friend on speaker. "How's California? How's Josh?"

"It's good! He's good! We're all good!" She giggled, the happiness with her new life evident in every exclamation.

"You sound really happy." Casey smiled and dropped her gaze to her lap.

"I am really happy, Case… but I miss you! How are things? How's Chicago? How's…" She hesitated.

"Oh, come on, you can say his name." Casey rolled her eyes. "Austin."

Mavis snorted. "Austin, apparently your new BFF now, right?"

"Oh, stop it. That's not fair and you know it!" Casey giggled, falling flat on the couch. She stretched her legs out and crisscrossed her ankles.

"It is too! He just like, moved in and stole you away from me!"

"Need I remind you that it was *you* who moved across the country?"

Well… I guess he did too?

"That didn't mean he had to move into my old apartment or into my old bedroom. It's kinda weird, isn't it?"

The initial excitement of the call floundered, the tone of Mavis's voice off-putting. Casey frowned as a knot formed in her gut, a restless defensiveness rising in her heart.

"Not really. He moved here for a job, Mavs. All I did was offer him a place to stay. He doesn't know anyone else in the city yet." She wrinkled her nose.

"You guys are just… really friendly. It feels weird to me," she admitted as her voice faltered.

"Well, I mean…" Casey hedged. "Isn't it better for you, though? That he's not in Rosewood right now?"

Mavis sighed. "For me? Yeah, I guess."

"You guess? Mavs, I know you have… er, *had* feelings for him. And he sure as shit still has feelings for you." Casey rolled her eyes again and returned to a sitting position.

"What has he said to you?"

"He doesn't have to *say* anything. I can see it, feel it." She frowned, tapping the speaker button again and bringing the phone back to her ear. "He's conflicted and confused."

"Case, tell me the truth. Are you guys, like…"

Well, the hell if I know!

Casey dropped her forehead into her left hand. "It doesn't matter. You're with Josh, right?"

"Yeah. I am. But that doesn't mean I don't care about Austin anymore. Or you for that matter!"

What the fuck is happening here?

"Look, I don't want to fight with you. This is stupid." She shook her head as a muffled sound in the hallway stole her attention.

"The only thing that's stupid here is if you're thinking about *dating* him. I can't let you do it, Case."

Anger flared, a sudden rush of contention hollowing out her heart. "I don't think you're really in a position to tell me—or him—who he can and cannot date."

"*Casey!*" she yelled. "My God! All I'm trying to do is protect you! And him! I don't want to see either of you get hurt!" She sniffled.

"Why would you think he'd hurt me?" Her gaze lifted to

the apartment door as something collided with the wall.

"Look, I've known him a lot longer than you have. And if he's still…" She swallowed. "As you say, hung up on me, then I just don't want you getting caught in the fallout, okay? Not after what happened to you last year."

The breath jammed in her throat, the words piercing her heart with a dull blade, impaling a wound still raw. She gulped.

"Look, it's simple. Men look for a rebound. I just don't want you to become the basketball."

Casey's gaze dropped to the couch cushion, Austin's eager response to her days ago resetting in her mind. *Was that all that was? A rebound?* Her stomach dropped, plummeting to the floor.

"That was the stupidest analogy I've ever heard," she whispered.

Mavis snorted. "Just keep your eyes open, okay? Don't get too close," she warned.

Silence filled the space between them as their words settled, biting into her heart.

"Hey, Case…" murmured Mavis. "He's not like us."

"Not like us?"

She sighed. "The Templetons. They just… they come from money. I'm not saying they're not good people. Because they are. But they just *see* things differently, experience the world differently. I've watched it my whole life."

An incoming call interrupted Mavis's voice. Pulling the phone from her ear, Austin's name flashed across the screen.

"I hear you, Mavs. I do." *Do I?* "But I'm sorry, I've gotta go. Lunch shift at Shaker. I have to go get ready."

"Promise me, Casey. Please? I don't want you to get hurt."

"Yeah. Promise. I'll keep my eyes open, all right?"

"Okay. I love you."

"Love you too. Bye." With shaking fingers, Casey ended

the call and accepted Austin's. "Hello?"

"Did I wake you?"

"Oh. No. I was just on the phone with... umm, the restaurant."

"I'm sorry. I didn't mean to interrupt."

"You didn't, no worries. What's up?"

"Can you meet me? I need your opinion on something."

Mavis's words lingered in her mind, her blunt warning slicing into her brain. *Screw it. Screw her. I'm getting really tired of her warnings.*

"Sure! Text me the address."

"Thanks, Cinderella."

Bibbidi-bobbidi-boo.

Within thirty minutes, Casey stood in front of a glass-walled skyscraper on Michigan Avenue. She peeked at her phone, double-checking the silver-plated numbers on the door with the address Austin texted her. *Yep, this is it.* She pushed her way through the revolving doors and stepped onto the shiny tile floor, its extravagant pattern looping and swirling her brain into a dizzy haze.

"Good morning, ma'am. Can I help you?" The receptionist shuffled a stack of papers, securing the corner with a paperclip.

"Umm, yeah, hi... I'm looking for suite 1260A."

The woman nodded. "Twelfth floor and hang a right." She pointed behind her to a pair of twin elevator doors.

"Thanks," muttered Casey as she headed around the desk. Her index finger stretched outward, tapping the call button. She grinned.

And how many germs were on that button, Austin?

The door to her right opened, and Casey hopped inside, tapping the number twelve on the panel. *Or that one?* With a click, the doors closed, just the faint notes of jazz music left to offer company. She surveyed the enclosure as the color gold screamed back. Everything from the plate around the buttons, to the excessively ornate walls, to the glittery gold streaks zigzagging through the carpet, shouted expensive—and wealth.

She staggered as the car lifted, each button lighting up as she rose higher and higher. *One... two... three...* Her stomach dipped. *Four... five... six...* Mavis's words rang in her ears. *Seven... eight... nine....* Her palms tingled as a sheen of sweat coated her brow. *Ten... eleven... twelve....* Casey huffed out a breath as the doors opened and a streak of the mid-morning sun blinded her.

Forcing her feet to move, she shielded her eyes and turned right, aiming for the slightly ajar door at the end of the hallway, the number 1260A stamped on the exterior. She exhaled, breathing out the nerves settling in her belly.

Why are you so nervous right now, Casey McDaniels?

"Just breathe," she whispered and pushed the door open, hurling Mavis's warning to the curb. A vacant office space with a floor-to-ceiling glass window wall met her gaze, flooded with sunshine throughout every inch of the room. Lake Michigan sparkled in the distance, the sun's rays reflecting off the water with beauty.

She stepped forward. *That view is fucking incredible!* As she navigated through the space, her gaze landed on Austin. Dressed in a navy-blue sport coat and silver tie, his left arm rested against the glass. The sun caught in his blond hair and illuminated the smirk on his lips. *But that view is even better.*

Distracted, her toe snagged the leg of a chair. It wobbled, threatening to crash as it bumped into an empty desk.

Austin's head snapped up. He grinned and dropped his arm from the window. "You always know how to make an entrance, don't you, Casey girl?" Winding his way in her direction through the maze of unused office furniture, he snorted.

Casey shoved the chair away. "If there's something to trip on, I'll find it." She giggled. "But Austin, that view..." She smiled and lifted her hand to point at the East window. "I mean, that's fucking incredible!"

"I know, right?" Austin stopped short before her. He leaned forward and pressed his lips to her forehead, melting her heart into a gooey puddle of mush deep within her chest. "I think this place is it, Case." A laugh tumbled from his lips as he lifted his gaze to return to the window.

"How did you find an empty suite on Michigan Avenue?" She squinted, shielding her eyes from the blinding sun.

"No idea. I guess Mrs. Harris has the inside scoop." He smiled, clasping her hand in his. "What do you think, though? This is it, right?" Austin tugged her toward the glass. The lake glimmered in the spring morning sunshine, Navy Pier smiling back in the distance.

"Well, I mean, you really can't beat this view."

"Way better than L.A.," he murmured. He squeezed her hand, sending a tingle to shimmy along her skin. "Should I do it?"

"Do what?"

"Sign the lease!" He laughed, a wide smile consuming his lips. The light caught the smattering of white lashes on his eye.

Her heart flip-flopped in her chest as the excitement bubbled from him, like a kindergartener ready to run out the door for recess.

"I don't think you'll find much better in this city." She tapped her finger to the glass. "But I'm no expert. My opinion doesn't mean too much." Casey snorted and tucked a curl behind her ear, dropping her gaze to the floor.

Austin scrunched his nose. "My dear Cinderella, your opinion means more to me than anyone else in the world right now."

Oh!

"Ahh! Mrs. Templeton! So lovely to meet you!" A woman in a brown pantsuit rounded the corner.

"Mrs. Templeton?" Casey whispered. The air escaped her lungs in one giant breath.

"Just go with it," he pleaded, raising his brow. His breath

tickled her ear as a grin tugged at her lips.

Mrs. Templeton, huh? Now that has a ring to it!

"Delighted to meet you too, Mrs.…." Casey extended her hand as the woman joined them at the window.

"Harris. Ellen Harris." Her fingers crushed Casey's in a handshake. *Ouch!* "So, what do you think?" She waved her arms at the view.

"Well, it's not called the Magnificent Mile for nothing." Casey grinned, slipping her aching hand back into Austin's. "It's exactly what my husband has been looking for." She squeezed his palm and avoided his face, fearful of the fit of giggles that would, without a doubt, overtake her if she caught his eye.

"Shall I draw up the papers?"

Austin nodded. "Well, since my wife approves, let's do it!" He smiled and returned the squeeze on Casey's palm.

"I should be able to have everything in order by about…" She tapped her watch. "Two this afternoon. Meet me back here then?" Smacking her gum against the roof of her mouth, she winked.

"Absolutely. Thank you, Mrs. Harris." Austin shook her hand.

"See you soon." She retreated, the heels of her shoes clicking down the hallway. *Clickety-clack, clickity-clack* until the elevator door closed.

"My dear husband. So kind of you to want my opinion this morning."

His eyes widened as an embarrassed grin cracked his lips. "I'm so sorry," he said with a snicker. "At some point, she just assumed I was married and started making comments about my wife, and I didn't know how to correct her without being weird." He shook his head and lifted his gaze again to the view of Lake Michigan.

"I just really didn't want anything to jeopardize this place, so I played along." His hand slid to her waist, his fingers tugging at the belt loops on her jeans. Pulling her body into his, he whispered, "Thanks for your help, Mrs.

Templeton."

The hesitation of the last few days seemingly disappeared as he leaned in and touched his lips to hers. The connection—electric and sizzling—returned her body and mind to the living room sofa.

If I'm a rebound, California boy… I won't stop you from scoring!

Dipping her hands beneath his jacket, Casey squeezed the muscles in his lower back. A groan escaped him as he deepened his kiss and toyed with the hem of her shirt.

Adrenaline hammered through her heart, his tongue exploring. Fueled by his sudden physical interest, her needy fingers worked, greedily yanking the jacket from his body. It dropped to the floor with a soft thud.

"Mmm… Casey girl," he murmured against her lips as he coaxed her right leg up and around his middle.

Shivers spasmed up and down her spine, and Austin cupped her bottom, scooting her body to a nearby desk. Her butt met the hard surface as he nudged her backward. Slipping from her foot, her right shoe fell—the weight of his body forcing her flat atop the desk.

"Mr. Templeton," she whispered in his ear as a frenzy of nerve cells imploded within her body, arousal clouding her brain with the touch of his lips on her neck.

With battered breath, he tugged at her jeans, unbuttoning until his hand grazed the top of her panties.

She moaned, stars erupting before her eyes as her back arched, desire flooding her system.

Austin returned his lips to hers as a single finger explored below the line of lace. Her skin, set ablaze by his touch, warmed, heat blanketing her body. A switch flipped in her brain, tuning out the cold wooden surface beneath her and the brilliant sunshine flooding the empty office. The physical space around them melted as her full attention rerouted, focused beneath the thin layer of lace separating them. She pressed herself into the force of his hand and groaned.

"So eager, Mrs. Templeton," he teased. His breath

tickled her skin as she shuddered beneath the weight of his body.

Casey inhaled, her heartbeat slamming into her ribcage as Austin's finger teased and then dipped inside her. The pressure set her skin ablaze, and her hand shot outward to steady herself. Her fingers collided with an ancient office phone, and it tumbled to the floor, the unexpected rattle lifting his spell of seduction.

"Hello? Hello?" A distant voice smothered the fire fueling the moment of passion. The voice echoed from the floor as Austin groaned and peeled himself from her body, replacing the receiver to the base with a soft click.

"Umm…" Casey dragged her hands along her pink cheeks and sat up, the warmth meeting her fingertips. She giggled and buried her face in her palms. "Oh, God."

Austin snickered and scratched at the stubble on his chin as his lips stretched into a wide grin. "Case… I, umm…"

Leaning back, she zipped and re-buttoned her jeans, willing her heartbeat to return to a normal pace and rhythm.

What the hell just happened? Were your hands just down my pants?

"Austin," she whispered, wrapping her arms around her body as she lifted her gaze to his and grinned. As she shook her head, her blonde curls tickled her cheeks.

He cleared his throat and bent down, scooping up his jacket and Casey's missing shoe. "You know, Casey girl…" He swallowed and pointed at the desk beneath her butt. "I think I'll put my office right here." Tapping the wood, he sank to his knees and slid her shoe back into place. "And this…" Austin lifted his gaze to hers. "Is definitely my new desk."

Her cheeks flushed as a dizzy spell overpowered her brain. His icy baby-blue eyes bore into hers as he stood and replaced his jacket. "Come on, Cinderella, let's get out of here while I still have the strength to control myself around you."

The breath caught in her throat.

I LOVE YOU TODAY

You can lose control like that anytime you want.

JULIE NAVICKAS

CHAPTER EIGHT

Austin

"The contractors are confirmed to start the renovations on Monday." Austin pressed the phone to his ear and leaned back in his seat. His gaze raked over the skyline from his new office. "There's some work to do, but they seem confident with a three-week turnaround."

"Well, keep us posted, kid. And hire yourself an assistant—or two. Just get 'em on the books before the end of the fiscal year, eh?" Steven Boyd's booming voice barked into the phone.

"There's about thirty-seven applicants in the pool right now." Austin leaned forward and scrolled through the growing list in his inbox. He grinned as another one popped in. "Make that thirty-eight."

"Loop Bernice in for the details, but just hire what you need."

Austin nodded and tapped the screen.

"I appreciate that, sir."

"Keep going, kid. You're doing great. Anything you need, just move on it. We trust you."

Austin swallowed, gulping down the compliments from

two thousand miles away. "Thank you," he choked out as a bead of sweat glistened on his forehead.

"Up and running by August, Templeton."

His eyes widened, glancing at the calendar. *Three months.* "That's the plan," he murmured, swallowing a bundle of nerves. "And I'll keep you updated on the construction."

"Sounds good. Enjoy the weekend."

"Thanks. You too."

Steven ended the call, and Austin dropped back in his chair. He sucked in a breath, replaying the conversation in his mind. His gaze surveyed the empty space around him. Within the last two weeks, a team had dismantled every cubicle and rolled out every chair. Austin tapped the surface of his desk with a grin. *Except for this piece.* His hand skimmed the surface, recalling the moment he claimed it for his own. *Cinderella...*

Snapping his laptop closed, Austin packed up his things, tossed his jacket on, and headed out of the suite for the weekend. Within minutes, the roar of the red line clattered down the tracks and stopped at the platform. He hopped into a crowded car and stuffed his hands inside his coat before taking a seat. *I love this city, but I really miss my Vette.*

The train stopped at Addison. Stepping outside, Austin headed down the rickety stairs of the platform as his phone vibrated in his pocket. He rounded the corner and cringed as Lauren's name flashed across the screen.

Shit. I owe you a call. Or three...

"Hello?"

"So, you are alive! I guess I owe Josh twenty bucks."

"Shit, I'm sorry, Lauren." He shook his head as the apartment building came into view. "I suck. I should have called you sooner."

"No... no... we all know you're busy. Just wanted to check in though. How's Chicago?"

He grinned. "You know, Lauren, it's good. Everything is just..." He lifted his gaze to the third floor of the building, automatically searching for Mavis's old room. But it landed on Casey's instead, her glowing red Christmas lights brightening the spring afternoon. "Really good." He snickered and sat down on the front stoop, his butt meeting the cold concrete.

"You sound happy, Austin."

I haven't felt this good in a long time.

"I am." He swallowed, recalling the moment Boyd and Bernstein offered him the job. As if they knew he *needed* it.

"We miss you though." Her voice wavered. "I miss you."

"I miss you too." He sighed. *I should have called you sooner.* "Umm... how're you? How's the restaurant?"

She snorted. "Still standing. Still a pain in my butt. You know how it is."

"And Mitch?"

"Umm, well you know. Mitch is Mitch. We'll push through it." She cleared her throat. "Oh! But hey, tell me about Casey. You know Mavs is still totally rattled that you moved in with her!"

Austin brought his hand to his heart, anticipating the squeeze at the sound of her name, the familiar tightening in his gut at the mention of his princess. He closed his eyes, waiting for the sorrow to spread.

"Austin?"

Opening his eyes, he dropped his hand to his lap and snorted, snickering into the phone. His heartbeat held steady—rhythmic and calm. *Well, how about that...* "Casey. You know, Casey is, umm... she's been really good to me. Good *for* me I think." He grinned and shook his head.

"You think you'll stay living with her?"

"I want to." He turned, staring through the building's door into the lobby. "You should come visit. Meet her and see the city. Want to?"

"Yes! Oh, that sounds so fun!" A shouting match echoed through the phone as something crashed. "Oh shit, I gotta go. Chaos in the kitchen!"

"Go ahead. We'll talk later. Love ya."

She groaned. "Ugh, love you too." The call ended, and Austin pulled himself from the step. After ramming his key in the door, he jogged up the stairs. His briefcase banged into the railing as the distant beat of an all too familiar pop song met his ears.

"Oh, God," he moaned, pushing the door open into the apartment. Austin stepped inside and cringed, the memories of Lauren's pre-teen years flashing through his brain.

Casey consumed the living room floor. Propped up on her elbows, she rested her stomach atop the carpet—her lips mouthing the lyrics as she bopped along to the nostalgic nineties beat. A flood of notecards and an open textbook surrounded her, and Austin grinned at the curls in her ponytail as they bounced from side to side.

"Dear Lord, make it stop." He dropped his briefcase to the table and removed his jacket and shoes—tossing his keys and wallet to the surface as well.

"No way!" Casey stretched, rolling from her belly to her back. "Don't you dare!"

On tiptoes, Austin hopped through the maze of notecards and gripped the knob to lower the volume on the ancient speaker. Justin Timberlake disappeared from the room as Casey rolled her eyes.

"I'm having flashbacks to my childhood."

"Oh, no way! You're an N'SYNC fan too?" She giggled. "I pegged you for a Backstreet Boys groupie."

Austin snorted and dropped to his knees. With a smirk, he crawled between her legs and planted a kiss on her lips. "You're tearin' up my heart. Everyone knows N'SYNC is the superior boyband." He shifted and pressed his lips to her neck, eliciting a sharp intake of her breath. "But if I have to listen to it any longer, I'm going to be the one running out of here singing Bye, Bye, Bye."

Her laugh filled the small space, each giggle tumbling from her lips a stitch on his once-broken heart.

"Like you could measure up to Justin Timberlake." She grinned, raising her hands to cup the back of his head. She tugged and pulled his mouth back onto hers.

A flurry of shivers sizzled along his skin as the weight of his body connected with hers. She moaned, running her fingernails through his hair, tightening her legs around his middle. "Trapped," she murmured with a smile.

Bracing his hands on either side of her body, he snickered as her thighs squeezed him in place. His palm met one of the notecards she'd flung across the floor. Peering at her print, Austin read, *State vs. Nation: what's the difference?* He flipped the card over. She hadn't answered.

"What're you looking at?" Casey frowned and pinched his side.

"This notecard. You haven't answered the question." Pressing his lips to her forehead, he pulled away.

"No, don't go!" she pleaded and gripped the collar of his shirt.

"Casey girl, what kind of tutor would I be if I seduced you instead of helped you study?"

Snorting, she climbed onto his lap. "I didn't know seduction was on the table. Tell me more." She dragged her finger down the length of his chest.

Austin smiled, pushing away the growing excitement her traveling finger incited in his belly. "Oh, I have a few ideas," he whispered and pressed his lips to the delicate skin beneath her ear. "But you have to study first." Lifting her body from his lap, he set her beside him.

"Oh, my God, you suck." She rolled her eyes and dropped her head against the couch.

Austin leaned forward, scooping up the notecards littering the floor. "You can suck something of mine later, but right now… political science it is, Casey girl." He grinned and pulled the *State vs. Nation* card to the top of the pile. "Come on, let's start with this one." He tapped the card, his cheeks reddening with heat at the glare she delivered.

"I'm not sucking anything of yours if you make me look at this stuff any longer."

Snorting, he lifted his gaze to the ceiling.

Well, if you're serious...

"When's your first test?" He threw his arm around her shoulder.

"Next Friday," she answered, snuggling back into him.

"We've got time then. How about this... let's go out tonight and have some fun and then we'll tackle this stuff together in the morning?" He inhaled, the now familiar scent of lilacs overtaking his nose from the top of her head.

She smiled. "What do you have in mind?"

"You pick." Squeezing her knee, he stood. "I gotta shower before we do anything though. Ten minutes, okay?"

She nodded.

Tugging at the buttons on his shirt, Austin yanked the material from his body. It brushed against his nose as he pulled it free from his arms. *What's that?* Pressing the shirt to his face, he frowned.

"Does this smell like smoke to you?" He held out the shirt with a wrinkled nose, and Casey cringed, ducking her head into her lap.

Burying her face in her hands, she whined. "I'm sorry! I know it's gross, okay?"

"Wait... you smoke?"

Eww, really?

She shrugged, still hiding her face. "It's a bad habit. I get it, all right?"

Austin sighed and rubbed at the muscles in his neck. "Umm... yeah." He frowned. "I guess I just didn't know that about you." His brain revisited the day they met. *But you did have a lighter.*

She jumped from the floor, her bare feet pounding past him and into the kitchen.

He followed, rounding the corner as she tugged a pack of cigarettes and a lighter from her purse and dumped them both into the trash.

"I quit. I promise." She wrapped her arms around her body, the tips of her ears turning pink. "Mavis was always on me about it too. I swear, I only do it when I'm just a little stressed."

Austin inhaled, his gaze running the length of her defeated, embarrassed form. Instinctually, he stepped forward and wrapped her in his embrace.

She fell into his chest and sighed. "Did I completely gross you out?" she whispered, pressing her lips to his skin.

A shiver snaked through him at the tickle. "Not even close." With a squeeze of her hips, he pulled away. "But for what it's worth, I'm glad you just quit."

She nodded and rubbed her hands along her arms.

"Ten minutes, okay?" Stepping backward, Austin pushed the door open to the bathroom and gripped the faucet. Hot water burst through the pipes as he nudged the door closed and yanked off his remaining clothes.

Her voice called from the kitchen. "Bleacher seats for twenty bucks in center field?"

"My wallet is on the table! Use the blue card!"

Go, Cubs, Go!

Casey shuffled through the crowd, leading Austin to their seats in center field. The lights, the music, the trademark ivy, and the enormity of the fandom brought to life had his heart palpitating. His butt plunked down on the bleachers beside her as his gaze soaked in the historic magic of Wrigley Field, Casey's larger-than-life obsession.

Wrapping his arm around her waist, he tugged her body closer to his as the sky darkened in the spring evening. His foot crunched a stray peanut shell, and an empty hot dog wrapper blew across their toes in the gentle breeze.

"What do you think?" She turned, tilting her face upward as a smile consumed her lips.

"Well, it's definitely not Dodger Stadium."

She giggled and wrapped her arm around him in return. "You're right. It's even better."

Agree to disagree.

The game started and the Cubs took an early lead at the bottom of the first inning against Baltimore. The wind wafted the scent of popcorn through the air, and Austin turned, spotting a beer vendor.

"Thirsty?" He nudged Casey in the side and pointed.

"Always." She smiled, seemingly resistant to tear her gaze from the field.

Pulling a twenty-dollar bill from his wallet, Austin handed it to the vendor and accepted two foaming cups of golden liquid. His lips split into a grin as he handed Casey a cup. "Please tell me this isn't…" He cringed.

"You know it is." She roared with laughter as her hand dropped to his knee and squeezed. "I mean, it's kind of like our thing now though, isn't it?" She tapped her cup to his. "Cheers."

Austin nodded and brought the cup of Old Style to his lips, grimacing as the liquid met his tongue. *I guess it is kind of our thing.* The memory of Old Crow returned to his brain. *And just where would I be without you right now?* He smiled and gripped her tighter. "Cheers, Case."

A boo hissed through the ballpark as Chicago allowed Baltimore to score a triple on a fielding error. The crowd groaned as Casey shuffled her feet, frowning into her beer. "E5," she muttered.

This girl puts me to shame.

He grinned and nudged her in the side. "So, umm… can I ask you a question?"

"Ask away."

"What would you think about my sister coming to visit?"

Casey smirked. "The one who loves N'SYNC? Absolutely!" Her hand returned to his knee and dragged along his thigh.

"She was like twelve when she was into boy bands. Not an adult like you." He snorted, his gaze falling to her hand. She rotated her thumb in small circles, the sensation warming his body in the cool evening.

"Oh, whatever. I won't buy us tickets to the Backstreet

Boys tour then."

"I thought you were an N'SYNC girl." Her thumb stopped, and disappointment squeezed his heart.

"I mean, they're the only ones still touring." She giggled and leaned her head against his shoulder. "But I'd love to meet your sister, Austin. She'll know all your embarrassing childhood secrets."

The crowd erupted in cheers as each of their fellow bleacher ticket holders flew from their seats. A homerun ball bounced into the stands four rows away and a mob of drunken men dove for the ball.

"I don't have any embarrassing childhood secrets."

Casey straightened and gulped down the rest of her beer. "Umm, yeah right. We all have something that makes us cringe."

He dropped his empty cup into hers. "All right, fine. You tell me one of yours and I'll tell you one of mine."

She tapped a finger to her cheek and lifted her gaze to the sky. "Hmm… okay well, you know how I'm a total klutz?"

"The defense rests."

Casey rolled her eyes. "All right, so my mom thought it would be a good idea to put me in ballet lessons when I was like seven. And I kid you not, I single-handedly destroyed the entire recital. Swan Lake became a swan shitshow. I tripped two minutes into the routine and took down the whole line of dancers and some decorations."

With a snort, he leaned forward and pressed his lips to hers.

Nothing about that is hard to imagine.

She giggled. "All right, it's your turn. Don't think your kisses will distract me, sir." She smiled and poked him in the chest.

Austin laughed, capturing her hand in his. He planted a kiss on the tip of her ring finger. "You have to promise me that you'll never tell anyone."

With her hand still caught in his, Casey raised her pinky

in the air. "A pinky swear is serious business. It's a promise for life." Her brow rose in jest.

Latching his pinky around hers, Austin returned his gaze to the field. The Cubs led Baltimore by one in the sixth inning.

"Take it to the grave, Casey McDaniels." He huffed out a breath. "My mom made Josh and me take ballroom dance lessons in junior high." His eyes widened at the admission.

"Oh, my God, Austin!" She cackled, tipping her head back with laughter. "You know, that makes a ton of sense. You were way too good a dancer at Old Crow!" She raised a finger to her eye and brushed a tear of amusement away.

Austin elbowed her in the gut. "All of my Tuesday evening waltz adventures with Mrs. Pennington have really paid off." He grinned. "If you're lucky, I'll teach you the Texas two-step one day." His cheeks burned with embarrassment.

She snuggled into him, resuming her grip on his thigh. "Actually, I hope my luck doesn't hold out for that one."

"You'll be sorry, Casey girl." A jolt of pleasure raced along his skin as her fingers explored higher, the light scrape of her nails doubling his heartbeat. Adjusting his hat, he turned to find her blue eyes staring at him. "This was a good idea. Thanks for bringing me here."

"Well, you're not a true Chicagoan until you've seen a game at Wrigley." She flicked the brim of his hat and smiled. "And don't even ask about that other team to the South," she added.

Austin wracked his brain, digging deep into his limited knowledge of baseball. *Why can't you like basketball?* "Oh, umm... the White Sox, right?"

"Shh! You can't say that out loud here!" She pressed her index finger over his lips.

He pecked the tip of her finger with a kiss. "Sorry," he breathed. "I'm a Dodgers fan, remember?"

"And it's the worst thing about you, Mr. Templeton."

A chorus of "Take Me Out to the Ballgame" boomed

throughout the park, the seventh-inning-stretch celebrations interrupting their spirited disagreement.

"When did that happen?" Casey wrinkled her nose and scanned the ball field. "You distract me too much."

An elbow to his right side jabbed him in the gut. *Ouch!* Austin turned as the woman beside him pointed toward the field at the gigantic screen above the scoreboard. His eyes widened as his and Casey's image stared back, squarely tucked within the shape of a pink heart, the words *KISS CAM* emblazoned in bold.

Casey roared with laughter and yanked his hat from his head. Her bright blue eyes sparkled in the stadium lights, her gaze hovering over his mouth. Leaning in, Austin pressed his lips to hers as the fans erupted in cheers, their claps freezing the moment. The lights faded. The cold bleachers melted away, and all that existed was the quirky girl in his arms, the girl who had unknowingly mended his soul with the stitch of a baseball. He deepened the kiss, bathing in the sweet contentment consuming his heart.

I think I'm falling for you, Casey girl. Hard... and fast...

Austin gripped her hand as they walked down the sidewalk. The streetlamps illuminated their steps, casting shadows on the pavement as they strolled the nearly deserted path in the early morning hours. After eleven innings, Chicago had pulled out a victory.

"What did you think of your first Cubs game, California boy?"

"You can't call me a Chicago fan yet." He pulled her hand to his lips and pressed a kiss on her soft skin. "But I can't complain. The company exceeded my expectations."

She grinned as her cheeks flushed. "I will admit, I've never been to a game where I found myself more interested in the person sitting beside me."

His heart fluttered. "Well, Miss E. Banks, I think that might just be the highest compliment you can give me." He smiled and tugged the keys from his pocket, pushing the small gold one into the lock. "After you." He held the door open.

Casey stepped inside, climbing the stairs as her hands glided along the railing. On the second floor, her feet faltered.

"You okay?"

She turned. "You know, Austin, I don't think I've, er... said the words." As she shook her head, a curl fell from her ponytail into her face. "I'm really glad you moved here," she whispered.

The breath caught in his throat as the words fell from her lips.

"I was pretty depressed when Mavis told me she was moving." Pulling away, she started to climb again, dropping her gaze to the dirty stairs. "And I never thought I'd find someone to take her place. But you kinda have."

Ignore the irony...

His heart leapt from his chest as he followed, his hand reaching for hers. He gripped her fingers as they arrived on the third-floor landing. "And I haven't even made you a cheesy sandwich yet. Some roommate, I am."

She grinned, unlocking the door and pushing it open. "You did promise me a cheesy sandwich, Chef Templeton." She winked as Austin tugged her hands into his chest, resting them above his heart.

"I'll make you a cheesy sandwich, but I want to tell you something too."

She nodded.

His pulse quickened, adrenaline hammering through his bloodstream as her doe-like eyes searched his soul. "I know we kid with each other a lot, but I need you to know." He ran a thumb along her bottom lip. "You're not just a roommate to me. You never really were."

She licked her lips.

"The day I met you, I'd never been at a lower point in my life. And it was like you were just standing in the stairwell, waiting for me. Waiting for us…"

She smiled. "More like trip—"

He pressed his lips to hers as he tugged her inside and shut the door. Her purse dropped to the floor with a thud as her leg lifted to wrap around his middle. "Austin…" she murmured against his mouth.

A shiver ran through him as her fingernails raked his hairline. "My Casey girl…" He dropped his hands to squeeze her butt, lifting her small body into his arms, the pressure grating against his pelvis and fogging his brain.

He carried her down the hallway and backed into her darkened bedroom, lit solely by the Christmas lights in the window. He stumbled, stubbing his toe on an unknown heavy object. "Shit. Ouch!"

"Sorry! It's my textbook!" She giggled. "I told you political science wasn't a good idea."

He snorted and set her on her feet, tugging his leg upward to rub his toe. "Yeah, but it's kinda what brought me to you," he whispered, dropping his foot back to the floor. He lifted his shirt up and over his head. It fell, covering the offending textbook.

"I guess it's not all bad then." Her gaze raked over his bare chest.

Drawing her body closer, Austin gripped her hands and pressed them to his heart. He dropped his forehead to hers as her fingers explored, each fingertip ice cold to the heat radiating from his body.

With a grin, he tugged at the hem of her shirt until she raised her arms. He lifted the soft material from her body, pulling it free until she gasped. Pressing his lips back to hers, he unhooked her bra and cupped her breasts.

She groaned, dropping her head back as his palms glided over her nipples. "Mmm… Austin…" she whimpered. "More."

Warmth thundered through him, the purr of her plea squeezing his heart and wringing it dry until every ounce of adrenaline in his system flooded his veins.

Her hands dropped to the zipper on his pants. The pressure in his groin built, growing and mounting with each ragged breath she took. Anticipation roared through his bloodstream as her fingers fumbled with the button and dragged the zipper down. She tugged the material from his hips, letting it fall to his ankles.

"Casey…" he whispered as she sank to her knees, taking his boxers with her.

His breath hitched as her fingers encased the length of him.

"You did say I could suck something of yours later," she whispered.

I'll never ask you to study again…

The air escaped his lungs as her mouth closed over him. He groaned, threading his fingers through her hair as she moved, shockwaves of pleasure exploding inside each nerve cell in his body. Her lips brought goosebumps to his flesh, chilling the sweat glistening on his skin. Closing his eyes, he worked to right the dizzying sensation invading his brain. He choked on the air in his lungs and gently nudged her back. "I'm… uh…" he moaned. "I'm not gonna last very long if you keep doing that."

She pressed a kiss to his belly and snickered. "Another time," she whispered and rose, guiding him to the bed.

Casey fell backward as he gripped the zipper on her jeans. He tugged, yanking the material from her legs. The red glare of the Christmas lights cast a hazy glow over her pale skin as he trailed his tongue down her torso. Pausing at the tattoo on her waist, Austin grinned and lowered his lips to press a kiss onto the outline of a royal-blue bear cub.

"Mmm," she moaned, arching her back. "Now you know, Mr. Templeton."

With a smirk, he tugged at her panties until they fell to the floor with the other discarded clothing. Heat surged through his body as he moved on top of her, positioning himself between her knees, pressing his arousal to her entry.

He groaned, a panicked thought slamming into his brain.

"Case, do I need…"

Her breath tickled the side of his neck. "No, I've got us covered," she whispered. Arching her back again, she pressed herself against him with impatience. "Austin, please," she begged.

"Always so eager, Casey girl," he murmured. His eyes closed as he slid into her.

She inhaled, the air catching in her throat as she moaned, the sweet sound of his own name ringing in his ear.

Euphoria clouded his brain as he pulled out, the pressure mounting with each entry. He moved, increasing the speed as her fingernails bit into his back, each pinprick digging deeper the faster he moved.

Casey called out his name as her body erupted in shivers beneath him. With a final breath, he spilled himself inside of her, following her quick lead. His heart softened, his soul opening to encase her own, bonded by the moment fueled by passion and desire.

"My sweet Cinderella," he murmured and rolled to her side. Pressing a hand to her heart, his fingers rose and fell with each breath she took. "You okay?" he whispered, brushing a stray curl from her face and tucking it behind her ear.

"Starving. I'm ready for my cheesy sandwich." She grinned and closed her eyes.

Austin snickered and pulled her closer, pressing his nose into the field of lilacs. Her head rested on his chest, and within seconds, her breathing slowed to a rhythmic pattern as she drifted off to sleep.

"Falling hard and fast, Casey."

She didn't stir.

Closing his eyes, he nodded off, contentment and happiness settling in his heart.

JULIE NAVICKAS

CHAPTER NINE

Casey

Austin pushed a plate of warm pancakes in front of her. "Eat. You need a good breakfast."

Her stomach churned, the sugary scent of the syrup nauseating.

"I can't. I'm too nervous." She shoved the plate away with a frown.

"Casey girl, come on, you know this stuff. Backward and forward." He pushed the plate back in her direction. "Besides, it's just a test."

She rolled her eyes. "Yeah, to you! Mr. Do Everything Perfectly."

He snorted. "Huh?"

"Never mind."

Austin leaned forward, resting his elbows on the kitchen counter. "You're smarter than you give yourself credit for, Casey McDaniels."

She shook her head. "Hardly. You should see my high school transcripts."

"High school doesn't matter." He grinned, chopping a pancake on her plate in half with a fork.

"Maybe not to you. What were you... like valedictorian?"

He snorted, shoving a bite into his mouth. "Salutatorian." He winked. "Josh beat me."

Good Lord. I was joking.

"Oh, God." Casey tugged her hand through her hair, a fresh wave of anxiety stabbing her in the gut.

"Look, Case. All that matters right now is you." He pushed the perfectly cut-up pancake back in her direction. "And you need a good breakfast this morning." The right side of his mouth tugged upward in a smile.

With a roll of eyes, Casey picked up the fork and stabbed a bite, the gooey syrup oozing to the plate. She stuffed it in her mouth and the sugar collided with her tongue.

Oh, these are Heaven.

"Good?"

"You know they are." She shoved another bite in her mouth and smirked, wiping the stray syrup from her chin.

He tapped the counter and grinned, turning to attack the dirty dishes. "It's backed by research, you know. Higher test scores are linked to a healthy breakfast."

She stuffed another bite in her mouth and chewed. "Healthy?"

"All right..." He snorted. "Let's amend that to *tasty* instead." Snickering, he dried the frying pan with a dishcloth and returned it to the corner cabinet. "I have to run, beautiful." Stepping around the corner, he planted a kiss on the top of her head. "But I know you'll do great."

"If you say so..."

"Don't forget, Lauren's flight gets in at eleven. Text me when you're done, and I'll meet you back here, okay?"

Casey nodded, forcing a smile on her lips. "Can't wait to meet her." Her stomach dropped.

Austin snagged his briefcase from the dining room table, pulled his keys from his pocket, and opened the door. "Good luck, Cinderella." He smiled and stepped into the hallway, pulling the door closed behind him. His key twisted in the lock as his footsteps disappeared.

And just where is your fairytale magic when I need it?

The little blue Ford rolled into a parking space. Casey yanked the keys from the ignition and sighed. No matter how sweet Austin's efforts, the nerves in her belly still sparked like the frayed end of a wire.

First this stupid test… and then meeting Lauren… yikes! Today is gonna be a rough one.

She pulled her curls into a ponytail as raindrops smacked against the windshield. Leaning back, she exhaled as the morning's events washed over her.

"Salutatorian?" she muttered. "You were probably top of your class at law school too." She stared out the window at the front sign on the brick building, her eyes skimming over the bold orange letters of Harold Washington Community College.

How the hell are you even interested in me, Austin?

Casey blew out a breath and tossed the keys in her bag as her heart stalled, the sickening, sudden realization squeezing the air from her lungs. *God, I could use a cigarette right now.* Her fingers brushed against a piece of paper in her bag and she tugged, revealing Austin's handwriting.

Good luck today, Casey girl! You'll do great! Top of the class, no doubt.

XOXO
Austin

Casey scowled, his confidence in her churning the pancakes in her stomach as she rammed the note back into her purse. *It's just a test.* His words drifted over her, grating at her soul as his image appeared standing in a glass window on the twelfth floor of Michigan Avenue. "You're right, Austin. To *you*, it is just a test."

JULIE NAVICKAS

She swallowed and yanked the car door open. Sprinting through the rain, she tugged at her hood until she reached the front door. Her wet shoes squeaked against the tile in the main hall as she headed to her classroom and grasped the doorknob.

"Ready or not," she whispered, pushing it open and navigating to her seat at the back of the room. And within minutes, Dr. Lavine dropped the exam on her desk, Casey's heart thudding to the floor as twelve pages of test questions looked back.

She swallowed, fighting the vomit rising in her throat. Every high school exam she'd ever taken flashed before her eyes, the anxiety from each test pooling in the pit of her stomach.

I'm just so bad at this stuff!

She sighed and lifted her gaze to her neighbor. Her pencil flew across the page, hastily filling in bubbles on her scantron sheet with quick answers. Casey rolled her eyes and heaved out a sigh, slouching in her seat as a familiar bout of insecurity settled in her heart—her sworn enemy.

Pressing her pencil to the paper, the tip flew into oblivion. *Fucking great.* She rummaged in her bag, wrapping her fingers around another pencil as the back of her hand brushed against Austin's note. With a small shake of her head, she scratched her name onto the page and looked down at question one. *True or false: States are cultural entities while nations are political.*

She wrinkled her nose, waiting for Austin's smart and sexy lawyer voice to invade her mind with the nuances of a nation-state. His methodical explanation reclaimed her brain and she bubbled in false.

Stealing another glance at her neighbor, Casey frowned.

"Are you okay, Miss McDaniels?" Dr. Levine leaned forward in his chair, his gaze peering down the aisle of students to the back row.

Oh shit! He thinks I'm cheating!

Casey nodded and dropped her gaze back to her own

paper. With a sigh, she powered through the multiple choice and true-false questions as Austin's explanations and examples replayed in her mind with each flip of the page. After an hour, she turned to the essay. Pressing her pencil back to the paper, she wrapped up the test with a five-paragraph essay about the practical application of a political science course on her future career.

She turned in the exam and rushed to the door, ready to sprint across the parking lot. *Lauren's flight lands in less than an hour.* But as her hands pushed open the building's main door, her phone vibrated in her back pocket with a text. Jim's name appeared with the schedule for the next week at The Broken Shaker. Casey eyed it, scrolling through the double shifts she'd begged for to accommodate a couple of free nights while Lauren was in town.

"Ugh," she groaned, ramming her hood back over her head. Casey pushed open the door and jogged back to Mavis's car, throwing her body into the front seat as the rain lessened to a steady drizzle. She swallowed, willing the unease away as her phone rang.

Austin.

"Hello?"

"How'd it go?"

"Umm… I mean, I think I did okay." She stuffed the key in the ignition and waited for the engine to hum to life.

"I'm sure you did great, Casey girl. But ah, hey… I'm running late. Can you swing by and pick me up at the office instead?"

"Yeah sure, no problem. I can be there in about fifteen minutes."

"Great. See you soon… Oh! And Case, Lauren can't wait to meet you." Austin ended the call.

Casey swallowed, dropping her phone into the cup holder. Her hand fell to the gear shaft, cupping the faded material with a dab of blue nail polish. She grinned.

Mavis.

"I miss you, Mavs," she whispered as her feet pressed

into the petals. Shifting into reverse, her best friend's voice wafted to the forefront of her brain. *He's not like us. The Templetons… They see the world differently.* Her warning echoed in her ears as she pulled up to the stop sign.

What if Lauren doesn't like me?

Disquiet crept back into her mind, wrapped in a blanket of doubt and self-pity. Her gaze lifted to the building as she continued down the road. "Harold Washington Community College," she whispered to herself. "Not exactly impressive…"

The last month of her life looped on repeat through her brain, the fairytale story of her heart falling for the man with white eyelashes. Glancing back up at the community college sign again, the air caught in her throat. "I hate that you're right, Mavs."

Insecurity followed her as she turned left and hit the highway.

"I'm a safe driver, Austin."

He snorted, pulling his gaze from the line of stop-and-go traffic at O'Hare International. "Casey, you duct taped the rearview mirror to the windshield." He tapped the newly repaired mirror, professionally adhered to the center of the window with perfection. "That's not exactly within my definition of safe driving."

"Ugh, whatever." She glowered and rolled down the window from the passenger seat as the sun peeked through the clouds for the first time that morning.

Austin squeezed her thigh. "You okay?" He pulled the sunglasses from the top of his head and dropped them on his nose.

"Umm, yeah. Why?" She tipped her head back, letting her cheek rest against the seatbelt strap. Her heart flipped in her chest, toying with the revelation that struck her earlier.

What do you see in me?

The traffic came to a standstill. "You seem weird. Talk

I LOVE YOU TODAY

to me."

"What if your sister doesn't like me?" The words vomited from her lips, tumbling outward in a rush.

He grinned. "That's what you're worried about? That she won't like you?" He snorted. "Case, she's gonna love you!" He squeezed her leg again.

Unease gripped her gut and she frowned. "You're gonna make me say it, aren't you?"

He wrinkled his nose. "I'm so confused. Say what?" The traffic inched forward, and he released the brake, the car jerking forward ten feet before stopping again.

"I mean… I'm just not really like you, or her. I'm afraid she won't *approve* of me, you know?" Casey dropped her gaze to the floor, peering at the seam about to split in the toe of her shoe.

"*Approve* of you? What the hell are you talking about?" He yanked the sunglasses from his face and dumped them in his lap.

She huffed out a breath. "Austin, come on. You're like this hot-shot lawyer. Your brother is a freaking doctor. And your sister owns this fancy restaurant in Los Angeles. I don't even know what your parents do… but geez. I'm a fucking bartender taking gen eds at community college!" The distress poured from her lips, every ounce of insecurity tumbling from the truth in her heart.

"Where the hell did that come from?" Austin widened his eyes, reaching over to grasp her hand. He tugged her fingers to his lips and pressed a kiss to her palm. "Casey girl?"

Tears burned the back of her lids. "Never mind, just ignore me," she choked out. "It's just something stupid Mavis said."

He shook his head and furrowed his brow. "First off, do me a favor and never listen to Mavis." He tugged at her hand. "And second, there's not a chance in hell I'm going to ignore you." Austin squeezed her fingers, pressing her hand into his heart. "Tell me what's really bothering you here."

Anger flared, a mounting realization stirring in her soul. "I'm not good enough for you, Austin Templeton."

"Who are you? And what did you do with my girlfriend?"

Casey rolled her eyes and pulled away.

I sound like a freaking psychopath right now.

"Casey," he whispered, reaching over to squeeze her hand. "Look at me. Please?"

With her sleeve, she wiped the offending tears away from her cheeks and turned. His head swiveled, working to balance the heated conversation and the line of traffic as the terminal approached.

"You are absolutely everything to me, Casey girl. In every way that matters, you are my equal." He tugged her hand back to his lips.

She scrunched her nose. "Be real, Austin. You're like this wealthy, sexy, successful man with a glass castle on Michigan Avenue. And I'm just this paycheck-to-paycheck bartender failing general education courses at community college. You see the difference, right?"

"Is that what this is about? Your test today?"

She scrunched down in her seat and rested her knees against the dashboard like a child. "No… I don't know. I just can't help thinking that your family won't like me, that you should be with someone better. Someone more accomplished."

The car crept beneath the overhang of the terminal. "Case, hear me when I tell you that you're flat-out wrong on this." He took a deep breath and exhaled. "People like you, people like Mavis… you're survivors. I had every advantage growing up. I fully admit that." He steered the car into an empty spot beside baggage claim five and six and waved to his sister. "If anything, you're *better* than me. You've accomplished way more." He leaned over and placed a kiss on her damp cheek. "Let's talk about this later, okay?"

Casey nodded and unbuckled her seatbelt. Plastering a false smile on her lips, she opened the door.

What did I just do?

"So, Casey, have you lived in Chicago long?" Lauren shoved a bite of the Cheesecake Factory's signature cobb salad in her mouth before wiping her lips with a satin napkin.

"Oh, yeah, umm for a while now." Casey sipped on a cocktail in the afternoon sunshine—every seat and table taken on the popular restaurant's patio. "I moved to Wrigleyville about eight years ago, but I grew up on the north side of the city. Lawndale. Er, North Lawndale."

"Is that far from here?" Austin squeezed Casey's knee below the table.

"Like a half hour. My mom still lives there."

He nodded, shoving the drink menu away from him.

"What made you move?" Lauren slurped from her straw, stirring the melting ice around in her glass.

"Oh… well, after my dad passed away, I just needed a change of scenery. And living downtown made it easier to find a job."

Austin tugged her hand into his lap and gripped her fingers. "I didn't know that." He squinted.

With her free hand, Casey pulled her drink toward her, sucking at the straw until only the ice remained. "Umm, yeah. Sorry, kind of a heavy topic, you know?"

The waiter reappeared at Casey's side with another round of drinks on his tray.

Thank God.

"Two more pineapple mojitos." With a grin, he set the two glasses down in front of Lauren and Casey. "And another water for you, sir?" His eyes widened as he pointed to the half-empty ice water in front of Austin.

He shook his head. "No thanks, I'm good."

The waiter nodded and shuffled away to a neighboring

table with a raised brow.

"I'm on the clock," muttered Austin with an eye roll.

A grin tugged at Casey's lips, watching the mild embarrassment tinge his cheeks pink.

"Do you ever stop working?" Lauren smiled, pulling the pineapple garnish from the glass and popping it in her mouth.

"On rare occasions, I can drag him to a Cubs game." Casey laughed and winked as Austin leaned forward, propping his elbows on the table.

"Cute, ladies. Go ahead, gang up on me." He tugged his phone from his pocket and scanned the screen with a frown.

Casey rolled her eyes. "So, Lauren, have you been to Chicago before? Anything you want to see or do while you're here?"

"I haven't! But I would love to see Millennium Park and the Bean. Oh! And Buckingham Fountain, Navy Pier..." She checked off the list on each of her fingers. "And the lookout platform on Willis Tower too."

The touristy of all tourist attractions.

Casey forced a smile on her lips. "Everyone just calls it the Sears Tower still."

"Well, look at our little expert tour guide." He tugged her hand to his lips and pressed a kiss to her skin as his phone vibrated, catching the edge of the ceramic appetizer plate in the center. It rattled, colliding with the aluminum tabletop. Austin frowned as he scooped it up.

"Everything okay?" Lauren pointed to the phone.

"Umm, yeah. Let me just take this real quick." Austin pushed his chair back and pressed the phone to his ear as he stepped away from the table.

Lauren grinned, her dark hair catching in the breeze. "He's really happy here," she said, tucking the long strands behind her ears.

"Huh?" Casey shifted her legs, banging her knee into the corner of the table. The contents shook. "Oh shit! Sorry!"

Lauren giggled and leaned back in her seat. "It's all over

his face. He likes you. He likes this city."

Her body warmed, heat rising to her cheeks at Lauren's sweet admission. "He's umm, found a lot of success with the new office so far, I think."

Lauren smiled, tugging her mojito to her lips. "It's more than just work though. I think it's you, Casey." She turned her head, eyeing her brother across the patio. "He'd kill me for telling you this…"

"Telling me what?"

Lauren dipped her head down, leaning in toward Casey. Pineapple clung to her breath as she spoke. "Austin had a really rough few months before he moved here. I'm not sure how much he told you, but he had it pretty bad for Mavis. And he didn't handle it well when Josh…" She sighed, widening her eyes as she peered back at him. "It was hard to watch."

Casey nodded. "Yeah, umm. Mavis kind of filled me in." She sucked down the cocktail in full. "And Austin's been pretty upfront about it all too."

This is so awkward!

"He seems better now though. Back to his old self." Lauren reached across the table and squeezed Casey's hand. "Thank you."

Her heart faltered, the insecurity consuming her earlier in the day slowly evaporating as the mojito tipped her brain upside down.

Lauren tugged her hand back as Austin returned, ramming his phone into his pocket. "I'm sorry." He sighed and stuffed his hand in his wallet, digging out the infamous blue credit card.

"Everything okay?" Casey asked, accepting the card he held out.

"Yeah, yeah, no big deal. But hey, I'm sorry. I have to run back to the office real quick. Can I meet you guys in about an hour?"

Casey nodded. "Yeah, just text me. I'll tell you where to meet us."

Austin grinned and leaned forward, pressing his lips to the top of her head. "If you're at a Backstreet Boys concert, you're on your own."

"Are they in town?" Lauren straightened as a smile tugged at her lips.

"God, I hope not." Austin snorted and stepped away. "One hour!" he called over his shoulder as his feet carried him up the steps toward Michigan Avenue.

"Eh, I'm more of an N'SYNC girl anyway." Lauren shrugged and drained her glass as Casey handed Austin's credit card to the waiter.

"They are the superior boyband." She snickered. "Austin told me you were a fan."

Lauren giggled and tilted her head to the side. "You guys talk about weird things."

Laughing, Casey gripped her stomach as the waiter returned and dropped the receipt on the table. "Thanks for coming in, ladies. Enjoy the rest of your day!" He winked and walked away.

As she scooted her chair back to stand, the metal legs grated against the concrete. "Come on. Let's start with Millennium Park. You can't come to Chicago without taking a picture in front of the Bean."

Lauren smiled and looped her arm around Casey's as they left the patio, following in Austin's footsteps toward Michigan Avenue to hail a cab.

And to think I was nervous about meeting you.

CHAPTER TEN

Austin

"But you said three weeks *total*." Austin cringed, dragging a hand through his hair as he peered into a hole in the ceiling.

"That was before we learned we had to rewire the entire suite." The lead contractor, Mike, tugged at a discolored beige wire. He ran his finger over the casing and snorted. "This is original to the building, typical for an early nineties build but a total fire hazard today." He raised his brow.

Austin sighed. "How long?"

"I'll get my guys out here. Another week or two depending on availability."

Austin nodded and inhaled a deep breath. "Look, I'm on a tight deadline. I'll pay you double to be the priority."

"I'll call you Monday and work you into the schedule for next week." He extended his hand, and Austin gripped it.

"I appreciate that." His gaze shifted to the center of the room and the exposed 2x4s. "Walls?" he asked, pointing at the wood.

Mike grinned. "I can slap those up in a day."

"Slap 'em up? I gotta have clients in here by August

first."

Mike shrugged. "It's June."

"I know." *I must sound like a whiny entitled asshat right now.* "I've just got what feels like a million other things to do, staff to hire and clients to source. This space is just step one. And I can't do anything without it." Austin exhaled, mentally running through the growing to-do list as his stomach sank with the unexpected setback.

Mike readjusted the ball cap on his head, white paint flaking from the brim and falling to the carpet. "We'll keep at it." He bent forward and scooped up his leather toolbelt, slinging a screwdriver into a free loop. "Have a nice weekend, man."

His work boots pounded away across the suite, disappearing down the hall.

"Yeah… nice weekend." Austin sighed and slouched toward his office. With a groan, he dropped into his chair and opened the timeline he'd created, counting down to August.

His fingers tapped at the keyboard, pushing back every date by two full weeks. "Damn it," he muttered, saving and closing the document with a grimace. "How the hell can a rewire take that long? That can't be right."

Am I getting screwed?

Austin yanked his phone from his pocket, instinctually dialing Mitch.

He answered immediately. "Is her phone broken?"

"What?" Austin wrinkled his nose. "Who?"

"Lauren. She won't answer my calls or texts. Did she get there okay?"

What the hell?

"Umm, yeah, she's fine. I just had lunch with her. She didn't mention anything about her phone."

She texted me when she landed.

He snorted. "Well, I guess she's ignoring me then."

Austin squinted, his gaze falling to the floor. "What's going on with you guys?"

Mitch laughed. "Don't worry, dude, I'm sure Lauren will give you an ear full this weekend." A voice echoed in the background. "Hang on a second, will ya?"

"Yeah."

Mitch's voice disappeared, replaced by monotonous pounding in the distance.

I caught you at work, didn't I?

"Okay, sorry." The noise disappeared as Mitch seemingly left the job site. "What's up, Austin? You didn't call to talk about my wife."

"I was calling about rewiring an office, but—"

Mitch cut him off. "What about it?"

"Umm, well, the suite I secured needs to be fully rewired. My guy says it's a two-week job. It can't really take that long, can it?" Austin leaned forward, poking his head around the door to peer back into the missing ceiling tile again.

"How big is the space?"

"About 19,000 square feet."

Mitch snorted. "And you think two weeks is too long?"

A wave of heat crashed over him, embarrassment flooding his body at his lack of knowledge. "Well, yeah…"

"Austin, I'm not an electrician, but it sounds like you've got yourself a good team if they can knock that job out in just two weeks."

Oh.

Austin sighed. "All right… it is what it is."

"How's the job? How's Chicago?"

Despite the growing to-do list in front of him, Austin smiled. "It's good actually. All of it." He stood and stepped toward the window. Lake Michigan stared back, sparkling in the afternoon sun. "I'm sorry, I should have called home sooner."

"Eh, you're fine. I hear you're a Cubs fan now."

Austin snorted, a grin tugging at his lips. "Not yet."

"I got a hundred bucks on the Dodgers the next time they play Chicago."

The probability of a win ran through his mind, pulling

stats and figures from the nonsense Casey seemed to spew about the team night and day.

The Cubs are the better team right now.

"I'll take that bet." Austin smiled, a piece of home settling back into his heart. He cupped the back of his neck as the tiny, buried pieces of Rosewood called from his soul. "Oh, and umm, hey, I guess I have to start planning a bachelor party. What do you think?"

Mitch snorted. "Well, it's Josh… so a strip club and illicit drugs for sure."

A bubble of laughter burst from his belly. He snickered into the phone, allowing the absurdity of Mitch's suggestion to consume him.

"You know my brother so well."

"Better than you, dude." He barked out a laugh. "Back room at Highside. Pizza. Beer. Basketball game."

"Probably more his speed."

"A bit." Mitch sighed and cleared his throat. "Hey, Austin?"

"Yeah?"

"Can you make sure Lauren has a good time this weekend? Just… make sure she sees everything she wants to and all that?"

"Yeah, of course." He frowned. *What's going on with you guys?* "She's with Casey right now, probably checking off the first place on her list."

"Okay… thanks." He exhaled, his breath cracking the connection on the phone. "Umm, I gotta get back to work. But talk soon, bud."

"Talk soon, Mitch."

He ended the call.

Austin blew out a breath and returned to his seat, his head swimming. "Something's up with you guys," he muttered, waking his laptop from sleep mode and vowing to pull some truth from Lauren this weekend.

His eyes skimmed the executive summary he'd started that morning with every intention of sending it off to Steven and Rodger by the end of the day. He checked his watch, the hour he promised the girls slowly ticking away.

Not gonna happen.

He groaned, pulling up the paperwork Bernice needed for the two new assistants he'd hired. His fingers tapped away, filling in bubbles and checking boxes until his cursor hovered over the submit button. He clicked it with a sigh and shuffled his notes as his eyes glossed over the list of business tax liabilities he had to research, the workers' compensation package he needed to choose, and property and casualty insurance he needed to secure. And the list continued.

I have to keep working.

With a frown, he picked up his phone and opened a text to Casey.

JULIE NAVICKAS

CHAPTER ELEVEN

Casey

"It's seriously just a huge bean!" Lauren tugged Casey's arm, pulling her along the crowded path toward the iconic Chicago sculpture. Her fingertips grazed the surface.

"If Austin were here, he'd be gagging watching you touch that."

A fit of giggles fell from Lauren's lips as she doubled over in laughter. "You *do* know my brother!" She smacked her hand against the Bean again, dragging her fingers along the surface with a wide, rule-breaking grin. "And believe it or not, Josh is actually way *worse* than him."

Casey snorted. "I don't believe that for a second."

"Believe it." She smirked and yanked Casey to her side, raising her phone to snap a photo. "Say cheese!"

Lauren took the picture as Casey smiled, her heart resurfacing from the pool of insecurity she'd drowned in all day.

"Seriously, so funny..." Lauren murmured as she grinned and stared at the silver sculpture.

"Its real name is Cloud Gate. I read somewhere that eighty percent of the surface reflects the sky." Casey

113

JULIE NAVICKAS

scrunched her nose and eyed the Bean closer.

"Oh, that's really cool!" Lauren hunched over and walked beneath it with the interest of an explorer on an adventure. "What's back there?" She pointed to the opposite side of the park.

"Oh, uh, just the pavilion. There's probably some live music going on or something right now." Peeking at her watch, Casey shrugged. "Want to check it out?"

"Sure!" Waddling from beneath the Bean, Lauren looped her arm back into Casey's. "Lead the way, lady!"

Folk music collided with their ears as they marched across the grassy field and down the stone steps to the pavilion. Casey led Lauren to the main level and chose the fifth row of red plastic seats beside the stage.

"How's this?"

"Perfect!" Lauren dropped her butt into a chair and plopped her bag on her lap. "I love it here," she admitted. "I've always wanted to visit this city." She stretched her arms up and leaned back, the sun's rays dancing on her tanned face.

"Why haven't you?"

Lauren snorted and rolled her eyes. "Because Mitch's version of a *vacation* is like a secluded cabin in the Northwoods of Wisconsin."

Casey giggled, a childhood memory of her and her older sister Cassie diving into a lake of a Wisconsin campground resurfacing. She grinned, nostalgia touching her heart.

"So, how long have you been married?"

"We got married in Vegas a little over seven years ago, but I've known Mitch basically my whole life." She rolled her eyes. "High school sweethearts, kinda."

"Well, that's really sweet, isn't it?" Casey snorted. "My high school boyfriend, Eric is in prison for dealing drugs." Her eyes widened. "I guess I lucked out there, didn't I?" She blanched.

"I'd say so! Yikes!" Giggling, Lauren toyed with her wedding ring, spinning it in circles on her finger.

The ping of a text message caught her ear, barely audible from her bag. Casey snagged her phone and pulled the screen to her face to read, *Hey beautiful, I'm so sorry. I'm gonna be stuck here for a little while longer. Are you girls okay?*

Casey snuck a peek at Lauren, watching as she pulled her long, dark hair into a ballerina-like bun. With a smile, the last shred of anxiety in her gut melted away. She tapped out, *We're totally fine! I love your sister!* She added the kissing face emoji and pushed *send*, dropping her phone back in her purse.

"Well, Austin is stuck at the office, so that means you're stuck with me."

Lauren laughed. "I'm not stuck with you. I'm enjoying your company!" She elbowed Casey in the side with a smile. "Besides, I didn't really come to see my brother."

"You didn't?"

She shook her head. "Can I tell you a secret?"

"Umm yeah, sure." Casey furrowed her brow, twisting her body to face Lauren.

"It's not that I didn't miss Austin. I did. But honestly, I came because I really just needed a few days away from Mitch." She hung her head, scraping the bottoms of her sandals along the concrete.

"Oh! Well… umm, yeah. Everyone needs a break once in a while, right?" Her eyes widened.

Lauren laughed. "Yeah… a break." She sighed and hopped to her feet. "But hey, if Austin's going to spend the day being a stuffy lawyer, let's go do something fun!"

"What do you have in mind?" *Please don't say Buckingham Fountain. Please don't say Buckingham Fountain…*

A mischievous grin curled Lauren's lips into a smile. "Let's day drink. I'll spill all of Austin's secrets!"

Spill, Lauren, spill…

Casey plopped into a metal chair on the back patio at Dark Horse.

"Oh, this place is perfect!" Lauren sat across the table beneath a royal-blue umbrella. "We're in Wrigleyville, right?"

Casey pointed over Lauren's shoulder and nodded. "Our apartment is about three blocks that way." Dumping her purse in the empty seat beside her, she pulled a menu to her lap and opened the plastic-covered page to the weekly specials. "Friday… eight-dollar domestic pitchers. You in?"

"Let's get two." Lauren grinned and set her bag beside Casey's. She leaned back in her chair, tilting her face to the sun.

"You don't need to convince me." Casey winked at the waiter as he approached the table. She pointed to the list of specials. "Two pitchers of Miller Lite please."

"How many cups?" He scratched their order onto a small notepad, eyeing the two empty chairs beside them.

Lauren laughed and tugged a pair of sunglasses from her bag. "Just two." She smiled. "I'm on vacation."

"Two it is, ladies." He snorted and walked away.

Casey giggled and propped her feet up on a chair. She leaned back and sighed. "You know, usually I'm the one pouring the beer. This is a nice change."

"Have you been bartending long? That's how you met Mavis, right?"

Casey nodded. "About eight years." *God, has it been that long?* "And yeah. Mavs worked at The Broken Shaker before me. She trained me on my first shift and the rest is history." She smiled despite the twinge in her gut. Casey shrugged. "I miss her."

With a sigh, Lauren tilted her head. "Before everything you know, *happened*… Mavis was my best friend too. I know what it feels like to lose her."

Yeah, I guess you do.

The waiter returned, setting the two full pitchers of beer on the table with two plastic cups. "Enjoy, ladies!"

"Thank you!" Casey snagged the cups and poured. "You must be happy to have her back now though."

"Oh, absolutely." She accepted the cup Casey offered and brought the beverage directly to her lips. She sipped and smiled. "This is so good."

Casey gulped and wiped her mouth with the back of her hand. Nodding, she smiled.

"So, can I ask? How did you and Austin get to be...?"

Casey's cheeks flushed, warmth rising in her body. She lifted her gaze to Lauren's and her brown eyes stared back.

"Umm... I guess I'm not really too sure. He was obviously here when Mavis moved out. Then we hung out that night and just texted dumb stuff to each other for a few weeks until he got his new job." Casey drained her cup and reached for the pitcher. "Oh! And he offered to help me with my political science course this summer. He's like... way smart."

Lauren rolled her eyes. "Tell me about it. Imagine being the little sister of the brilliant Templeton twins." She snorted. "Now let me tell you, that's a tough act to follow." She tipped her head back and drained her cup too.

Casey grinned and refilled. "I can't even imagine. Valedictorian *and* salutatorian, I hear?"

With another gulp of beer, Lauren winced. "Don't remind me." She shook her head with a laugh. "What about you? Do you have any siblings?"

"Yeah, I have an older sister, Cassie. But we haven't talked in a while."

Lauren frowned. "Oh, I'm sorry. I didn't mean to—"

"No, no, you're totally fine. She's in jail, so we kinda lost touch." Casey cringed, bringing the cup back to her lips. *Why did I just tell you that?* "And... I'm making myself sound crazy..."

Lauren smiled and stretched her arm across the table. She squeezed Casey's fingers. "You're not crazy, Case. I'm sorry, I didn't mean to make you uncomfortable."

Her cheeks flushed red again, the embarrassment swirling in her gut. "No, no... don't apologize. My family is just a little *messy*." Her gaze lifted to the sky as Mavis's warning swirled in her brain again. *The Templetons… they just see things differently.* "I haven't really even told Austin anything about my family yet," she admitted.

"Austin is really understanding about literally everything. He processes things differently, never any judgment."

Casey nodded. "Yeah, that's true." She sipped again. "I really envy how close you all are."

Lauren smiled, slouching back in her seat. "I do love it, but twin brothers come with a bit of drama." She tipped her beer in Casey's direction. "It's actually been really nice not to have to listen to them fight lately."

"Yeah, I bet. I just saw a tiny bit of it that one weekend." Her eyes widened with recall.

"I seriously thought Josh was going to murder Austin." She drained her cup and reached for the pitcher, pouring the last of the golden liquid. "And honestly, I think I could have murdered him myself after what he did, going after Mavis like that."

Casey's stomach dropped as jealousy roared in her veins. "He really felt something for her."

"But that's just it, Casey." She leaned forward, resting her elbows against the aluminum table. "Austin has never really had feelings for *any* woman before. I mean, he's dated… like, a lot, but everyone's just been a fling. And then out of nowhere, he just professes these deep feelings for Mavis. He'd hidden her away for a long time."

Casey swallowed, regret filling her heart at her eager willingness to hear all of Austin's secrets.

Lauren shook her head and gripped Casey's fingers again. "I'm so sorry. I'm scaring you." She squeezed, tugging her hand. "But it's different with you, I swear. I can see it already. He cares for you too."

And now you're placating me…

Casey tugged her hand from Lauren's grasp and reached upward, yanking out her ponytail. "Oh, umm. Yeah, no worries. I mean, we're still really new." Pulling the hair tie from her wrist, she secured the mop of curls again. "And

Mavis kind of already warned me."

She squinted. "Warned you?" Lauren's brow furrowed.

"She's just being protective of me, that's all."

That's not all and you know it.

Lauren tilted her head, her gaze boring into Casey. "You know, sometimes I wonder if Mavis…" She shook her head and dropped her gaze to her lap.

"Still has some feelings for Austin too." Casey completed her thought.

She nodded. "For a lot of reasons, Casey, I'm really glad he moved here. Glad he found you." Lauren smiled. "A part of me wishes it was permanent."

Her stomach rolled, sloshing around the beer in her gut. "Permanent?" Casey squinted and pressed a hand to her belly.

"Well yeah, once he's got this office established, he'll be made a partner at the law firm. And he'll move home to Rosewood."

An invisible hand reached into her chest and squeezed her heart, crushing it with the force of a steamroller to fresh pavement. The blood drained from her cheeks as the truth spilling from Lauren's lips settled into her soul.

Of course, he'll move back to California. It's his home.

"Are you okay?"

Casey forced a smile on her lips and coughed. "Oh! Yeah, sorry! Just swallowed funny…" She dragged her fingers along her throat. "This beer isn't very good."

"Actually, I love it! I never drink this stuff!" She drained her cup and set it on the table with a grin. "This place is a lot of fun! You're a lot of fun, Casey. Thank you for bringing me here."

Casey nodded as Lauren poured the first drink from the second pitcher. "Oh, for sure… good times." She swallowed the rest of her cup and pushed it toward Lauren.

Enjoy it now, Lauren, because it's apparently just temporary. I'm just temporary.

JULIE NAVICKAS

CHAPTER TWELVE

Lauren

Lauren twisted the knob, the last drops of hot water dripping onto her head. She stepped from the shower and toweled off, the dull ache in her brain still pounding. *That's what I get for day drinking yesterday!* After ramming her body into clean clothes, she stepped from the bathroom in a cloud of steam and tossed her pajamas into her suitcase before heading into the living room.

"Hey." Lauren slouched into the empty seat beside Austin, snorting as her butt sank deep into the cushion.

"You have to tuck your feet underneath you." His gaze whizzed across his laptop screen as his fingers tapped away at the keyboard.

"Okay..." Lauren rearranged her legs. "I guess that's a little better."

Austin smiled. "Hang on, I'll be done in just a minute."

Lauren nodded. "No rush." Her gaze wandered around the apartment, taking in the plain white walls and the collection of mismatched furniture. The lace curtains rustled in the breeze, the bottoms frayed and fading yellow. Returning her gaze to Austin, Mavis clouded her brain and tugged at her heartstrings. *Eight years… holed up and hidden away right here…* Everything in the room carried her story, carried her heartbreak, carried her survival. A shiver ran down her spine as she eyed her brother.

Do you see her here too?

"Are you okay?" He snapped his laptop closed and set it on the floor beside his feet. Furrowing his brow, he turned to her.

"Are you? All you've done is work since I got here."

He sighed and ran a hand through his hair. "You're right. I'm sorry." He nudged the laptop further away with his toes. "I'm done. I promise."

She snorted. "You're fine. I know you've got a list of shit to do."

With a grin, he tapped her knee. "A list of shit for sure. But still, it's no excuse. You came to visit and I'm being rude."

Lauren shook her head, her gaze intent on the curtains dancing in the breeze. "Where's Casey?"

"She has the lunch shift. She'll be back around four, I think. Guess you're stuck with me today." He snorted and elbowed her in the side. "I'm not an expert tour guide like her, but I'm sure I can still find your Buckingham Fountain or whatever water park it was you wanted to visit."

She giggled and shoved him back. "It's not a water park, you idiot! And besides, I'd rather wait for Casey. I still have nightmares about your directionally challenged skills on the 405."

Austin rolled his eyes, playfully tossing a throw pillow to her lap. "I was like sixteen."

Her palm deflected the pillow as it tumbled to the floor. "Still. I'll wait for Casey."

"All right, fine, whatever… What do you want to do then? Just sit on the couch and stare at each other all day?"

"Not all day." She shrugged. "But I do want to talk to you while we're alone." Lauren shifted, angling her body to face him.

His right eyebrow raised. "About?"

"You." She nudged him with her feet. "How are you?"

Austin wrinkled his nose and frowned. "You've been here for like a full day. Haven't we been over this already?"

"Come on, Austin." Lauren folded her arms across her chest and glared. "I mean it. I want to know how you really are."

"Are you my therapist now or something?"

"Haven't I always been?" She grinned, flashing her perfect set of white teeth.

With a sigh, Austin dropped his hand to her foot and squeezed. "Lauren, I'm good. I really am. I told you, moving here was a good choice."

"I know the job is good. And you're having fun with Casey. But you know what I'm asking you here." Her gaze dropped to her hands as she picked at the pink nail polish on her thumb.

"Do I?"

"Mavis, Austin. I'm asking you about Mavis." Her hands stilled.

"What about her?" He frowned and removed his hand from her foot.

"She's marrying our brother in less than a month. You may have run from home, but you can't run from reality."

"That's what you think I did? You think I ran away?" He slouched against the armrest and heaved out a heavy breath.

"Didn't you?" Her eyes widened. "I mean, you did leave, but you kinda ended up in her bed anyway, didn't you?" Lauren tapped the wall behind the sofa and tilted her head toward his bedroom.

Austin slumped backward and groaned, cupping the nape of his neck. "What do you want me to say here, Lauren?"

"The truth. Are you over her?"

He turned, his tired gaze meeting her own. "I'm trying, okay? I really am." He smirked and tilted his head. "But if you want the truth, I'm always going to feel something for her. We're connected, always have been. It's hard to just push those feelings away completely." His palm dropped to the cushion with a smack.

"And Casey?"

He smiled, the growing grin on his lips releasing some of the concern and unease from her heart.

"Casey is absolutely fucking amazing." He snorted. "She's exactly what I needed."

"You're right." Her toes nudged him in the gut. "She's perfect for you, you know?"

"Subtle." Austin rolled his eyes, turning his head to grin at her. "But I think you're right."

"What happens to her though?"

He squinted. "What do you mean?"

"When you make partner and move home. What happens to Casey?"

His body shivered as his gaze fell to the floor. "You know, you're asking really obnoxious questions today."

"As your therapist, it's my job." She leaned forward as her stomach dropped, churning angst with yesterday's cheap beer. "August first, right?"

Austin shook his head. "That's just when the new office opens. Boyd and Bernstein never told me…" He shuddered, dragging his hands along his cheeks. "Don't make me think that far ahead, okay? The fucking paint color isn't even picked out yet."

Lauren nodded. "I earned my paycheck with this session, didn't I?" she whispered, pulling her legs inward to tuck them against her body.

He stood and shuffled to the window. Drawing back the curtains, he eyed the passing train cars, their clatter roaring into the tiny apartment. "Can we just let this one go for a bit? Go grab a cup of coffee or something instead?" He turned to her with pleading blue eyes.

Forever conflicted. Exactly what I was afraid of.

She nodded. "Yeah, let me grab my bag, okay?"

Austin swallowed, turning back to the window as Lauren

rose from her seat and tiptoed out of the room.

She padded down the hallway and pushed the door open to Austin's bedroom. Lifting her purse to her shoulder, she yanked her phone from the charger on the nightstand and scanned the screen.

"Mitch…"

Her heart sank, falling into the empty void inside her chest as she scrolled through the growing list of missed calls and text messages from her husband. With a sigh, she tossed her phone into her bag and left the room.

Fuck him.

Austin's foot held the apartment's door ajar. Stuffing his phone in his pocket, he glanced up and yanked out his keys. "Ready?"

"Yep."

His foot shifted and the door closed in her face. "What's wrong?"

Lauren rolled her eyes as her breath caught in her throat. "Nothing. What are you doing? I thought we were going to get coffee." She sidestepped him and gripped the doorknob.

"Come on, Elsa. You just emerged from my room a frigid ice queen. What the hell happened?"

"Let it go, Austin." She raised her right eyebrow and glowered.

"Uh-uh. You made me come clean." He nudged her backward to the dining room table. "Now it's your turn, sis."

With a sigh, she dropped her butt into a chair, all remaining air escaping from her lungs. Tears welled behind her eyes as she blinked, battling the burn. "I'm fine, Austin. Really."

"Tell me about it anyway." He squeezed her shoulder as he stepped around the table and into the kitchen, turning the little coffee pot on. He winked and tugged Casey's unidentified plastic can of coffee grounds toward him. "Trust me. This coffee is just as good as Starbucks." He shook the container with a grin.

Lauren snorted and dragged her fingers beneath her eyes as she moved from the dining room chair to the barstool at the kitchen counter. She sniffled as Austin hit the *start* button on the little machine and turned to open the refrigerator.

Tell him. Just tell him.

She opened her mouth and swallowed, the words catching in her throat as her heart shattered, bursting into a million tiny pieces deep within her chest, the truth of her words ready to draw blood.

"I think Mitch wants a divorce."

His head smashed into the freezer as his body jerked. "Fuck. What?" Austin emerged, rubbing his head with a stick of butter in his hand. "What did you just say?"

Lauren hung her head. "You heard me," she whispered, pressing her eyes closed.

"I'll fucking kill him." The butter dropped to the counter with a thud. "I'll fucking kill him!"

The tears betrayed her, leaking down her cheeks like Poseidon himself ordered them to flow. "Austin, he's just… tired of me." She sniffled, wiping at the tears with her palms.

"*Tired* of you? Lauren, you guys have been together since we were all in high school." He pressed his hands onto the counter, resting his body weight against them. "Hell, kind of even before that…" The coffee pot beeped, and he pressed the glowing button to silence the noise. "I'll kill him," he muttered again, shaking his head.

"Oh, stop." Lauren wiped her nose with the back of her hand. "Like that would help anything." She straightened and inhaled a deep breath.

"Lauren, what the hell?" He bit his bottom lip. "How? I don't even know what to say."

She shook her head. "Even I don't know what to say. But no one else knows yet." She cringed. "Can we just keep this between us for now?"

Austin sighed and rounded the counter. His arms surrounded her, pulling her into safety and squeezing her into comfort. "What happened?" he whispered.

She groaned and pulled away, wiping another river of tears from her face. "He just doesn't love me the way he used to and he's tired of trying."

"Tired of trying to love you?" Austin retreated to the kitchen and tugged mugs down from the upper cabinet. "I don't understand."

"This is so weird talking to you about this."

"Why? It's just me." He poured the brown liquid into the mugs with shaking hands, sloshing drops onto the countertop. Frowning, he wiped the stains away with a soapy dishcloth.

Lauren sucked in a breath and closed her eyes. "We've been trying to start a family, and it's just not working."

"Oh." His body stilled, the coffee carafe hanging in the air halfway back to its home. "Umm…"

"See, it's weird." Lauren buried her face in her hands, the heat rising to warm her cheeks. Through the gaps in her fingers, she watched as Austin returned the carafe to the coffee pot with wide eyes.

He shook his head and swallowed. "Maybe just pretend I'm not your brother for a minute or something." He stuffed his head back into the fridge, pushing bottles and containers aside to grasp the cream.

Lauren snorted as he straightened and pushed the door closed. "Austin, relax. I'm not going to tell you the *details* of our bedroom." She snagged a mug of coffee and the cream. With shaking fingers, she poured and mixed the swirling contents with a spoon. Her eyes glazed over as her heartbeat slowed, the silence of the room calming—an open window to vent frustration. "I think we're just at the end of the road."

"Should I talk to him?" Austin wrinkled his nose, panic rising in his voice.

A bubble of laughter burst from her belly as fear grew in his eyes. "Oh, God no!" Bringing the mug to her lips, she winced at the hot liquid. "If he knew I was telling you any of this he'd be mortified." Her eyes widened as she set the coffee down. "Wouldn't want anyone to think his er—*parts* weren't working…"

Austin nodded. "Yeah… okay."

The pent-up secrets and silent frustration shattered the shields around her heart, the weight of the heavy discomfort tumbling from her lips in a rush of fumbled words. *Sweet Austin, the keeper of all our secrets.* "I just don't know what to do anymore! When one person wants a divorce… you get a divorce!"

He nodded. "I mean, yeah, but Lauren, you guys really can't be at that point yet." His gaze fell to a crumb on the counter. Brushing it to the floor, he shook his head. "I just talked to him yesterday."

Lauren coughed, choking on a gulp of coffee. "You did? Why?"

"Doesn't matter. Just a dumb question about electric. But Lauren…" He reached across the counter and gripped her hands. "When I talked to Mitch, he wanted me to make sure you had fun this weekend, that you saw everything you wanted to see. He even thought your phone was broken because you hadn't called him." He squeezed her fingers. "I work with divorce clients every day. Believe me, Mitch didn't sound like one of them."

She hung her head, her gaze resting on her brother's fingers blanketing her own.

"I know he still cares, Austin. It's like what you said about Mavis. You can't just get rid of feelings you've had your whole life. But Mitch… I think his feelings have just *changed*."

Lauren pulled her hands away and scooped up her mug, staring down into the brown liquid. The steam tickled her face, the coffee warm and delicious in her hands. But the longer it sat, the cooler it would become… until cold and unappealing entirely. She swirled the contents, wrinkling her nose as some stray coffee grounds floated to the surface. The steam lessened as the silent minutes ticked away.

And as she sucked down the last of the liquid, her gaze settled on the grounds coating the bottom of the mug— soggy, unappealing, and ready to be discarded.

Just like my marriage.

Lauren folded her clothes and shoved them back into her suitcase two days later. Drawing in a deep breath, she exhaled, the weight of her crumbling marriage stuffed back into her luggage as her flight home loomed.

"Just make it through the wedding, Mitch…" she whispered. "We can't ruin anything for Josh or Mavis."

From her bag, she tugged out their wedding invitation and cringed, having found zero strength over the course of her visit to hand it to her brother directly. With a sigh, she pulled a pen from her purse and scribbled on the envelope.

Austin, we'll get through it together.

Lauren propped the invitation on the bedside lamp. She zipped her suitcase closed and hauled it off the bed, and with a quick fluff of the bedspread, she left Austin's bedroom and departed Chicago.

CHAPTER THIRTEEN

Austin

Austin scrolled through the seemingly endless flight options as the monotonous sound of a screw gun drilled into his brain. He peeked through his newly erected office door to see another piece of drywall go up down the hall. With a grin, he exhaled out the bundle of nerves that had taken up a permanent residence in his belly ever since the small setback in his timeline.

Getting closer.

His gaze scoured the calendar on his screen, zeroing in on July ninth as it drew nearer. He swallowed, frowning at the impending wedding date as his heartstrings involuntarily tightened. Austin exhaled and closed his eyes, willing the dip in his stomach to disappear. "Princess..." he murmured, balling his hands into fists. The familiar longing for her love washed over him, returning for the first time in several weeks with full force. Mavis appeared before his eyes, clad in a long white dress, a smile playing across her lips as she whispered his name. The green of her eyes pierced his soul, squeezing his heart with forbidden love.

"You're a goddamn fool, Austin Templeton." *After all*

this time, why am I still doing this? A groan escaped his lips as his elbow bumped into a picture frame on his desk. It fell forward, clattering against the surface of the wood. Guilt swirled in his belly as he scooped it up, locking eyes with the commemorative Kiss Cam moment from the infamous night at Wrigley Field. He ran his index finger over the glass, resting his fingertip over Casey. "My sweet Cinderella," he whispered, propping the frame back into its place. He blew out a breath and willed the ghost of lost love away from his heart. "I need you, Casey girl," he whispered. "Now more than ever."

His gaze rested on the photo, pulling him back to the moment they locked lips in a sea of cheering fans. He smiled, allowing Casey to reclaim his heart—her quirky habits and silly antics tripping into the age-old emotions of sorrow and defeat. Forcing the ancient feelings back into a box deep within his soul, Austin mentally locked it shut with a key labeled *Mavis*.

"Casey…" Austin exhaled, dragging his fingers along the growing smile on his lips. And with a snort, he scooped up his phone and called her.

"Hello?"

"Hi, beautiful. Do you have a minute?"

"Umm, yeah. Hang on one second." Papers shuffled in the background, followed by a clank and a muffled curse. "Okay, sorry. What's up?"

Austin grinned. "Where are you?"

"The library. I forgot to put my phone on silent. Apparently, it's frowned upon if you make any noise whatsoever." She snorted.

"Well yeah, Case, it's a library."

"Eh, whatever. What's up? Need something?"

Austin leaned back in his seat, his heart rebounding from the momentary relapse of confusion. "I'm looking at flights for the umm, wedding." He cleared his throat. "When did you request off work again?"

"Hang on, let me check…"

The image of her disorganization grew in his mind as the shuffle of papers met his ear again.

Constant chaos.

"Okay, umm, Jim gave me Thursday through Sunday off. I close on Wednesday night though, so nothing crazy early." She snorted.

He smiled, scanning the flights for the best options. "How about 11:20 AM out of O'Hare Thursday morning?" He scrolled. "And then 2:44 PM on Sunday out of L.A.?"

"Sounds good to me."

"Booking it now." Austin clicked and confirmed, pulling his wallet from his back pocket as he selected two seats together on each flight. "Hey, when will you be home tonight?"

"Like an hour, maybe? I need to swing by the bank."

"Okay, what do you feel like having for dinner?" The flight confirmation popped into his email. With a roll of his eyes, he stuffed it into a folder in his inbox without opening it.

"Champagne and a cheesy sandwich." She laughed.

"Champagne, huh? And what are we celebrating?"

She giggled. "My amazing tutor. He helped me get an 'A' on my test."

"Casey!" His lips twisted into a smile as his cheeks warmed, a flood of excitement filling his chest. "That's incredible! I'm so proud of you."

"All you, sir. There's no way I would have gotten that grade without you."

He shook his head. "When are you gonna realize just how smart you really are, Casey girl?"

"Oh, stop it," she hedged. "I'll umm… see you soon, okay?"

"Can't wait, Cinderella." He ended the call and set his phone down with a grin. "Champagne, a cheesy sandwich, and a boost of confidence for you, Casey."

With a deep breath, Austin returned to his laptop, closing out the tabs of unused flight options until an ad caught his attention on the right side of the screen. He snickered as a silly throw pillow with a Chicago Cubs pattern appeared. "Perfect," he whispered, pulling his credit card back out and placing the order. Another confirmation pinged in his inbox as he dragged a hand through his hair with a smile. He tilted his head and shrugged. "May as well get a new couch while I'm at it." And ten minutes later, a new blue couch appeared in his inbox—confirmation of delivery within two weeks.

No more sunken butts for us, Case.

Smoke infiltrated his nose the moment he reached the third floor. Gripping the doorknob, he pushed the apartment door open and met the ear-piercing screech of the fire detector.

Standing on top of a dining room table chair, Casey waved a red dish rag in front of the screaming device until it quieted, smoke still billowing from the frying pan on the stove.

Austin dropped the grocery bags onto the kitchen counter and held out his hand as Casey hopped down. "What happened?" He eyed the unidentified, blackened to a crisp *meal* on the stove.

"I suck at cooking. Like… really suck!" She giggled and snuggled into his arms with the dish towel still in hand.

"What the hell is it?" Austin twisted their bodies and pointed at the frying pan.

"Nothing edible."

He tightened his hold, pulling her small body into his until she melded into him like the fit of two adjacent puzzle pieces.

"Why don't you leave the cheesy sandwiches to me, Chef McDaniels?"

She snorted. "I guess I'm a sous chef for a reason." Tilting her face upward, she grinned and glided her thumb along his bottom lip, silently begging for his kiss. Austin leaned down and pressed his mouth onto hers. The moan tumbling from her lips fueled him, her fingers tugging at the knot in his tie—a welcome invitation.

Adrenaline flooded his body as he gripped her hips, the friction of her skin against his triggering a shiver to zip along his spine. Her mouth pulled from his, moving to trail kisses along his jaw to the tip of his ear. Heat thundered through him, anticipation coursing through his veins as she shifted and sank her teeth playfully into his earlobe.

"I'm hungry," she whispered.

He grinned, dropping his hands to cup and squeeze her butt cheeks. "Hungry for what, Ms. McDaniels?" he murmured, dragging his hands along her body to rest on her breasts.

She giggled, each bubble of laughter melting his heart as regret seeped from his soul. *Why do I let myself even think about Mavis when I have you, Casey girl?*

"Food first, sex second." She smiled and pulled his hands off her chest.

Austin closed his eyes and rested his forehead against hers. "Counterproposal," he whispered. "Sex first, food second." He dropped his hands back to her butt and squeezed.

Poking him in the chest, Casey laughed. "That's your counterproposal? I thought you were this hot-shot lawyer in a courtroom."

"You don't need a courtroom for estate planning—and rarely for divorces, my political science extraordinaire." His arousal diminished as his stomach growled.

You win. Food first.

"You did promise me champagne."

"In the bag." He pointed toward the counter. "You pour, I'll cook." And with a smirk, Austin dumped the unidentified, burnt to a crisp *meal* in the trash.

What the hell was that even supposed to be?

"Oh! This is fancy shit right here!" Casey pulled the champagne from the bag, her eyes twinkling with excitement as she read the label.

Austin rolled up his sleeves and filled the sink with hot soapy water, dropping the frying pan in the bubbles. "It's not every day we get to celebrate an 'A' on an exam." He winked and picked up a sponge.

She rolled her eyes. "You act like it's a big achievement." Casey tugged at the cork and frowned when it didn't budge.

"It is a big achievement, Case. You're always so down on yourself, diminishing your schoolwork." Eyeing her struggle with the cork, he pulled his hands from the soapy water and toweled them off.

"Austin. It's *community* college. Save your pep talk." With a wrinkled nose, she shoved the bottle across the counter in his direction.

He wrestled the cork free with a muscled tug and pushed it back. "Say what you want about it, but it's a solid step toward your first degree." He dipped his hands back into the soapy water and continued his attack on the pan.

"First degree?" Casey raised her brow as she moved around the counter to open a cabinet door, snagging two champagne flutes from the top shelf. She blew the dust from the plastic and dragged a finger along the one with a suspicious crack down the middle.

"Yeah, of course. You said you were almost done with your associates. A bachelor's degree is next." He snagged the flutes from her hands and cringed, tossing them into the sink and rinsing them clean.

"And then onto law school!" She chuckled and accepted the clean cups. Filling them to the brim with champagne, Casey admired the bubbles as they fizzed to the top.

Austin rolled his eyes and circled the counter, gripping her upper arms until she turned to face him. He pressed his lips to hers. "I'm not trying to pressure you. I just know you're smart and you should keep going." He handed her a champagne flute, tapping his own to hers. "To you, Casey girl. Congratulations on your exam."

She sipped and swallowed, her eyes darting back and

forth as she pulled the cup from her mouth and set it back on the counter. Biting her bottom lip, she lifted her gaze to his. "Maybe you're right, Austin."

"I'm rarely wrong." He grinned, moving behind the counter to pull bread and butter from the grocery bag. "What do you think, Case? If you could do anything, what would it be? What's the dream job?" Austin pulled a knife from the drawer and spread butter across the first slice of bread.

She huffed out a breath, tracing the cracks in the countertop with her fingers. "Did you always know you wanted to be a lawyer?"

He tossed the first piece of buttered bread into the clean frying pan. It sizzled as he increased the heat and layered a slice of cheese on top. "Unless you count the brief phase when I was six and wanted to be a garbage man, then yes." He turned, pulling out the utensil drawer to rummage for a spatula. He tugged one free, and with wide eyes, grinned at the large bite that had been taken out of the rubber.

Casey snorted as her cheeks flushed pink. "Totally Mavis's." She shook her head as she reached for it, pulled it from his hands, and tossed it into the trash can. "Try that one." She pointed to the drawer beside the fridge.

Austin searched, pulling from within an intact spatula, and smiled. He flipped the sandwich, revealing a crisp, golden brown piece of bread—not one drop of cheese out of place.

Casey scrunched her nose and eyed the sandwich. "Do you ever do anything less than perfect, Austin Templeton?"

"Huh?" He snorted and reached for a plate in the cabinet.

"Seriously. It's kind of exhausting." She rolled her eyes and drained her glass with a large gulp.

"Are we back to this again?" He flopped the perfect sandwich onto a plate and pushed it in her direction. "It's just a sandwich, Case."

Her gaze dropped to her lap, her fingers busy picking

pieces of lint from her shorts.

With a sigh, Austin leaned forward on the counter. "Do I do anything less than perfect?" he whispered. "Need I remind you of the reason we met?" He took a bite of her sandwich with a raised brow. "Believe me, I do plenty wrong."

Her face fell as she sucked in a breath. "I'm sorry. I didn't mean—"

Austin raised his hand. "I know you didn't. I just wish you'd tell me what's really wrong here." He drained his glass and refilled both their flutes. "Because I know it's not this tasty sandwich that's upsetting you."

She smiled and picked it up, stuffing the first bite in her mouth—the warm cheese coating her tongue in gooey goodness. "It's good."

Austin reached forward and wiped the stray cheese from her bottom lip. "I know. I told you I make a mean grilled cheese." He grinned and pulled back. "I mean it though, Case, you can tell me what's bothering you. Talk to me."

Setting her sandwich back to the plate, Casey dropped her elbows to the counter, her fingers twisting the two small silver studs in her ears. She huffed out a breath and lifted her eyes to his. "Where do I start?"

"This moment. What's bothering you most?"

She snickered. "Oh. Well, I'm floating through life with no direction, barely surviving school." She shrugged. "I pour drinks for strangers every night... Oh, and I'm totally falling for you when I know you're just going to leave in a few months." Her eyes widened as her gaze fell to her lap.

Falling for me...

Austin's heart hammered in his chest as he reached across the counter and grabbed her hands, squeezing her fingers. "And just where do you think I'm gonna go, Casey girl?" he whispered, pressing his lips to hers.

His soul smiled, kicking the box of feelings for Mavis deeper into the void, further away from his heart.

"Home. You'll go home, Austin. While Lauren was here,

she reminded me that this whole thing"—she waved her arms around—"is just temporary. You're going to be made a partner at your real law firm and move home to California."

Austin sighed, internally wrestling with the truth—and likelihood of her words. *Nothing's for sure yet.* "First of all, don't ever listen to my sister." He grinned, squeezing her fingers again. "And second, I decide where I live and what job I work, okay?"

She nodded but pulled back, picking up her champagne and swirling the liquid around.

"You never answered my question," he whispered, eyeing her. "What do *you* want, Casey McDaniels?"

She bit down on her bottom lip and sucked in a deep breath.

"Campaigns." The word fell from her lips in a rush. "I want to be a campaign manager for local politics or something."

The first bit of confidence I've ever heard you speak.

"No one in my entire life has ever asked me what I wanted to do... or who I wanted to be," she whispered. Her eyes glistened with tears as a sad smile grew on her face.

Austin inhaled, soaking in the beauty beaming from her lips and the confidence radiating from her heart. He returned her grin. "Then it's about damn time someone did."

The breath caught in her throat as she rose from her seat and circled the counter. Her hand grasped his tie, coaxing him backward into his bedroom. She grinned as her butt sank to the bed, wrinkling the perfectly smoothed bedspread. With a giggle, she yanked her shirt from her chest and dropped it to the floor.

Food first, sex second. You don't break promises, do you, Casey girl?

Anticipation returned, flooding his system and fueling arousal to hammer through his bloodstream, coursing through his veins as he tugged his shirt from his body. Her fingernails tickled his skin as he nudged her backward onto his pillow, coaxing her legs to fall open. Easing his body onto hers, he crawled on top of her and sighed, bathing in the moment and readying his heart to love.

Austin closed his eyes as his lips pressed into the side of Casey's neck. His heartbeat increased, banging wildly in his chest with ferocity, pumping rhythmically. Each heartstring—each heartbeat intertwined with Casey's in perfect unison as she squirmed beneath him.

Pulling his lips from her skin, he dropped his palm to her heart and gazed into her eyes. Rampant thoughts clouded his brain. *This feels different.* Warmth washed over him, blanketing his body in the growing connection they shared. *You feel different, Case.* She smiled and draped her hand on top of his. Her fingers squeezed as his name fell from her lips. "Austin," she murmured, letting her lids flutter and close.

Austin swallowed, his heart skipping a beat as his brain shouted the truth. The moment for the words had arrived, the words that had undeniably settled in his soul since the moment she fell into him on the staircase—ready to be spoken out loud and deposited into the heart of the woman beneath him.

"I love you, Casey," he whispered. His breath caught in his throat as he searched her eyes, searched her soul, longing for her to return the words living in his heart.

"I love you too, Austin." Her whisper fueled him, burning his skin with desire as he tugged at their remaining clothing, each second one too many before he could slide inside her and solidify their connection.

She moaned when he entered her, each breath ragged in his ear, each exhale a groan of ecstasy and plea for more. The blood pounded in his ears as every nerve cell in his body activated. His name dripped from her lips with repetition, inciting a deepening carnal pressure to build with intensity.

Her fingernails dug into his back, each prick a point of pleasure. Casey tightened her legs around his waist, arching her back to meet his speeding rhythm. His vision clouded as she shuddered beneath him, a sigh of climax in his ear as he followed her lead, releasing his relief inside her.

His body calmed, resting on top of hers as they fought to catch their breath, basking in the afterglow of love. Austin pressed his lips to her neck, trailing kisses along her soft skin and branding the words *I love you* into her soul.

Casey's eyes glistened as he rolled off of her and pulled her to his body, snuggling into her essence. Her hand rested on his stomach as she dropped her head onto his chest.

As he breathed deeply, a field of lilacs bloomed beneath his nose. Austin inhaled, committing the scent to long-term memory, committing the moment to his heart.

Because it's the first time in my life that I understand what true love is.

He sighed as her body relaxed, drifting off to sleep in his arms. His eyes closed, giving in to the exhaustion, giving in to the moment before pain pierced his heart.

But why did it have to happen in Mavis's old bed?

JULIE NAVICKAS

CHAPTER FOURTEEN

Casey

Her reflection mirrored back, sliced in half by the large crack down the middle of the glass. She twirled, her yellow maid of honor dress flowing in the breeze as the material slid an inch down her chest.

Casey snorted and yanked the dress back up. "Why did you have to pick a dress with no straps, Mavs?" With a grimace, she turned to her jewelry box and tugged the lowermost drawer open. Her fingers brushed against a strand of pearls in her search for pins. "Oh! Grammy's pearls!" She pulled them free, running the delicate necklace along her fingers as she clasped it around her neck.

Returning to the mirror, she grinned. *Perfect.* "And less money I have to spend on jewelry..."

She snorted and resumed her search for pins, tugging some free from the depths of the middle drawer. Casey contorted her arms, working to stuff pins in the gown at odd angles. With a laugh, she rammed the last pin in the fabric and returned to the mirror for a final spin.

The dress stayed firm to her chest. "There," she announced to herself. "Now I won't flash anyone—and I just saved about a hundred bucks on alterations." Casey stepped back, eyeing the final look. She reached upward to tuck her curls behind her ears, her finger brushing against her naked left earlobe.

Shit! Where's my earring?

Her gaze fell to the floor, searching for the silver stud amidst the chaos of dirty clothes, school notebooks, and mismatched flip-flops. Casey scrunched her nose, forcing her brain to recall the last moment she had it. *I had it in the library. I had it at dinner.* Her heart lurched. "Austin's bed!"

Her bare feet padded down the hall to the dining room where Austin sat, camped out in his usual spot as his fingers flew across the keyboard.

"Hey, have you seen my earring?"

His gaze lifted from the screen, a grin growing on his lips. "What're you wearing?" He leaned back in the chair and tugged his reading glasses from his face, dropping them to the table.

"Oh, just the ever-so-practical, three-hundred-dollar, one-time-wear-only, maid-of-honor-dress." She performed an exaggerated twirl and stumbled over her own bare feet.

Austin snorted. "I cannot wait to see what you do on the dance floor."

Her eyes widened as a smile cracked her lips. "And in heels too!"

He laughed. "Did you forget? Ballroom dance expert right here."

Casey tapped her forehead playfully. "How did I forget I was dating Fred Astaire?"

Austin grinned and stood. "In all seriousness, you look stunning, Casey." He reached for her. "Absolutely beautiful," he whispered. His hands ran the length of the yellow fabric as his lips trailed down her neck, planting soft kisses on her bare skin.

She shivered.

"But I can't wait to take it off you," he murmured, lifting the chiffon to expose her butt cheeks. He squeezed, tugging at her lace panties.

Casey giggled and pressed her hands to his chest. Heat washed over her as the light from the window caught his eyes, the feathering of white on his lashes accentuated by the sun's afternoon rays.

You're freaking irresistible, Austin Templeton.

His fingers traveled up her back and gripped the zipper.

"It's pinned in a thousand places, so don't get too excited yet, sir." She giggled as his face fell. "But after the wedding, you have my permission to rip it off me."

"It's a deal." He grinned and leaned forward, pressing his lips onto hers as his fingers threaded through her hair, skimming her ear.

"Oh!" She pulled away. "My earring."

"Hmm?" His eyes popped open.

"I think I lost my earring in your bed last night. Can I go look?"

His laptop pinged on the table and his attention rerouted. "You don't need to ask me, Casey girl."

She took two steps down the hall and turned, her gaze raking over him. He'd replaced his glasses, and his fingers tapped away at the keyboard as his eyes scoured the screen. Casey shook her head.

Men and their two-second attention spans.

She gripped the knob, pushing the door open to his bedroom. In true Austin fashion, he'd made the bed and had a stack of folded laundry resting near his pillow. She ran her hand across the top blanket. *Nothing.* Casey sighed, lifting the tower of clothes to the nightstand. The lamp wobbled as an envelope fluttered to the ground, the words, *Austin, we'll get through it together* returning her gaze.

"Get through what?" She frowned and squinted at the unfamiliar handwriting. With a quick glance at the door, she bent down and yanked out the glossy cardstock inside. It tumbled to her lap as the loopy cursive reflected the sunlight on the gold inlay.

Dr. Joshua Michael Templeton
&
Mavis Marie Benson
request the honor of your presence
at their wedding
on the ninth of July
at one o'clock in the afternoon
The Templeton Manor
Rosewood, California
Dinner & dancing to follow
Black tie required

A pain seared in her gut, gnawing at her insides. She sank to Austin's bed and eyed the note scrawled on the back of the invitation. "We'll get through it together," she whispered, dragging her index finger along the note. "Lauren?" she whispered. "Why?"

She swallowed, fighting back the bile rising in her throat as more questions danced through her mind. *Why would he need help getting through the wedding? Unless...* Casey shook her head, stuffing the invitation back in its envelope as the pit in her stomach deepened. *What did you tell her, Austin?*

Casey dropped her gaze to the bed, the recall of last night settling in her heart, his admission of love pouring into her soul. She ran her hand over his pillow, pulling forth the memories of the love they created no more than twelve hours prior. She heaved out a breath as her eyes caught the red smear on the wall—Mavis's blood from the night she fainted, the night that set everything in motion.

She dragged her fingers atop the stain. "It always comes back to you, Mavs." A swell of anger flared in her heart, jealousy roaring through her bloodstream. Her fists clenched, creasing the invitation in her hands.

"Did you find it, Case?" Austin called from the dining room, jarring her back to reality. She jumped from the bed and dropped to her knees, running her hand along the floor beneath the bed. The silver stud caught her palm on the second pass, and she snagged it with half a smile.

"Yeah! It's here!" she called, rising to her feet. She replaced the envelope on the nightstand and moved the stack of laundry back to the bed. With a sigh, she left Austin's room and the offending note, tiptoeing back down the hall to her own bedroom.

Casey returned to the mirror and shoved the silver stud back into its home. With a step backward, she surveyed herself once more and frowned at her reflection. Her stomach churned, anxiety swirling in her gut once again.

Do you still have feelings for her, Austin?

"Because if you do… you're doing a bang-up job hiding it from me."

"When're you flying in?" Mavis tied a piece of white lace ribbon into a bow and picked up the hot glue gun.

"Oh, umm, Austin booked our tickets. Hang on." Casey propped the phone up against her pillow and yanked the iPad from the stack of clutter on her desk. Stifling a mid-morning yawn, she tapped away in search of flight times. "We leave O'Hare at 11:20 AM on Thursday… so, that's what? Like two o'clock your time that we land?"

Mavis nodded. "Perfect. I'm kind of nervous for this bachelorette party Lauren has planned. I'm glad you'll be there, Case." She smiled and dropped the bow.

Lauren.

Her anxiety-inducing note hammered against her heart, unease gripping her gut. Casey forced a grin on her lips. "It's just a party."

Her eyes widened on the tiny phone screen. "Just a party, but my soon-to-be mother-in-law will be there. She doesn't exactly like me anymore."

"She used to?"

Mavis nodded. "I mean, she always seemed to when I was a kid."

"So, it's just her that's making you nervous?"

I have to get to the bottom of this. What if it's not just Austin who still feels something?

Mavis pressed her lips together. "Among other things I guess."

"Like?"

She shook her head and picked up another piece of ribbon. "I mean, I'm nervous it'll rain on our wedding day. I'm nervous I'll trip walking down the aisle." She shrugged. "But that's normal, right? Every bride feels that." Her fingers twisted the lace into an intricate knot.

Tread lightly here, Casey!

"What about Josh?"

Mavis snorted. "Case, I've wanted to marry Josh since I was ten." She rolled her eyes. "He'll tell you the same." The ribbon fell from her fingers as she frowned. "Why would you ask me about him?"

Casey scrunched her nose and pulled her gaze away from the phone, a new flood of anxiety running rampant through her bloodstream.

"Damn it, Casey! Is this about Austin again?"

She tugged the phone farther away from her face and dropped her head back onto her pillow. "Maybe..." she muttered.

"What about him? Because I have to be honest here. I'm really not too interested in whatever it is you want to say." She rolled her eyes.

Uh-oh. What does that mean?

Casey huffed out a breath. "Well interested or not..." Her stomach dropped, sinking into the center of the mattress.

"Is that why you're asking me about Josh?" Her voice softened as she tugged the phone closer.

"Ugh..." Casey smashed her face into the pillow, dragging her cheeks across the soft material.

What am I getting myself into here?

"I'm in love with Joshua, Casey. There's really nothing else I can say about it. And I'm really not sure why you keep bringing up Austin. You know he's…"

"Know he's what?" Casey challenged.

"Complicated."

"Well, you got that right." Casey huffed out a heavy sigh and closed her eyes, letting Austin's essence encase her soul. She smiled, inhaling the imagined scent of sandalwood. "But he's also absolutely incredible… kind… gentle… and perfect."

"Oh, my God! You fell for him."

Casey rolled her eyes. "Well, you did too, girlfriend!"

"I told you not to get involved, Casey!" Her head dropped into the palm of her hand, her fingers kneading her temples. "I specifically told you not to! God, there are so many reasons!"

Like you still love him?

Casey sneered. "You're not my mom."

"No. I'm not, but I may as well be. Damn it, Casey! Why?" she scolded.

"Oh, please! Give me a break here, Mavs." She exhaled and tugged her body upward to rest against the wall.

Mavis scrunched her nose and dropped her chin to her chest. "Does he love you back? Is that what this is? You telling me that you guys are what, like a couple now?" Her head snapped up as a smile grew on her lips. Josh appeared on the screen, pressing a gentle kiss to her forehead—a Templeton trademark.

"Hey, Casey! How are you?" he asked, tugging the phone from Mavis's hands.

"Hi, Josh… umm… all good. Just catching up on girl talk." She plastered a smile on her lips, one usually reserved for customers with fat wallets.

He smiled and handed the phone back to Mavis. "Well, then I'm interrupting."

"No, no! Actually, I gotta run anyway. Lunch shift in twenty," she lied. "I'll see you love birds soon, okay?"

Mavis's eyes widened. "Casey McDaniels, don't you dare—"

Casey tapped the red button on her phone, eager to end the conversation as a pile of guilt and confusion jammed in her throat. She swallowed, forcing away the discomfort as a knock on the door interrupted the sour mood she'd ended the call with.

"You awake, Casey girl?" The knob twisted, and the hinges creaked as Austin pushed the door open. The weight of his body met the bed, snuggling in beside her as the scent of sandalwood blanketed the room, the smell intoxicating. "Still in bed, Sleeping Beauty?" His breath tickled her neck as a shiver raced up her spine.

"Wrong princess," she murmured. "But I'll still take true love's kiss." Her eyes closed as she exhaled away the aftermath of her conversation with Mavis.

"And I'll take that happily ever after." His fingers glided along her cheek as he turned her face toward his body and pressed his lips to hers.

A familiar wave of exhilaration washed over her, her heartbeat quickening at his tender touch. His left hand ran the length of her thigh beneath the covers as a moan escaped her mouth. Heat descended on her like a summer day's humidity.

Do you even know what you do to me, Austin?

"Hey, come with me. I've got a surprise for you."

Her eyes popped open as he moved, shifting to hop from the bed. "Must be one hell of a surprise if you just turned down the strong possibility of morning sex."

"Surprise first, morning sex second." He winked and tossed a sweatshirt to her lap.

"This better be good," she muttered and padded down the hallway on his heels.

His butt plopped down on the couch, and his feet automatically tucked beneath him. She dropped to the seat beside him as he propped his laptop on her legs. Her eyes scanned the screen, skimming for the elusive surprise.

"What am I looking at, Austin?" She squinted.

His voice boomed. "An internship, Case!" He snagged

the computer back from her lap and pointed to the screen. "The mayor of Chicago is up for reelection next year, and she's hiring interns to help run her campaign. You have to apply. This is a freaking phenomenal experience!"

Casey's lips smashed together, regret settling in her stomach—icing on the cake of uncertainty. *Of course, you'd find something like this.* Tugging the sweatshirt closer to her body, her anxiety rebounded and burned a new hole in her gut.

"She's hiring for everything. Social media managers, event planners, promotions, communications—all of it," he continued, his gaze still glued to the screen. Excitement burst from his body as his fingers tapped away at the keyboard, scrolling through the application. "Do you have a résumé saved somewhere? We can apply right now."

She swallowed and winced as the words left his lips. "And by résumé, do you mean a piece of paper that just says *bartender* in big bold letters?" Casey rolled her eyes. "Or maybe you want the one that says, *part-time community college student?*"

He frowned. "Oh, come on, Case, that's not all you have to include, and you know it." He sighed, tilting his head as his gaze returned to the screen.

"I'm not qualified, Austin. Look, I appreciate what you're trying to do here, but come on… I'm not who they're looking for." Her gaze fell to her lap as every ounce of confidence in her body drained from her system.

He wrinkled his nose and set the laptop on the coffee table. Draping his arm around her shoulders, he tugged her into his body, into the warmth radiating from his heart. "I just want you to be happy," he whispered. "My dad always told me… when you love someone, their success is your happiness too. And this just seemed like an easy way to get started on that path." He pressed his lips to her forehead. "I'm sorry if I'm upsetting you. It wasn't my intention at all."

She nuzzled into him, the morning stubble on his chin

scratching her cheek. "I know. And I'm sorry. It does sound like an amazing opportunity. I just have, like, zero confidence." Her face fell as her fingers searched for the missing drawstring on her sweatshirt.

He nudged her chin upward as his eyes found hers. "My goal here is not to pressure you. I just don't want you to miss out on an opportunity that makes a lot of sense for your future."

She shook her head and tucked her hair behind her ears. "I swear, Austin, between you and Mavis, you're the only reason I'm still in school and limping forward in life." Pulling her body from his embrace, she rose from the couch and staggered into the kitchen, seeking a cup of coffee. The brown liquid poured into the mug as the brew infiltrated her nose, the power of caffeine perking her dismal mood.

Austin sank onto the barstool at the counter and propped his chin in his palm. He sighed, raking his eyes over her—his lips motionless.

Discomfort settled in her stomach as the coffee slid down her throat.

Is this some stupid lawyer tactic? Stare at the defendant until they talk?

"Say something, Austin."

"Still your turn, Casey girl. You can't just throw a comment out there like that and then walk away." A half-hearted smile tugged at his lips.

"Ugh. You're fucking infuriating to talk to sometimes. Do you know that?" She gulped another sip, cringing at the burn on her tongue. "I didn't mean anything I said," she spit out.

He shook his head. "No, you did. And I want to know more."

"And I don't want to talk about it, all right? Can we please just leave it alone?"

He frowned and slouched in his seat, his fingers trailing along the edge of the counter. A sigh escaped him as his gaze lifted to find hers.

She cringed and slammed the mug on the counter. "Fine, Austin! Do you really want to know why I'm *still* in school? Why I'm not interested in a bachelor's degree or a fancy internship with the mayor?" Blood pounded in her ears as the pangs of tears threatened her eyes, a tidal wave of emotions crashing in her heart. Her vision fogged, clouded by the frustration and anger welling in her eyes.

"Talk to me, Case..." he whispered. "Tell me."

She dropped her hands to her hips as the first tears betrayed her lids and rolled down her cheeks. "I'm not like you. My family didn't have money. My parents never went to school. My father died of an overdose when I was seventeen. My sister is in prison, and my mom wants nothing to do with me." The words tumbled from her lips, spilling the secrets of her soul into the man before her. "Graduate high school, get a job, and get out of the house. That was it." She shrugged and jammed her hands into the pockets of her sweatshirt. "And honestly, Austin, when Mavis pushed me to actually try to go to school full-time last year, I fucked it up. Among other *things*, I couldn't balance a job and all the classes. And Mavis always picked up my slack. Always supported me through..."

Her voice wavered as her fingers dragged across her stomach, the still fresh memory of miscarriage squeezing her heart. She shook her head. "Never mind. Just never mind." Casey picked up the coffee carafe and refilled the cup as a fresh wave of tears trickled down her face. She hung her head and swallowed the swell of emotions bubbling forth from her belly.

His arms encircled her, tugging her into the safety and comfort of his body, accepting her secrets, ready to be stored in his heart for safekeeping. His warm breath tickled the top of her head as he squeezed, threading his fingers through her hair. "I'm so sorry, Casey. I shouldn't have pushed you to tell me all that," he whispered.

She sobbed, pressing her face into his chest as embarrassment crashed around her.

"Mavis made you keep taking classes?" he murmured in her ear.

The embarrassment morphed into fury, spiraling and spewing with rage as it coated her heart, piling onto the frustration she shared with her *best* friend. Jealousy fueled the sudden blaze of fire in her soul, each flame licking at her wounded pride.

Fucking Mavis. It's always about fucking Mavis with you!

She pulled away, yanking her body from his grasp. "I pour my soul out to you, and you're going to focus on fucking Mavis?" Her voice quivered as she swiped at the tears, running her hand beneath her nose.

He shook his head. "No! Case! That's not who I'm focused on!" His eyes widened as he reached for her.

She swatted him away, backing into the corner. "You are though, Austin! Don't you see it? It always comes back to her!" Casey wrapped her arms around herself as shivers cascaded along her body.

"That's not true," he stammered, his gaze falling to the floor.

"Just last night, you told me you loved me."

His eyes flew to hers. "And I do, Casey. I wouldn't have said those words if I didn't mean them." He blew out a breath and dragged his hands through his hair. "What is happening here?"

Lauren's note paraded through her mind again, the onset of uncertainty.

I have to know. I have to know if you're over her. I have to know what you told your sister.

"Austin, are you over her? Are you still in love with Mavis?"

The question hung in the air, filling the space between them—stabbing holes in the heart of newfound love.

His face fell, an unnatural stillness overtaking his body before he smacked his lips together and stepped back, stuffing his hands into his pockets. The hurt in his eyes ripped holes in her soul.

"You know, Casey…" He grabbed his keys from the dining room table and shuffled toward the apartment door. His hand grasped the knob as he looked back over his shoulder. "I've been truthful with you from the first day I met you. I may be a lot of things, but a liar is not one of them. When I told you I loved you last night, I meant it. I'm sorry if that's not enough." He pulled the door open and left the apartment, the lock snapping with a soft click.

Her stomach dropped, the pit in her belly swallowing the remains of her heart. She shook her head as the tears pooled, sliding down her cheeks like a river. The silence rang in her ear, each passing second a new stab to her gut.

"You didn't answer my question. Do you still love her?" she whispered before her knees gave out and she sank to the floor.

JULIE NAVICKAS

CHAPTER FIFTEEN

Austin

"Do you want a coffee?" Casey dropped her neon-pink bag onto an empty stretch of faux leather seats at gate 3B.

"Umm, yeah. Thanks." Austin dumped his stuff on the floor and settled into the block of seats. Through the smeary window, his gaze sought the empty tarmac, the minutes ticking away as their flight to California loomed. With a sigh, he yanked his computer from his bag and opened it across his lap. The device powered to life as his stomach twisted, each knot tightening in his chest.

"Okay, be right back," she announced and marched away.

His eyes followed her through the crowd, a smile spreading across his lips as she stumbled where the carpet met the tile of the walkway. Casey disappeared into the sea of hurried passengers, her flip-flops slapping away across the floor.

Austin released a heavy exhale, rubbing the muscles in his neck. His heart hadn't quite repaired from the blowout fight they shared a week prior, their relationship strained and tested for the first time. *I owe you an apology, Cinderella...*

He shook his head and dropped his gaze back to his computer, focusing on the spinning pinwheel as the airport's crappy wi-fi network appeared.

You called me on the very thing I hate most about myself, Casey girl. And none of it is fair to you.

"Dammit, Mavis," he muttered as the internet connected. His eyes closed as he dropped back in his seat to allow the memories of last year to flood his brain. Her voice reverberated in his soul, her admission of love squeezing the air from his lungs. "You loved me back," he whispered, dragging his hands along his cheeks. "You really did…" A moment of epiphany rippled through his body. *I watched you struggle, Mavs, torn between me and Josh.* He snorted, realization gripping his heartstrings. *And now here I am in the same struggle. You or Casey?*

The day he moved to Chicago rebounded in his memory as he turned again to stare out the window. The plane pulled up to the gate as a smile tugged at his lips, the recall of Casey crashing into his battered heart, unknowingly helping him navigate his conflicted sense of self. He hung his head. "You deserve better, Casey girl…"

I owe you something better.

Blowing out a breath, Austin opened the mayor of Chicago's webpage, Casey's information pre-populating into each box. His heart lurched as he reviewed the materials he'd secretly pieced together for her over the last week, praying she'd change her mind before the deadline to apply.

Her butt hit the chair beside him, the scent of fresh coffee wafting to his nose.

"Here you go." She pushed the coffee into his hands.

"Thanks, Case," he murmured, angling his laptop away. He leaned over and pressed his lips to her forehead as a field of invisible lilacs overpowered the coffee and stale air of the airport.

"I'm sorry," he whispered.

She shook her head as her free hand squeezed his knee. "Don't, Austin…" A frown tugged at her lips. "Come on, we already talked about all this."

His heart sank. Her willingness to overlook his biggest flaw rattled his soul.

"It's me who should apologize to you… *again.*" She swallowed, shuffling her feet to hide her toes beneath his bag. "That morning, I umm, took a lot of my crap and insecurities out on you. It wasn't fair. I asked you something very unfair."

A flurry of warmth descended on his body, her words slashing at his heart. Leaning forward, Austin set his coffee on the floor and wrapped his arms around her, drawing her closer to his body. He shook his head. "Case, I forced you into it. All of it. I shouldn't have pushed your buttons like that." His laptop slipped from his knees, and Austin lunged to save it, the mayor of Chicago beaming her wide smile directly at Casey.

"Looks like you're not done pushing though." She pointed at the computer screen and grinned.

Shit!

His fingers clasped the top of the screen, ready to snap it closed. "I, umm…" he stammered before her hands yanked the device from his lap.

"Wait. Is this a *completed* application?" Her eyes skimmed the screen, her fingers scrolling through his words.

His heart hammered in his chest, blood pounding in his ears with each scroll of her finger. "Case, before you get angry… I didn't submit anything!" He exhaled as his cheeks reddened. "I was just *thinking* through some potential answers. That's all, I swear!"

Her gaze lifted from the laptop, scanning his face with X-ray vision. "So, this is like, done?"

"I mean, yeah, but…"

She smiled and clicked *submit*, the little pinwheel spinning with gusto. The words *thank you for your submission* appeared on the screen. Casey shut the laptop and handed it back to Austin.

"Thank you," she whispered and pressed her face into

his chest.

Austin dropped the laptop to the seat beside him, pulling Casey fully into his embrace. His nose met her hair as he exhaled, breathing out a sigh of relief. "You're not mad at me?"

She nuzzled into him. "No. Actually, I just might love you a little bit more, Austin Templeton."

The overhead intercom crackled to life. "Ladies and gentlemen, we are now ready to begin boarding flight 1219 to Los Angeles, California. At this time, we welcome passengers in Group A to approach the gate. Please have your ticket and identification ready."

Their fellow passengers stood, stretched, and gathered their belongings, ready to make their way to the line forming at the gate. Austin reached down to collect his bag, but the sudden weight on his knee stilled his heart.

"Are we okay?" She squinted, the blue of her eyes clouding with a layer of tears.

He dropped his hand over hers and squeezed, lifting her fingers to his lips. He pressed a kiss to her soft skin and smiled. "Better than okay," he whispered, tugging her upward to stand.

She followed and scooped up her bright pink bag, draping the strap over her shoulder. With a gulp of coffee, she stepped behind him, dribbling the brown liquid down her chin.

Austin grinned as she used the sleeve of her sweatshirt to mop up the mess. "Come on. Let me show you home, Chicago girl."

For better or worse.

The car from the airport pulled into the driveway of Austin's extravagant red brick home. As the driver put the vehicle in park, Austin's breath caught in his throat staring out the window at the luxury bachelor pad. His stomach churned, but his fingers gripped the car door's handle, pushing it open as the familiar warm summer air of California kissed his skin.

"Oh, my God... this is your house?" Casey gulped and slammed the door. "Why would you ever move into my teeny tiny little apartment?" She held up her hand and allowed an inch of space to appear between her thumb and index finger.

After retrieving their bags from the trunk, Austin thanked and paid the driver and met Casey at the bottom of the porch steps. "Because you lived there, Casey girl." He grinned and pressed his lips to hers.

Her cheeks flushed pink as she grabbed her bag from his grasp, following him up the staircase to the front door.

Austin tapped in the keycode and stepped inside, his gaze zeroing in on his favorite chair in the living room—still there, still just as he left it. He swallowed, dropping his bag to the floor as unease gripped his gut. *How long have I been gone?* The familiarity of home didn't quite touch his heart the way it once did.

"Geez, Austin!" Casey giggled. "You have a freaking mansion!" Her fingers ran along the wrought-iron railing as she kicked her sandals off.

He cringed.

What are you going to think of Templeton Manor?

She walked the length of the foyer until her butt dropped onto the sofa in the living room. Slouching backward, she smiled. "I don't even need to sit on my feet here."

He shook his head and snorted, picturing the new couch he ordered, finally scheduled to arrive over the weekend.

You'll be so surprised when we get home!

"Holy cow!" She pointed behind him. "Is that your backyard?" Her eyes widened as she jumped from the sofa and darted past him to the sliding doors. "It's like the size of Millennium Park!" she called over her shoulder, stepping down onto the paved brick patio.

Austin followed her outside under the baking sun. He tilted his face upward, basking in the dry heat of

California—the muggy, humid summer weather of Chicago two thousand miles away.

"Geez, this must be a bitch to mow." Casey laughed as her feet padded through the luscious green grass. "My mom always made me pull weeds and mow as a kid and I hated every second of it. Just one reason I love city living." She unzipped her sweatshirt and looped it around her waist.

Stepping behind her, Austin ran his hands along her bare arms and planted a kiss on the top of her head with a sigh.

"You've never mowed it, have you?" she asked, turning to face him.

A smile tugged at the left side of his mouth as embarrassment snaked up his spine. His cheeks flushed red with more than the warmth of the sunshine.

"I've called you pretentious before, right?" She snorted. "I think I need a new word."

He scooped her small body up into his arms and carried her back to the house. "If it makes you happy, I'll cut each blade of grass by hand with a pair of kitchen scissors before we leave."

She giggled as he returned her feet to the cool wood floor in the dining room. "While that would promise a few laughs, you can save your time, sir." Tugging the collar of his shirt toward her, she pressed her lips to his.

Adrenaline surged through his bloodstream and goosebumps erupted on his forearms with a shiver of longing as her mouth moved against his. He pulled her closer, gripping her waist until her hands dipped beneath his shirt, the lazy graze of her fingernails skimming his skin.

Desire coated his heart as his name tumbled from her lips in a whispered, raspy rush, the depths of her soul calling to his own with urgency.

"What time do you have to meet my sister again?"

"Four," she murmured, nipping his earlobe with her teeth.

Fire blasted through his system, prickling and burning through his veins. Glancing at the hallway clock, he read

3:23 PM.

Oh, that's plenty of time, Cinderella…

"And I still need to shower and get ready," she added, dragging her tongue along the side of his neck.

Heat descended on his body, each nerve cell sizzling with growing anticipation. *Do you even know what you do to me, Casey?* A mischievous smile broke across his lips. "Have I not shown you the lovely two-person shower upstairs yet?" He pressed his growing arousal into her belly.

Her hands dropped to the button on his pants. "Sounds spacious. I'd like to see it," she whispered, trailing the zipper downward.

The smile on his lips widened as the sultry purr of her voice prioritized all blood flow to his pelvis. "Follow me."

The doorbell rang. "You're home!" Lauren's voice penetrated the front door, biting into the moment, each word slicing the plans of shower sex in half with a serrated knife.

A guttural groan of disappointment dripped from his lips as he dropped his forehead against Casey's. "No fucking way…" he moaned, closing his eyes and catching his breath.

She giggled, giving his hips one last longing squeeze before pulling away. "I think your sister's here."

Austin shook his head and tugged at the zipper on his jeans. "I'm gonna need a minute." His eyes widened as the smile on her lips grew. "Distract her for me?"

Casey nodded and smoothed her hair, stepping toward the front door with pink cheeks.

With another groan, Austin retreated into the kitchen and folded his torso over the cold quartz countertop, willing his body to calm.

Impeccable timing, Lauren.

From the foyer, Casey's voice greeted his sister as his eyes caught sight of the digital display on the microwave. 4:02 PM. Tilting his head to the side, the hallway clock reappeared, still reading 3:23 PM. "Ugh." He rolled his eyes.

Lauren's singsong voice floated down the hallway, the

excitement in his pants diminishing. With a stretch, Austin pulled himself from the counter and headed for the living room with heavy steps.

"You're home!" Lauren wrapped her arms around him with a squeeze.

"And you're right on time, aren't ya?" He locked eyes with Casey behind her back with a grin.

She returned his sheepish smile. "Oh! But that means I'm running late!" Casey tiptoed back to the foyer and snagged her bag, eyeing the second floor.

"First door on the right." He pointed.

She tripped on the third stair and barked out a laugh as she regained her balance, sprinting up the remaining steps. His bedroom door clicked closed, echoing in the quiet home.

"She's a walking accident."

Lauren giggled. "True, but I love her anyway. She's so good for you, Austin."

He rolled his eyes. "Always so subtle." With a deep sigh, he dropped into his favorite chair, instinctively curling his feet beneath him. He snickered and wiggled his toes.

"How was your flight?" Lauren sank onto the couch opposite him.

"Fine I guess," he answered with a yawn, stretching his arms over his head.

It's going to be a long night.

"Is it weird being back?"

He nodded, his gaze circling the room. A Dodgers ball cap looked back at him from the hat rack, and Austin grinned. "A lot has changed, I guess."

Lauren dropped her elbows to her knees, propping her chin in her palms. "Are you feeling okay about this weekend?"

You really don't disappoint, do you?

His gaze fell to the floor, waiting to see if the familiar squeeze on his heart would return. He inhaled, ready to battle the tightening sensation in his chest, but nothing happened. Lifting his gaze back to Lauren, he smiled. "Actually, I'm good."

"Yeah?" She tilted her head.

"A hell of a lot better than the last time I was here." He blew out a breath and gripped the arms of the chair.

Lauren nodded. "I see it." Leaning to the side, she snatched the throw pillow beside her and squeezed it tight to her chest. "Are you ready for tonight? Josh is like way nervous you're gonna force him to go to a strip club or something."

He snorted, picturing his twin in a seedy downtown L.A. strip club. *If I'm a little weird about germs, Dr. Templeton is a certified germaphobe in double-layered latex gloves.* He smiled. "The agenda is void of strip clubs," he promised.

"Well, what are you doing then?" Her eyes widened.

"You girls do whatever you want. And let us boys do what we want." He winked.

Lauren rolled her eyes, chucking the pillow at his head. "Fine then. Keep your dumb secrets." She giggled. "Should I at least expect Mitch to come home at some point tonight?"

Austin shrugged. "He can sleep here. I don't care."

A crash overhead thundered through the ceiling. He cringed, glancing upward. "Do your plans involve bowling balls by chance?"

A belly laugh burst free from her lips as she fell backward onto the couch. "Oh yeah, Mavis, our bowling champion!"

His cheeks turned pink as warmth flooded through him, the image of the girls bowling inviting a bout of giggles. "Casey slips on regular flooring. She doesn't need oiled floors or special shoes!"

Lauren laughed, clutching her side as tears clouded her eyes. "World's worst bridesmaid sitting right here if I planned a bachelorette party at Pinheads!"

Austin smiled and pulled his body from the chair. He stretched and looked upward at the ceiling, the laughter and comical image subsiding. "Well… whatever it is you have planned, just don't let Casey pay for anything, okay?" He pulled his wallet from his back pocket and handed cash over to Lauren. "I think four days away from the restaurant is a tight swing for her."

She shook her head and swatted the cash away. "Don't be silly. I'll cover it."

Austin pushed the money into her purse. "Humor me."

She rolled her eyes. "Whatever you say, boss." She tucked the money deeper into the bag and zipped it closed. "Oh! I have your suit in the car. Mitch picked everything up this afternoon. Let me go grab it." She stood and Austin followed her to the front door. "I've got cases of beer too that I'm supposed to deliver." She snorted. "Mitch means business tonight, I think."

Returning to the driveway Austin squinted and shielded his eyes in the blazing summer heat. "How have things been with you guys? Any better?"

Lauren shook her head and opened the trunk of her silver Lexus. "Just make sure he has a fun time tonight, okay?"

The trunk door lifted as cases of beer and brown bags of liquor appeared. "Fun, I can promise…" Austin pointed into the trunk. "But I can't promise a quality return condition with this kind of supplies."

She snorted as her phone rang. Pulling the device from her pocket, she frowned and pointed toward the house. "I'll be right back," she mouthed before accepting the call and walking away.

Pulling two cases of beer from the trunk, Austin retreated to the staircase and pushed the front door open.

"There you are!" Casey smiled, dragging her hands through her damp curls. "I came down and you were both gone."

"Sorry, Casey girl." He set the beer down and pulled her body into his. His fingers collided with the sheer black tank top hugging her skin, the little bear on her hip peeking out from atop her skirt. Austin groaned and pressed a kiss on her lips. "Proposal. Skip the party. Let's spend the night in my bed instead," he pleaded.

With an inhale, he lowered his lips to her neck, ready to breathe in the field of lilacs from the wet tresses. But his brow furrowed, and he scrunched his nose. "Wait, why do you smell like a man?"

She giggled. "Would you believe I forgot my bathroom bag at home? I had to use what you had in your shower... so I'm rugged mountain fresh tonight!"

He snorted. "Well, I won't have to worry about any men trying to steal you away from me." He wrinkled his nose, hampering a sneeze. "You'll smell just like them."

With a laugh, she snuggled back into his embrace and looped her arms around his torso. "Behave tonight. Don't get too crazy." She tapped her index finger against his chest, tipping her face upward to kiss the blond stubble on his chin.

"No worries, Casey girl. No Old Style in sight." He pointed to the cases of beer on the floor behind him.

She grinned and Austin snapped a mental photo of her, etching her beauty in his brain.

CHAPTER SIXTEEN

Lauren

"Just keep 'em coming, okay?" Lauren squeezed Miguel's elbow with a smile.

"Whatever you say, boss." He winked and backed out of the private party room's side door with an empty tray.

"These are delicious." Mavis brought the glass to her lips and sipped. "But dangerous!" She squinted, eyeing the drink. "What is it?"

Lauren giggled, heat rolling over her body in the crowded room. "It's the Mystic Mavis!"

Casey choked on the liquid in her mouth, setting the glass on the table as the aqua-tinted cocktail sloshed over her hands. "I'm sorry, the Mystic Mavis?" She snorted and wiped her sticky hands on a cloth napkin. "Eight years of bartending and not once have I made that for anyone."

Lauren gulped the rest of her drink, resting the empty glass on the table. "There's a reason for that. It's Pier Ninety Two's signature drink of the evening in honor of our beautiful bride."

Mavis smiled and dropped her gaze to her lap. "You didn't need to do that, Lauren," she murmured. Pink tinged her cheeks. "But it's really tasty!" she added, perking up as a new song came on. "What's in it?"

Casey held her hand up. "Hang on, let me guess." She took another sip and set the drink on the table, licking her lips. "Tequila for sure... lime... and honey?"

Lauren's eyes widened. "Damn! You're close!" She pushed her empty glass to the side. "Tequila, pear puree, agave, and lime."

Casey nodded and tossed back the rest of the liquid in her cup. "Well, I'll be taking this recipe home to Chicago with me! It's so good!"

The smile widened on Lauren's lips as her gaze circled the party. *Is everyone having fun?* She shifted in her seat, tugging at the hem of her dress. *Is the music too loud?* Brushing a crumb from the tablecloth, she straightened her napkin.

"Lauren, please stop stressing." Mavis smashed her lips together and tilted her head. "You've put together an amazing party. I can't thank you enough!" Reaching across the table, her hand covered hers and squeezed.

With a nod, Lauren smiled, her gaze still circulating the room at the small groups of women hovering around cocktail tables, sipping drinks, snacking on appetizers, and chatting.

"Seriously, Mavs is right! I can't believe you own this place!" Casey scooped up a fork and eyed the shiny silver. "I've never felt so fancy!" She dropped the utensil back to the table and dragged her fingers along the set. "I don't even know what all of these are for." She grinned.

Mavis leaned forward and pointed to each fork with a polished pink index finger. "Salad, dinner, and dessert." She winked.

"Why do you even know that?" Casey squinted and wrinkled her nose.

"Our little Bensons were subjected to one too many dinner parties at our house as children." Susan Templeton stepped to the side of the table and smiled, straightening the forks in front of Casey.

Lauren's gaze lifted to her mother as she pulled a chair from a neighboring table and placed it between Mavis and Casey.

Uh-oh.

Mavis straightened, twisting in her seat to face Susan. "Oh! Mrs. Templeton, have you met my friend Casey yet?"

The color drained from Susan's face as she smashed her lips together in a thin line. "You should probably just start calling me Susan, dear," she answered curtly, dropping her hand to pick at a non-existent piece of lint on her navy-blue dress. "But no, we haven't met. Though I hear my son is quite taken with her." A brilliant white smile replaced her look of indifference as she extended a rigid hand in Casey's direction.

"Oh! Umm... so nice to meet you, Mrs. Templeton!" answered Casey, gripping Susan's fingers.

"Charmed," she murmured, shaking her sticky hand.

Casey cowered and dropped her gaze as Susan released her hand.

"So... you're the one who stole my son's heart and sent him running across the country?"

Geez, Mom! Could you be any ruder right now?

Casey's knee slammed into the table and rattled the silverware. "Ouch! Oh! Umm, I mean, well..." she stammered, straightening forks again.

"Mom, you know Austin left for Chicago for the law firm. Casey didn't make him leave L.A." Lauren shook her head as a sudden boost of courage burst forth from her heart, the many Mystic Mavis drinks coursing through her bloodstream.

Susan sneered. "No, I suppose it wasn't *her* that made him leave, was it?" She pulled her glass to her lips and raised a pencil-thin eyebrow, rolling her eyes in Mavis's direction.

Mavis frowned, slouching forward in her seat as the air seemingly deflated from her lungs. Her lips mouthed the word *help* in Lauren's direction.

I'm on it.

"Oh! Mom, did you try the bacon-wrapped dates yet? They're new on the menu and you just have to try them! Miguel swears by them—best appetizer on the menu!" Lauren rose from her seat and pointed to the buffet, offering her hand to her mother.

Susan shrugged and stood. "Lovely to meet you, Casey dear." With a glance over her shoulder, her parting words dripped from her lips. "Mavis, enjoy your party tonight."

Oh, God.

Lauren wrapped her arm around her mom, tugging her toward the corner of the room and the tower of appetizers, leaving Mavis and Casey's lifeless stares behind.

"Mom! You're being so rude right now. Leave Mavis be," hissed Lauren. "And Casey is really perfect for Austin," she added with a small stomp of her foot. "He's really happy with her. Please give her a fair chance." She piled bacon-wrapped dates onto a plate and pushed it into her mom's grasp.

"What is it she does again?"

"Umm, same as me. A restaurant, Mom."

No need to share job titles.

Susan bit into a bacon-wrapped date, and a rare genuine smile spread across her lips. "Oh, these are good, sweetie!" Her gaze wandered in search of her friends. "Christina and Anna must try them!"

"Yeah! Don't let me stop you." Lauren shooed her mother away, releasing a heavy sigh as she raced back to her seat.

Casey blanched. "Holy hell, your mom hates me."

"Join the club." Mavis rolled her eyes and sloshed the melting ice around in her near-empty glass.

You guys aren't exactly wrong.

Lauren grinned as Miguel reappeared, setting three fresh Mystic Mavis drinks on the table. "No worries, Mavs. I'm not her favorite either." She lifted her eyebrows, bringing the fresh drink to her lips. "But welcome to the family anyway. Trust me, no one will ever outrank the miraculous

Templeton Twins."

Casey giggled and sipped. "Sore subject?"

"You have no idea…" Lauren brought the glass back to her lips and gulped, letting the sweet liquid touch her tongue and slide down her throat—willing the alcohol to take effect and release the stress on her heart.

Mavis downed her drink and shook her head. "Well, on that happy note, I should probably start thanking everyone for coming." She rose from her seat and stepped away, a slight wobble to her high-heeled step.

"You okay?" asked Lauren.

"Me?" Casey pointed to her chest. "Oh, umm… yeah for sure." She drained her cup again.

"I don't know about you, but I need something stronger than these girlie drinks. No offense to Miguel, but they're weak." A mischievous grin grew on her lips as she nodded her head toward the door. "Interested?"

Casey stood and dropped her napkin to the table. "After your mom, you don't need to ask me twice."

Lauren giggled and grabbed Casey's hand, leading her out the side door and into the kitchen. The smell of the evening's special, mushroom ravioli, infiltrated her nostrils as they passed through the prep station. Pulling a set of keys from her pocket, Lauren opened the door to the stockroom and stepped inside, tugging Casey behind her.

Casey's eyes scanned the tiny space, alight with excitement. "Every alcoholic's dream," she murmured, dragging her hands along the shelves of alphabetized bottles of liquor.

"Well, what'll it be?" Lauren stepped further inside, pointing at the many options.

"Umm, how crazy do we want to get tonight?" Casey's fingernails tapped on a bottle of Angel's Envy, her eyes glowing with sudden mischief.

Lauren's smile grew. "I mean, the boys are gonna get wild tonight, no doubt." She pulled the bottle of bourbon down and popped the cork. "I suggest we do the same." She held the bottle out to Casey. "You first, girlfriend."

Casey's hand closed around the neck of the bottle. "To Mavis and Josh… and their *happily ever after*." The bottle met her lips, and a dry cough followed her gulp. She sputtered, shaking her head back and forth. "Holy cow," she choked out.

"That good, huh?" Lauren tugged the bottle from her grasp and brought it to her mouth. Fire burned her throat as the liquid traveled downward, her body lurching at the warm sensation.

With a swipe of her hand, Casey brushed away the sweat forming on her brow, tugging the bottle back from Lauren. Two swigs later, her eyes swam with tears. "Oh, my God, it hurts! How do people drink this stuff?" She stared at the bottle and eyed the label.

Lauren shrugged. "Mitch loves it… just sips it over ice. I don't get it." She brought the bottle back to her lips with a grimace. And like the steam over the mushroom ravioli in the kitchen, her stress evaporated into thin air as the bourbon filtered through her bloodstream.

"Oh!" Casey giggled as she stumbled over the door jam. "We should take a picture and send it to the boys!" Pushing a stray curl away from her face, she staggered closer to Lauren.

"Ha! Yes! Let's do it!"

Casey patted her hips and pulled her phone from the waistband of her skirt.

Lauren roared with laughter. "You did not just pull that phone out of your underwear!" Tears clouded her eyes.

"Well, where else am I supposed to put it in this outfit?" Casey dissolved into her own fit of drunken giggles, moving closer to Lauren to snap a photo in front of the shelves of liquor. Opening a text, Casey tapped in, *Not one can of Old Style in this fancy place!*

"Old Style?" Lauren wrinkled her nose and clogged the cork back into the bottle, discreetly hiding it inside her jean jacket.

Casey snickered. "It's kind of a dumb joke between us." She smiled and tucked the phone back into her waistband. "Austin hates it!"

Lauren snorted and tugged the door open. She led the way back through the kitchen, passing Miguel with a wink and another squeeze on the elbow before re-entering the party.

"There you are!" Mavis sighed, folding her body over an empty cocktail table in the center of the room.

Casey cackled and stumbled forward. "How long have we been gone?"

Lauren dropped the bottle of bourbon onto the table and released a roar of drunken laughter. "Sorry, Mavs. World's worst bridesmaids right here!" She wrapped her arm around Casey's shoulders and pushed the bottle toward the bride. "But come on, catch up. The *real* party is about to start!"

Mavis smiled and yanked the cork from the bottle, her green eyes blazing with excitement.

CHAPTER SEVENTEEN

Casey

Casey stumbled up the steps, her eyes drooping with exhaustion. The ringing in her ears competed, and won, with the quiet 4 AM hour. Gripping the doorknob of the heavy oak front door of Austin's home, she pushed it open as the cab pulled out of the driveway.

Fuck, I'm tired…

The bright light of the chandelier flooded the foyer, the speakers in the living room blasting the smooth sounds of classic rock. Casey cringed and dropped her shoes to the floor as an unknown man rolled over on the couch in a deep sleep. A pillow fell, knocking into the coffee table, and an empty beer can tumbled to the carpet.

A chorus of rambunctious laughter echoed from the dining room.

"Oh, my God, they're still up?" she muttered, rubbing her eyes.

She stumbled down the hallway toward the rowdy male voices, each step bringing her closer to the powerful source of alcohol fumes dominating the house.

"Casey!" Josh slurred her name as she rounded the

corner and entered the brilliantly lit dining room. Playing cards tumbled from his hands, fanning out across the floor. "What're you doing here?" A wild grin broke free on his lips. "Aren't you supposed to be with my blushing bride?"

"Party's over, Josh. I left your blushing bride with her head in the toilet about twenty minutes ago." She giggled. "So, flushing, not blushing I guess."

Josh hiccupped as Casey slid into the empty seat at the table between the twins. The warmth of Austin's palm raked over her thigh as he leaned forward and planted a sloppy, wet kiss on her lips, the scent of scotch lingering in the air as he pulled away.

"Come on, I'll deal you in." Austin shoved a pile of cards into her hands, his head drooping forward like a rag doll. Leaning back, his elbow knocked into a half-empty beer bottle. The golden liquid coated the tabletop and soaked into the cards before dripping to the floor. Scooping up a wet card, he grinned and wiped it on his shirt.

"Oh, real nice, Austin." The dark-haired man beside him smacked him on the arm and tossed a pizza-stained paper towel in Casey's direction. He snorted, pulling his heavy eyes upward to meet her own. "And how about *my* wife?"

His stare searched her, the eerily familiar piercing green gaze biting into her soul. *And you are without a doubt, Mavis's brother.*

Casey flashed a smile. "Flushing a different toilet, Mitch Benson."

"Does anyone have a six?" Josh dropped another card to the floor, his eyes scanning the pile wadded up in his hands.

Mitch chucked the seven of diamonds into his lap and downed a shot of amber liquid. He grimaced and wiped his lips with the back of his paint-covered hand.

Casey eyed the seven of diamonds as Josh paired it with his six of clubs, resting it on a pile of stale breadsticks in the center of the table. She giggled. "Umm, what game is this?"

Austin swayed in his seat and passed a shot of clear liquid

across the table to his brother. "Go Fishy, Casey girl. You drink whenever you ask for a card or when you give a card."

A belly laugh boomed from her gut, the drunken trio of men playing a child's game of Go Fish squeezing her heart with pure amusement. She examined each of their faces, soaking in their silly smiles, tired eyes, and goofy grins.

It's only a matter of minutes before one of you falls from your chair and makes the floor your bed until dawn!

With a snort, she scooped up her cards and nodded toward the living room. "So how many cards did the guy on the couch ask for?"

Mitch dragged a hand through his hair and knocked the eight of hearts from the table with his elbow. "Scott has a new baby. Poor guy barely made it past eleven."

Casey smiled. Pulling the bottle of amber liquid in her direction, she fanned out her cards. "Who has a queen?" The smooth liquid invaded her mouth, trickling down her throat.

Austin handed her the king of spades. "My king to your queen, Cinderella," he answered, pulling the bottle from her hands and bringing it back to his mouth. He winked, flashing his baby blue eyes at her, the white tips of his lashes poignant under the harsh lighting.

Her stomach dipped, overriding the exhaustion blanketing her body. She grinned and scooped up his king, dumping it in the basket of bread.

"I think I have a full house." Mitch dropped his cards on the table with a proud smile and jabbed his elbow into Josh's gut.

Josh squinted, eyeing the row of cards. He barked out a laugh and plucked from the pile a business card tucked between the red and black royalty. "You're cheating!" he roared, flinging the business card across the table. His hand shot out, seemingly ready to return Mitch's jab, but his body tumbled from the chair instead, dropping to the floor in a fit of giggles.

Casey snickered as Mitch bent forward to help, his

attempt much like a toddler trying to pick up an object too heavy. He tripped, toppling over Josh as they rolled amidst the spilled beer and playing cards. Sliding from his seat, Austin joined them on the dining room floor, roughhousing as if they were all eight years old.

Casey dropped her head to the table in a fit of laughter, eyeing the beer slowly seeping into her hair. She snorted and closed her eyes with pure exhaustion, ready to let sleep take her. Shifting in her seat, her hand dropped atop the business card Josh had pulled from Mitch's hand. Reopening her eyes, the letters swam into focus, the words *divorce attorney* punctuating her brain. With a heavy jolt of realization, she swiped the card and pocketed it next to her phone, resting Dave Jensen's name in the waistband of her panties.

Shit. Lauren.

Casey woke to a vicious bout of nausea.

Death, please take me now.

She rolled, not daring to open her eyes, dreading the spinning room rollercoaster—a hangover guaranteed. Pressing her lips together, she swallowed the invisible ball of cotton in her mouth and cringed, the deep beat of a bass drum beating in her brain. She drew in a deep breath and heaved out a sigh, quelling the urge to immediately vomit.

A muffled moan met her ear, and she chanced a one-eyed glance at the mound of covers beside her. Austin unburied his body. His eyes popped open as a grin spread across his lips.

"Coffee. I'm gonna go make coffee." His fingers threaded through her hair as his lips pecked her forehead. He rolled away, bouncing to his feet before snagging a pair of sweatpants from his dresser and walking out of the room.

Casey rammed her eyes closed again, cowering beneath the covers. *How the fuck are you even moving right now?* But ready to move or not, her stomach lurched, and she raced to the bathroom, upending the last moments of their Go Fish game. She frowned and wiped the sweat from her brow. "Fucking disgusting," she murmured and squirted toothpaste on Austin's toothbrush.

Her tongue tingled with spearmint as she returned to bed, tugging the covers back up and over her face in a makeshift cave. The fresh scent of coffee reached her nose before the bed jiggled with the weight of Austin's body. His voice infiltrated her darkened hole of safety. "How're you feeling, Casey girl?"

She inhaled. "Like I just lost the game in the bottom of the ninth inning." She unburied her face, sweeping her gaze over Austin.

He lounged at her side, his left elbow propping his body up on the pillow. A steaming cup of coffee rested in his hand and a smile pulled at his lips. "Always baseball with you." He shifted the cup to his other hand as his warm palm caressed her cheek, brushing a curl behind her ear. "Fun night, huh?" He raised a brow and blew out a breath.

"I'm not even sure how you're awake right now. You boys had a shitshow in progress when I got back here."

He snorted and dropped his head to the pillow. "I don't remember you coming home." His fingers kneaded his forehead. "The kitchen is a fucking disaster." He grinned again and a giggle tumbled from his lips. "I have no idea what the hell happened down there."

"Go Fishy," she muttered, scooting her body upward to mimic his position. Casey reached for the coffee, and Austin handed it off to her with his eyebrows squished together.

"I'm sorry, what?"

"You don't remember playing Go Fish with Josh and Mitch last night?" She snickered and sipped the coffee. "Well, I mean, you at least called it Go Fish…"

Austin smiled and tilted his head. "Memory solidly unaccounted for, Cinderella." He scratched his forearm and reached forward, tugging her body into his bare torso. Lifting the cup from her hands, he set it on the nightstand.

Casey dropped her head into the crook of his arm and

inhaled, breathing in the scent of his body amidst the lingering smell of alcohol. Sandalwood penetrated her nose, the scent always intoxicating with comfort. She sighed. "Well, sir, what memories are accounted for? What did you boys do last night?" Her eyes closed, settling into the moment as Austin's face snuggled into her messy hair, his warm breath colliding with the top of her head.

"It wasn't supposed to be wild. We reserved the private room at Highside, had a few drinks, grabbed some pizza, and headed back here." He snickered. "Sounds really lame when you spell it out like that."

"Yeah, but it's probably exactly what Josh wanted. I bet he missed you."

Austin snorted and tugged the covers over his legs. "I will admit it's nice that he's speaking to me again."

"Well, it's like you said from the start... Moving to Chicago was a good idea. It gave you—and him—some dis—"

Austin's lips pressed into hers, tasting of coffee and fueled with urgency. Burrowing his hand beneath the covers, he squeezed her hips as a groan escaped his mouth. His fingers dipped below the waistline of her panties, his touch a guarantee of pleasure, but something scratched her instead.

His mouth pulled from hers as his hands uncovered the business card she'd tucked away hours before. He snorted. "Tell me I didn't just find a man's business card in your underwear, Casey McDaniels." Austin twirled the card between his fingers with amusement.

"Oh! Umm, yeah, I ahh, snagged it from the table last night." She wrinkled her nose and yanked the covers up to her face. "Mitch had it."

Austin frowned, his eyes flashing to the tiny card again. "Asshole," he muttered, crumpling it in his hand.

"The divorce attorney or Mitch?"

His brow furrowed. "Both." He smacked the card against his palm as his eyes sought the door of the bedroom.

"You grabbed this last night?"

"Yeah. Mitch had it in his pocket."

He nodded. "Can we keep this between us for now?"

"Yeah, of course." Casey squeezed his forearm. "You're not surprised by it though. Why?"

He shook his head but smiled as his gaze connected with hers. "Lauren mentioned it when she came to visit. I guess I just didn't really believe her, but this…" His voice trailed away as his fingers ran along the stubble on his chin. "How was she last night?"

Casey shrugged. "She seemed fine. We had a great time. Lauren even saved me from your mom." She smirked as his eyes widened.

"Oh, God, my mom was there?" He bit his bottom lip.

"Yeah. I don't think she likes me very much." She giggled, snuggling back into his body.

His arms tightened and pulled her closer. "Don't take offense to it. She's never liked anyone I've dated."

"Well, she really doesn't like Mavis too much either."

His body stiffened, the breath hitching in his throat at her words. "She used to, but I guess that was a long time ago," he muttered. His hand dropped, smacking against the mattress as his phone vibrated. He turned and snatched at the device on the nightstand, an immediate frown twisting on his lips as his eyes skimmed the screen.

"Everything okay?"

He nodded. "Umm, yeah. It's Steven Boyd. He wants me to stop in today while I'm in town."

"That's kind of weird, isn't it? He knows you're here for your brother's wedding."

Austin shrugged. "He and Rodger must just want a quick update on the office or something. No big deal. Will you be okay on your own for a bit?"

Casey flopped backward on the bed and smashed her face back into the pillow. "I think I can handle that." She closed her eyes and grinned. "Rehearsal at four, right?"

"I'll be back way before that, Cinderella." He leaned

forward and pressed a kiss to her nose before scooting out of the bed.

She eyed him, watching as he gathered clean clothes. The light flipped on in the bathroom, and the water turned on, steam billowing outward through the crack in the door. Casey grinned, and the pounding in her head subsided as she snuggled deeper under the covers.

The door creaked open, and Austin's head popped out, followed by his naked body. He winked. "I never did show you that spacious two-person shower, did I?"

Casey smiled as a shiver of excitement rippled through her body. "No, you didn't."

But you sure can now!

She leapt from the bed.

CHAPTER EIGHTEEN

Austin

Austin parked his car in the garage beneath City Hall in downtown Los Angeles. Snagging his briefcase from the passenger seat, he hopped out of his Corvette and patted the hood.

If there's one thing I missed about L.A. it was you, baby.

The view from the Chicago office flashed in his mind, Lake Michigan sparkling in his memory as he climbed the small set of underground steps to the lobby. His shoes squeaked across the dull gray tile, the swirling patterns of the Windy City office flooring zigzagging through his brain. He pressed the button for the thirteenth floor and stepped inside the elevator, pulling his phone from his pocket. Josh's name flashed across the screen and Austin read, *I feel like absolute horse shit. Can't remember half the night, but I'm sure it was fun! Thanks for the party, man.*

He smiled, the final piece of his heart thawing from the fallout of last year. Stepping from the elevator, he tapped out, *I don't remember much either, but Casey tells me we played a rousing game of Go Fish. Wild tale to tell the future grandkids about your epic bachelor party!*

Tucking his phone away, he stepped into the firm's suite. The fluorescent lights beat down on him, and claustrophobia clouded his brain. Austin frowned, picturing the floor-to-ceiling walls in Chicago as he wound his way through the maze of cubicles.

"Mr. Templeton! You're back!"

Austin's hand froze on his office doorknob as Bernice shuffled down the hallway with a stack of manilla file folders balanced precariously in her arms.

"Hey, Bernice! Just for the day." He smiled and wrapped his arm around her shoulders in a small hug.

"Oh, you're missed here, sweetie. But from what I hear you're doing great work. The big bosses are pretty proud of ya."

He swallowed and his cheeks warmed with embarrassment. Austin cupped the back of his neck as a sheepish smile tugged at his lips. "Well, I don't know about that." He adjusted the top few folders in her arms. "But I am trying. I really love it there. Chicago's a lot of fun."

A smile blossomed on her bright red lips. "Modest as always." She sighed, her gaze sweeping over his face. "Hope you love it here too." She squeezed his elbow and backed away.

Huh?

Austin shook his head and opened the office door. Scanning the empty space, he sighed. *Exactly as I left it.* His desk—clean and tidy—looked back, facing the chair in the corner on the west window. Physically, nothing had changed, but as the door clicked closed behind him, a chill raced along his spine, an eerie sensation gripping his soul.

Chalking it up to the hangover raging through his body, Austin dropped into his chair and smirked as Josh's response appeared. *Are you fucking kidding me? Go Fish!?!?*

He pounded out, *You'll have to ask Casey. I don't remember it either. Are you still at the house?*

A moment passed before Josh answered. *Yep, I just woke up. You're not here?*

Austin opened his laptop and logged in. Pulling up the firm's internal messaging system, he tapped out a note to Steven Boyd. Returning to his phone and Josh's question, he answered, *I had to run to the office. But I promise, I'll be at the rehearsal on time.* He hit *send* and sneered, adding to his final text. *Make sure Mitch is still alive. We might have to kill him together later.*

His laptop pinged and Austin peered at the note from Steven reading, *Welcome back! Conference room B, Templeton!*

His eyes glossed over the words *welcome back*, the letters inciting the discomfort in his belly to seep deeper into his soul. With a sigh, Austin scooped up his laptop and stood, glancing out the window at the L.A. skyline. He frowned and left the office, striding down the hallway to the infamous conference room B.

Austin knocked on the door as laughter met his ears. Sticking his head inside, he smiled. "Sir?"

"Templeton!" roared Rodger. "The prodigal son returns. Come in, come in!"

"Shut the door, kid." Steven waved him inside and tapped his fat fingers on the table.

His heart hammered, each beat threatening to escape his ribcage as he closed the door and stepped inside. He sank into the same seat he'd occupied when the Chicago job had been offered.

"Mr. Boyd, Mr. Bernstein, nice to see you both again." He leaned forward and shook the hands of both men.

"Likewise! Likewise!" boomed Steven, propping his elbows on the table. "Home for a wedding, yes?"

Austin nodded. "My brother's."

"Very good. Very good. Well, thank you for stopping in while you're in town." He glanced at Rodger and grinned. "We have a question for you that feels best to ask in person."

Austin gulped, swallowing the bile rising in his throat and fighting the wave of nausea brewing in his gut. He nodded and choked out, "Fire away."

Rodger twisted his fingers around his mustache and winked. "We're getting old, kid..." He leaned back in his seat and swiveled the chair back and forth.

"Hardly, sir."

Steven beamed. "Unfailingly kind as you are, Rodger is right. And kiddo, it's time we start to step back and begin putting the firm in younger—*capable*—hands." He tapped his fingers together as his gaze lifted to lock eyes with Austin's. "You're the future of this place, Templeton. We both know it, and it's time we make you a partner."

Austin's eyes widened, another bout of nausea sweeping his body and stirring the unease ripping through his stomach.

Holy fuck!

"I... umm..." Austin shook his head, the simple statement before him one he wished to hear since the moment he first accepted the job with Boyd & Bernstein at Law. He blanched and blinked his eyes. "I don't know what to say," he spit out.

"You say *yes*, boy." Rodger leaned forward and returned his fingers to his mustache. "Steven and I built this place from the ground up. And it has simply got to continue to be led by strong leadership. You have the education. You have a proven track record. And you have the experience— and expertise. That's it, Templeton! You're the future of the firm."

His brain dizzied, swimming in a thick fog as the words crashed in around him—the opportunity he'd wished for, hoped for. The promotion he'd fought for.

"Let our old bags of bones start to think about retirement knowing our legacy is in good, competent hands," added Steven.

The dream sat before him, the opportunity laid bare on the table, ready to be seized. Austin's gaze fell to the floor as uncertainty flooded his heart. *This is it, Austin! This is what you've always wanted!* He bit his lip and lifted his gaze back to Steven. *Then why doesn't it feel right?*

"What about Chicago? I'm not done." He shook his head, stupidly pointing out the window as if they could turn and see the unfinished work two thousand miles in the distance.

Rodger waved off the question. The hardware squeaked beneath him as he shifted his weight. "Don't worry about it, Templeton. We'll get Smith out there to finish up whatever it was you started. The future of the firm is *here*. In California. The money will always be in L.A. You know that." He frowned. "Hollywood divorce rates are sky high. You're just not gonna find that in the Midwest. It's a different specialty, still a market for our name, but we need your expertise *here*."

Steven nodded in agreement. "You're more valuable to us here. Your absence in this place is noticeable."

His heart shattered, the impact of their words crashing into his soul, a tidal wave of emotions swirling in his gut as Casey's face clouded the vision. He bit the inside of his cheek and tasted blood. Forcing a smile on his lips, he nodded. "That's umm, really quite the offer. I didn't expect any of this," he muttered, brushing the sweat from his forehead with the back of his hand.

"We should have prepared you for it sooner, kid, not sent you packing. That's our error." Steven crossed his arms over his chest and lifted his eyes to meet Austin's.

"Take the job, partner." Rodger tapped his hands on the table, matching each word for emphasis. "Boyd. Bernstein. And Templeton. *At Law...*" His hands rose, punctuating each word and popping his fists open and closed like fireworks in the sky.

An image of the sign out front appeared in Austin's brain, his name included beneath the two legendary founders.

I've wanted this for so long.

Austin inhaled, sucking the air into his lungs, feeding oxygen to his brain. "When do you need an answer?"

Steven squinted. "You need to think it over?"

Austin nodded and bit his bottom lip again. "I'm sorry. It's the wedding…" He dropped his face into the palms of his hands and dragged his fingers along his cheeks. "There's just a lot going on. It's hard to absorb it all."

"Monday then. Take the weekend and call me Monday." Steven eyed him, dropping his hands to the table.

His legs went numb—the blood flow in his body seemingly at a standstill—frozen in the moment with his brain and stunned alongside his heart. Austin wiggled his toes and stood, bracing himself against the table. He nodded and extended his hand for another round of handshakes.

"Thank you for the opportunity," he murmured and retreated to the door.

"Templeton?"

Austin turned, his gaze falling on Rodger.

"Your career started here, and it can end here too." His words sliced into his soul, the veiled threat bouncing off his heart and inciting shivers to skyrocket through his body.

Austin nodded and left, staggering down the hallway toward the safety of his office. He slammed the door and twisted the lock. As he dropped into his chair, the weight of the conversation rested heavily on his psyche. "Holy fuck," he choked out and closed his eyes, willing the pounding in his head to disappear. "What just happened?"

His phone vibrated in his pocket, and Austin tugged it free, expecting Josh's name to reappear.

But it didn't.

His eyes clouded over, his vision darkening as his heart leapt, lodging deep in his windpipe. He read the message, *I need to see you, Austin.*

Swallowing the vomit rising in his throat, his lips betrayed him. "Princess?" he whispered before losing the battle and upending his stomach in the wastebin beneath his desk.

CHAPTER NINETEEN

Casey

Casey opened her eyes and stretched, yawning in the early afternoon sunlight. She rolled and stuffed her face into Austin's pillow. Running her fingers along the soft bed sheets in his empty spot, she sighed.

"California boy…"

She giggled, summoning from her memory the silly grin on his lips playing Go Fish in the early hours of the morning. "I love you," she whispered and gripped the edge of the bed.

Her mind returned to the blowout argument they shared, all her feelings of insecurity and unworthiness deposited into the ether, an invisible wedge jammed in the middle of their budding relationship. She shook her head and replayed his reactions, repeating his responses in her brain. "You still never answered my question though…"

She clenched the sheets in her hands and balled her fingers into fists. "I know you love me," she whispered, breathing in the scent clinging to his pillowcase. "But I need to know what you still feel for her too."

With a groan, Casey sat up and dropped her feet to the

floor. The warm rays of the sun danced across her toes as she surveyed Austin's room. She observed the ornate furniture and décor, everything in the space clean and organized with perfection.

The sunshine caught the glass of a picture frame on the chest of drawers. Rising to her feet, Casey crossed the room and brought the photo to her nose. She grinned and gazed at the teenage version of Austin in a royal-blue and gold high school football jersey. *Well, there's no mistaking you, is there?* As she dragged her finger over him, her gaze drifted to the other familiar faces standing beside him. Without a doubt, the teenage versions of Josh and Mitch wrapped their arms around Mavis and Lauren.

A sudden pain gripped her heart as she returned the frame to its home. *I envy you, Austin Templeton. All that you had … all that you still do have.* A shiver ran along her spine, leaving a trail of jealousy in its wake. "Where do I fit?" she whispered, eyeing herself in the mirror. No matter the reassurances he spoke, he had a life in California—a beautiful, supportive family and a promising career, nothing but success earmarked for his future.

She sighed and shook her head, pushing aside the sinking feeling in her gut as her phone pinged. Shying away from her pity party, she crossed the room and reached for the device on the nightstand. An unknown email address flashed across the screen, the word *Congratulations!* grabbing her attention. With a deep breath, she clicked it open.

Dear Ms. McDaniels,

Congratulations! You have been selected to fill one of the campaign manager internship positions with the Office of the Chicago Mayor. We were quite impressed with the application you submitted and the promising skillset you'll bring to the team.

We invite you to schedule your orientation by clicking here.

Thank you for your passion and dedication to local politics. We look forward to working with you soon.

Sincerely,
Veronica Smalling
Human Resources Manager
Office of the Chicago Mayor

Casey reread the email three times, allowing the words to slowly penetrate her brain. *Oh, my God. They actually want me?* The breath caught in her throat as her heart hammered in her chest. "Austin!" She giggled and with shaking fingers, scrolled to locate his name in her contacts list.

She held the phone to her ear. One ring. Two rings. Three rings. Then four. Casey ended the call, disappointment pooling in her belly. She opened a text to him instead and typed out, *I hope you'll be back soon! I have something really exciting to tell you!* She added her favorite winking face emoji and clicked *send*.

But nothing happened.

Casey shrugged and frowned at her phone.

It's okay. You're just busy. You'll call me back soon.

With a sigh, Casey stepped inside Austin's closet and slipped on a pale-pink sundress amidst a line of suit jackets. After snagging a pair of strappy sandals from her bag, she pinned her blonde curls away from her face with bobby pins and applied a light layer of makeup. She left Austin's bedroom with her phone held tightly in her hands—still no response to boot.

The sounds of cans crunching, and bottles clinking met her ears as she moved down the staircase. *Is that you, Austin?* She followed the noise to the kitchen until a tidal wave of disappointment crashed into her body.

Mitch tossed an empty pizza box in a trash bag.

Oh. It's you.

He smiled and lifted his gaze from the mess littering the counter. "Couldn't leave this place a total dump." Flattening a beer box, he winked, his chin rising to gesture in her direction. "You look really nice."

"Do you even remember who I am?"

Mitch snorted. "Vaguely?" His hand rose to scratch the back of his head. "Casey, right?"

She nodded with a false smile. "Nice to meet you, Mitch."

May Austin screw you over if you decide to divorce Lauren.

He scooped another pile of trash into the bag and tucked his shoulder-length dark hair behind his ears. "You too," he hedged. "So, umm, you ready for the wedding and stuff?"

Casey stepped forward and turned on the faucet, tossing a dish rag under the flow and wringing it out with a squeeze. "Yeah, for sure. Are you?" She ran the wet rag across the counter until Mitch dropped his hand over hers.

"Hey, you don't need to clean. We made the mess, not you." He tugged the cloth from her grasp. "Besides, you don't want to get beer stains on your dress." His gaze fell to her stomach.

Following his line of sight, she shrugged, eyeing the new wet smudge on her belly. "Eh, it'll dry. And it's not like I have anything else to do. Austin left hours ago."

Mitch wrinkled his nose and dropped the rag on the counter. "Where'd he go?"

"The office. He got a text this morning from his boss… er, bosses," she corrected. "They wanted him to stop by while he was in town."

He snorted again and tied the trash bag closed. "A meeting with the bosses. Well, I don't envy him." He winked and tapped his forehead. "Killer hangover."

"No kidding." Casey giggled and attacked a dried spot of marinara on the counter with the cloth. "I have no idea how he just hopped out of bed!"

"Bastard." Mitch laughed and stepped across the room to open the side door. He tossed the bag of trash into the garbage bin as Casey's phone pinged.

"Finally," she muttered, snatching her phone. Austin's name flashed across the screen. *I'm not going to make it back before the rehearsal. Can you grab a ride over to the Manor from Mitch or Josh if they're still there?*

She bit her lip, dismay radiating from the pit in her stomach.

"Something wrong?"

"Oh, umm. I mean, I guess not. Austin isn't going to make it back here before the rehearsal. Can I ride over with you?"

Mitch nodded. "Yeah, of course. Let me just finish up. Fifteen minutes?"

Casey forced a smile on her lips, pushing the unease in her heart away. "Cool. Thanks. I'll go grab my stuff." She stepped away from the counter and left Mitch to collect the last evidence of the party.

Something's wrong. Austin didn't even acknowledge what I said.

Her feet met the bottom stair as she tapped out a response that read, *Okay sure, no problem. Love you.*

She slouched upstairs and gathered her things. Stepping from the room, Casey sighed and rolled her eyes, retreating to make the bed as guilt wracked her body. "Wouldn't want to give you an ulcer or anything," she murmured, haphazardly flipping sheets around. Her fingers glided over his pillow and a sigh escaped her lips.

You're probably just hung up in a meeting. I'm being weird for no reason.

Gripping her bag, she tiptoed out of the room and down the staircase.

"Ready?" Mitch jiggled his keys and reached forward to take her bag.

"Ready," she answered and handed off her things. "Thanks."

The heat beat down as she followed him outside, opening the door to his Ford F-150. The leather seats baked in the sun, and Casey squirmed in her seat, struggling to avoid touching her skin to the black interior.

"Sorry!" Mitch cranked on the air conditioning and grinned. "Never been to California before, have you?"

Casey shook her head. "Nope. True Midwestern girl

right here."

"Chicago, right?" He put the truck in reverse and backed out of the driveway, heading south down the empty street.

"Guilty." She grinned, adjusting the vent on the dashboard. "How about you? You always lived in Rosewood?"

Mitch nodded and tapped the lever to spray the windshield with cleaner. The wipers danced back and forth in synchronization. "Pretty much. Did a few tours of duty with the Navy for a few years, but I've been back ever since."

"Oh! I didn't know you were in the Navy!"

He glanced in her direction. "Yeah, for about three or four years."

"I had a cousin in the Navy. He was stationed out in Norfolk."

Mitch nodded and tapped the brake at the stop sign.

"San Diego for me."

Casey raised her shoulders and grinned. "Makes sense." She nodded. "How about deployment? Where'd you go?"

He turned onto a larger road, leaving Austin's neighborhood behind. "I saw ports in Japan, South Korea, Hawaii, and the Persian Gulf once too."

A whistle sailed from her lips. "Geez, maybe that's what I should have done after high school too. I've hardly ever left the state of Illinois, let alone seen another country." She turned her head, her gaze drifting out over the fields of wildflowers racing past.

"There's a whole world out there." He smiled, turning to meet her gaze.

"What brought you back then?"

A smile grew on his lips as his eyes returned to the road. His cheeks tinged pink and his fingers gripped the steering wheel tighter. "Lauren," he murmured.

Casey nodded, her smile matching his. "I know I hardly know any of you guys…" Her heart lurched as she swallowed. "But I can tell how much she loves you. You're really lucky."

His lips disappeared, flattening into a thin line as he steered the truck into a private driveway. The wrought-iron gate flanking the path was adorned with intricate pale-yellow bows, each ribbon floating in the breeze.

"Lucky..." he whispered as Casey's eyes widened, the Templeton Manor appearing through the line of weeping willows.

"Holy fuck!" Casey turned and dropped her jaw at the grand Victorian mansion. "This is where you live? This is where Austin grew up?"

Mitch parked the truck in the driveway and killed the engine. He shifted and turned to face her. "Casey, can I let you in on a little secret?"

She nodded and closed her mouth for the first time since the truck left the road.

"I'm not saying the Templetons aren't good people. They absolutely are." He huffed out a breath and shook his head. "But take it from me, or Mavs, no matter what you do... you just never quite seem to fit in, or measure up to any of 'em." He reached over and squeezed her knee. "Austin's a good guy. But just keep your eyes open, okay?"

Mitch left the truck, his warning hanging in the slowly warming vehicle.

"My eyes open..." she repeated. Casey pulled the handle and hopped down, following him to the front porch.

Never quite seem to fit in, or measure up to any of 'em. With a deep breath, she stepped inside Templeton Manor, Mitch's words resonating in her heart like none ever before.

CHAPTER TWENTY

Austin

This is fucking stupid. This is so fucking stupid.

Austin stepped forward, his shoes crunching the grains of sand as he left the safety of the parking lot and headed for the woman sitting alone on the picnic table, her wild dark curls whipping in the gusts of ocean wind like snakes striking their prey.

"Turn around, Austin," he whispered to himself, pleading with the sole remaining ounce of sanity left in his brain. "Just go home." His feet faltered, his brain battling with his heart. He eyed her, watching as she reined in her hair and fastened it into a low ponytail with a white ribbon. Austin shook his head and sided with his heart. *Just see what she wants. You owe her that.* He moved forward, each footfall bringing him closer to his personal Garden of Eden's forbidden fruit. Heaving out a heavy breath, he reached the table, his heart sinking as his lips parted. "Princess?" he whispered.

She turned, the deep green of her eyes penetrating his soul, her heart calling out to him from the ghosts of a war zone.

His chest pounded, the blood speeding through his veins with ferocity. Austin gulped and swallowed the fear erupting in his gut at the sight of her, a surge of repressed longing rippling through his body as his eyes met hers.

"Hey, you." She patted the wooden seat beside her. "Thank you for coming," she whispered.

Austin shook his head and exhaled the heartache he loathed. The remaining pieces of his soul still belonging to her roused from the rubble surrounding his damaged heart. "Why am I here, Mavs?"

Her hand stilled on the tabletop. "Because I knew you'd come."

Austin bit his bottom lip and dropped his gaze to the sand as the truth struck him.

I'll always come.

"I shouldn't be here though. *We* shouldn't be here."

She slumped, the air expelling from her lungs in a rush.

"Does Josh know?" he pressed.

Mavis shook her head.

He rolled his eyes and dragged his hands through his hair. Massaging the back of his neck, he frowned as the weight of her silent answer drowned him.

I'm so tired of this.

"I'm gonna go. This is a bad idea." He stepped away, shuffling his feet through the sand as pain swirled in her eyes.

"Austin! Please…" she begged, rising from her seat. Her arms wrapped around her body, her signature self-hug deflating the courage fueling his words.

His heart caved, wringing itself dry, squeezing from the center the love that lay hidden beneath lock and key.

Dammit, Mavis.

"Why?" he whispered, stuffing his hands into his pockets.

A sob fell from her lips as her body shook, the warm rays of the sun losing the battle to the shivers wracking her skin. "I need to apologize to you."

The wind whipped at his face, the dry heat beating against his cheeks. He shook his head and pressed his lips together. "We've already had this conversation."

"We haven't though. Not face-to-face." She ran her fingers beneath her eyes as they filled with tears, trickling down her cheeks with the same intensity hammering in his chest.

The broken teenage girl from his dorm room fought free from his memories, piercing his brain with the emotional upheaval her words caused the night she reappeared in his life—the start of all the secrets and the catalyst for love in all the wrong places.

I can't help myself.

Austin heaved out a breath and stepped forward, pulling her into him. His arms squeezed and wrapped her shaking form into the warmth of his body. "Please no tears, Mavs," he whispered in her ear. "Come on, not today."

She sniffled and pressed her face into his chest. "That's just it, Austin. It has to be today."

Huh?

Austin dragged his hand along her back, his fingers catching in the lace of her white sundress as her words swirled in his mind. He frowned, breathing out the never-ending complexity of the woman in his arms.

"I'm sorry for the way things are between us. I ruined everything we used to share," she choked out between sobs. "I'm so stupid, Austin. And I'm just so sorry—for every part that I played."

Her apology impaled his heart, her words biting into his soul. He sighed and closed his eyes, letting his face fall to the top of her head. He nuzzled his nose in her hair and the scent of coconuts settled in his nostrils, the smell breathing life into the past. Austin inhaled, ready to dance with the echo of heartache only Mavis could cause, but a field of lilacs bloomed in his brain instead.

Casey.

She smiled at him in his mind, falling into his arms in the

stairwell with a lost shoe. Her laughter bubbled, captivating his heart, relieving the pressure of sorrow, and releasing the residual feelings left in his soul… placed there by the woman in his arms.

Austin exhaled and his grip loosened, each finger clinging to Mavis's body slowly releasing. He pulled away as her gaze lifted to meet his.

"Austin?"

He stared into the depths of green, into the pools of the past, into the days the dragon reigned, standing tall and proud in the tree fort atop the imaginary Lonely Mountain, the princess hidden amidst his treasure.

"The road goes ever on and on…" he whispered, dropping his gaze from hers. A grin tugged at his lips, and his heart softened, the weight of the past beginning to melt with dragon fire.

She frowned and wrinkled her nose. "Tolkien, Austin? Really?" She snorted and stalked away, dropping back into her seat at the picnic table. "I'm laying my heart out bare here, and you quote me some garbage from *The Lord of the Rings*."

He grinned as his cheeks flushed. *It's from the Hobbit too.* "Don't insult Bilbo Baggins, Princess."

She rolled her eyes as he sank to the seat beside her, draping his arm over her shoulder and scooting his butt away from the gouge in the wooden bench. His fingers raked along her skin as she leaned into him and heaved out a heavy sigh.

The pressure in his chest lessened, the memories of the past lifting from the fog that had endlessly clouded his heart. The childhood fairytale crumbled in his mind, each piece of the memory fracturing as understanding slowly seeped through the cracks.

I loved you yesterday, Princess. But today…

He turned and pressed his lips to the top of her head. "Why all this now? In like forty-five minutes, you're supposed to practice walking down an aisle to my brother."

Her hand fell to his knee, her fingernails grazing over the material of his pants. She sat in silence, her eyes staring outward toward the ocean as her breathing returned to a normal rhythm.

"Why now?" he whispered again.

She inhaled and closed her eyes, opening her lips to let the words fall. "Because when I marry Joshua tomorrow, my heart can't be split in two anymore." Mavis swallowed. "I'm having a hard time letting you go. *For good*." She cringed, squeezing her eyes shut. "I'm having a hard time letting go of *us*... or at least... what could have been *us*."

You still have feelings for me too?

His heart stilled as his eyes closed, her admission of the truth an invitation for the memories to return, crashing into his brain. Her lips on his, bathed in love beneath the secrets of the world. Swimming in the depth of her words, reality crashed in around him. Their relationship, the love they shared, the pull toward each other... Every part of her swirled in his soul until his eyes opened.

The memories faded as the sun beat down, forcing droplets of sweat to appear on his forehead. With the back of his hand, he swiped at the moisture and grinned.

"Was there ever really an *us* though, Mavs? Did we ever really have a chance?" Austin rose from his seat and tilted his head to meet the sun. The rays fried his skin, baking his soul in the heat as the weight of the conversation snaked along his spine. He inhaled, breathing in the salt hanging heavy in the air. It circulated in his lungs, cleansing and refreshing. With a smile, he turned toward her. "Just a make-believe dragon and the princess he captured."

She shook her head. "Was it all make-believe?"

Austin tapped his watch and sighed. "You have about thirty minutes to decide that."

Her body straightened, and her gaze swept over his face. She stared, seemingly lost in the depths of her heart, searching her soul for the truth as the seconds ticked by.

"It was real for me, Princess," he whispered, a small

smile tugging at his lips. "But I think…" Austin pulled his arms to his head, cupping his palms at the base of his neck. He grinned before his gaze settled on hers. From the bottom of his heart, the truth finally fought to set itself free. "I think…

Her cheeks flushed as her lips parted. "A black arrow then."

Austin pressed his hand over his chest, the slashes in his heart stitching together with the finality of her perfectly inspired Tolkien analogy, closing the chapter on their childhood and closing the door on a relationship that would never be, that could never be.

And for the first time in my life, I'm okay with it.

"Mavis Benson, you'll forever be my Princess. But I think we both know that whatever we could have had together, it's all part of our past now. Neither of our hearts belong in two."

She stood and tiptoed across the sand to stand beside him. Her fingers interlaced with his as she turned to stare out at the ocean. "The road goes ever on and on," she whispered.

"Down from the door that it began," he answered and squeezed her fingers.

Peace washed over him, a sense of calm crashing into his body. He breathed, letting go of the turmoil and confusion that had wracked his soul for the better part of his life. With his sigh, a smile bloomed on his lips as the door of forbidden love closed and locked for the last time. The tide raced forward on the sand as the gulls screeched overhead, and Austin turned, ready to release the princess from the captivity of his heart.

Her gaze lifted to his. "How about one last secret?"

Oh, God, what now?

"For old times' sake," she added with a grin.

He snorted. "Yours or mine?"

A crease formed along her forehead. "You mean you have one?"

Austin rolled his eyes and sighed. "You could say that."

Her fingers tightened on his palm as her elbow banged into his side playfully. "Go on, then, sir. Our last secret is for you."

A shiver chilled his skin, shooting through his system as the words fell from his lips. "Boyd. Bernstein. *And Templeton*. At Law."

Her hands covered her mouth as her eyes widened, her gaze boring into him. "Oh, my God, Austin! Are you saying?"

He nodded. "Partner." His stomach recoiled, the second round of hangover nausea threatening the moment. Austin swallowed and ran his hand across his belly.

"You're not smiling," she whispered, tugging his hand back into her own. "You're not happy."

Austin shook his head and squeezed her fingers. "The job is here, Mavs. In California."

Her body stilled as his secret and his gut-wrenching decision settled in her heart. A gasp escaped her lips as her phone rang on the picnic table behind them.

They turned, eyeing the innocent bag on the tabletop. "I think our time's up," he whispered.

She swallowed, and her hands gripped his tie, forcing his gaze to return to her own. "Chicago," she muttered. "Casey?"

Austin sighed and shifted, scooping up her bag from the table. He draped it over her shoulder and frowned. "My secret's safe with you, right?"

She nodded, and Austin turned, pulling her behind him as they walked toward the parking lot in silence, the ghost of forbidden love resting in a grave beneath the sand.

JULIE NAVICKAS

CHAPTER TWENTY-ONE

Casey

"More wine?" The metal bottom of the chair grated against the brick patio as Austin stood. He reached forward and gripped her empty glass as his lips pecked her forehead.

"Sure, thanks." Casey eyed his retreating figure as he slid the glass door open and disappeared into the house, leaving her alone in the Millennium Park-sized backyard of his home. The crickets chirped in the quiet evening as a summer breeze ruffled the skirt of her pink sundress. She sighed, the pit in her stomach intensifying.

What's wrong with you, Austin?

She frowned and pulled forth from her memory the stoic expression he wore all throughout the rehearsal and dinner. With a swallow, she re-tasted the dry wine clinging to her lips as Austin reappeared. He slid the patio door closed with his foot, each step forward echoing the name *Mavis... Mavis... Mavis* in her mind.

It has to be her. It has to be the wedding that's bugging him.

"Here you go, Casey girl." He set the wine down in front of her and brought his glass to his lips. With a sigh, his gaze fell to the floor as he swallowed.

"All right. Clearly, you're not going to tell me willingly, so I have to pry. What's wrong with you?" She leaned forward and propped herself up on her elbows, her chin dropping into each open palm.

He snorted and rested his hands behind his neck. "Nothing. Just been a long day, that's all." He winked.

"You're a lot of things, Austin Templeton, but a liar you are not." She returned his wink and tilted her head, a curl falling free from her pin.

A grin appeared as he leaned forward and snagged her hand, pressing a kiss to the inside of her wrist. "You belong in a courtroom, Attorney McDaniels. Using my own words against me is one hell of a closing argument."

A shiver raced along her skin, inciting goosebumps to appear on her forearms. "Who said anything about closing?"

Austin smiled and tugged her hand. "Come here."

Gladly.

Casey fell into his lap, breathing out the raw anxiety fueling every heartbeat in her chest. She snuggled into his embrace and rested her head beside his. Pressing her lips to his cheek, she closed her eyes.

"I missed you today," he whispered and tightened his grip around her body. "I'm sorry I was gone for so long."

"Why were you then?" She trailed her fingers along his jawline, reveling in the familiar scratchy sensation the stubble on his chin offered.

He shifted and toyed with the fabric of her dress. His fingers squeezed her thigh, traveling upward to her waist.

Heat enveloped her, a pull in her groin flushing her cheeks with warmth. The breath caught in her throat as his fingers pinched her skin, tugging the waistband of her panties.

"I haven't seen anyone in that office for a few months. I just got caught up, you know?" He pressed a kiss to the top of her head. "And I wasn't exactly firing on all cylinders either," he purred in her ear.

Casey giggled and dipped her hand inside the collar of his shirt. "The way you bounced out of bed this morning, you'd never know." Her fingers dragged along his neckline, popping the top button on his collar.

He shivered and captured her hand, planting a kiss on her palm before wrapping it in his own, resting their intertwined fingers on his chest.

"Oh! Didn't you have something you wanted to tell me? You texted me something this afternoon…" He freed her fingers and dove into his pocket to pull out his phone. "What're you excited to tell me, Cinderella?"

Her eyes skimmed his screen as a jolt of forgotten excitement gripped her body. *The internship!* She straightened and reached across the table, snagging her glass of wine. "I got an email from the Office of the Chicago Mayor. They offered me an internship!" She snorted. "Whatever the hell you said in that application… Well, they picked me, Austin!"

His body went rigid beneath her, his muscles tensing as the breath caught in his throat. He swallowed and squeezed his eyes closed, then open. "Case, uh, wow, that's wonderful news! I'm so proud of you. You'll be great." His lips disappeared into a thin line as his gaze returned to the floor.

What the actual fuck?

"Okay, umm. I really thought you'd be, like, way more excited than this." She scooted off his lap with an eye roll.

"Hey, where are you going?" His brow furrowed, forcing a deep *V* to crease his forehead. His hand shot out and grabbed her waist, his palm radiating heat, gently tugging her backward.

"Austin, I don't know what's going on with you, but you've been acting super weird since the rehearsal. You pushed me to apply. Fuck! You applied *for me*! And now that it's actually happening, your response is, *you'll be great?*" She sneered. "What the hell happened to you today?"

She locked eyes with him. Even in the twinkle lights of the patio, his eyes returned nothing, the glimmer of his baby blues lost to the secrets of his silent mind.

"Tell me this isn't about Mavis."

Her heart skipped a beat as her bold words dripped from her lips. Scrunching her eyes together, she swallowed as the seconds ticked away, each cricket's chirp a knife slowly assaulting her heart.

"I saw her today," he whispered, biting his bottom lip.

Casey rolled her eyes. "Umm, yeah, so did I. We sweated our assess off in that stupid meadow together."

His gaze lifted from the floor, the smattering of white lashes catching in the glow of the light. He opened his mouth as if to speak, but the words didn't follow.

Oh, God.

Her heart hammered in her chest, her blood pounding through her veins as a dizzy spell left her breathless. She swallowed and forced down the wine threatening to return from her belly.

"I…" he stammered and gripped the arms of the chair. "I saw her before the rehearsal… alone."

Casey squinted, her eyes unwilling to leave his face as she sank back into her chair. "Before the rehearsal," she repeated, bringing the glass of wine back to her lips.

"It's not what you think though."

She drained the deep-red contents in a single gulp. "And what do I think, Austin Templeton?" Replacing the empty glass on the table, she folded her arms across her chest. Her brain ran rampant, searching her memory for a clue, her heart landing on their collective late arrival at the rehearsal. "God, I'm a fucking fool," she murmured.

He dropped to the ground between her knees. Gripping her arms, Austin pried them apart, his sudden muscled tug stealing her breath. "I'm the fool, Casey girl. For ever letting myself fall for her." His lips pressed a kiss to her palm. "I met her at the beach to say goodbye. We *needed* to say goodbye, for good this time. It's over. All of it."

His eyes clouded, sparkling under the twinkle lights as he stared up at her. His fingers tightened around her hands, squeezing as if willing her to understand the complexity of emotions swirling in his heart.

She swallowed and leaned forward, tugging at the sad form of his usually confident body. His head rested against her heart as her fingers cupped the back of his head. Her eyes closed as his breath hammered against her chest. "I should have told you where I was. And what I was doing, Casey." His lips pressed into her skin, his tongue tasting her. "I said goodbye. That's it."

"Did you *kiss* her goodbye?" A groan escaped her, the fog of the wine clouding her brain, toying with the fraying edges of her heartstrings.

He pulled away and shook his head. "No."

A sigh burst from her lips, sailing into the air between them. "Then why—"

His mouth covered hers. The dry bite of Merlot swirled along her tongue as he moved against her, nipping at her bottom lip. His hands squeezed her waist, digging into the fabric of her dress.

She gulped for air, lifting her face to the night sky, his breathing heavy on her neck.

"I don't understand," she gasped. "Is that it? That's why you're acting so weird?"

He pressed another kiss to her neck before pulling away, sinking back to the brick patio floor.

"You're scaring me, Austin." Sweat coated her body, the chills of desire battling with the still warm temperature of the summer night. She groaned and tipped his chin upward until their eyes locked.

He froze, his stare penetrating her soul.

That's not it.

"Casey, I was offered a new job today." He gulped, his Adam's apple bobbing up and down.

"Okay..."

Spit it out!

"Boyd and Bernstein... they asked me to join them as their partner."

A smile grew along her lips, her heart returning to a

steady rhythm as a bubble of laughter released from her belly.

"Fuck! Austin, that's incredible!" She sank to the floor beside him, pushing her chair away as the metal raked across the brick and toppled over.

He fell backward under her weight, the first true smile breaking free on his lips since the steamy shower they shared that morning.

She kissed him and straddled his body on the patio floor. "I'm so happy for you, Austin!" she whispered, gliding her hands over his cheeks. "Congratulations, California boy—"

He inhaled, the smile disappearing from his lips as his eyes found hers. He stared, searching her heart until Lauren's voice crashed into her mind. *Once he's made partner, he'll move home to California.*

The breath left her, escaping her lungs as she sank backward. Her ears rang, disrupting the symphony of crickets, each rub of their little legs falling short as the blood raged through her body, coursing through her system until the adrenaline of the moment subsided. A cold sweat broke out across her forehead.

"The job's here, isn't it?"

He tucked an escaped curl behind her ear as his head tipped forward, pressing his forehead against hers. "It's here," he whispered.

Casey swallowed, understanding gripping her heart and squeezing her soul. Her lungs deflated, all air escaping her body as the weight of his words rocked the only thing in her life worth smiling for.

I can't ruin this for you.

Clearing her throat, Casey summoned the sole ounce of courage in her body. And with a forced smile, she opened her mouth. "Then here, you'll stay," she whispered and pressed a kiss to his lips.

After all, when you love someone, their success is your happiness too.

CHAPTER TWENTY-TWO

Austin

Austin stretched out his arm, ready to pull Casey into the warmth of his body beneath the blankets, willing her to snuggle in beside him, her soft breath kissing his skin. His fingers searched, brushing up against a piece of paper where her head should have rested.

Opening his eyes, he pulled the note closer to his face, Casey's childlike print blurring before his eyes. Swinging his hand out, he snagged his reading glasses on the nightstand and dropped the frames on his nose. He gripped her note as something black coated the tips of his fingers.

He frowned, rubbing his thumb and index finger together. "Is this… is this eyeliner?" he whispered, wrinkling his nose. Austin snorted, sinking back beneath the covers as his gaze flew across the makeup-adorned page, her words left in charcoal gray.

Austin,

Lauren picked me up. We had early hair and make-up appointments and I didn't want to wake you. You tossed and turned all night.

I'm so proud of you! You're going to make an incredible partner, even if it leaves you a Dodgers fan for life. I'll never convert, but this Chicago fan wouldn't mind seeing the stadium when the Cubs are in town.

Meet you at the altar. I'll be the one in yellow.

XOXO,
Casey girl

"When the Cubs are in town," he read aloud to the empty bedroom.

You think you're gonna move here to be with me, Casey girl, don't you?

Austin rubbed the back of his neck and frowned, swallowing the suspicion churning in his gut.

And what about school? And your new internship? You're finally chasing your dream.

"I can't let you do it, Case," he muttered, tossing her note to the nightstand. He dragged his hands down his cheeks and smacked his palms on the blanket.

He sighed, allowing his heart to pick through the unease flooding his body. His career pulled him, dragging him to the thirteenth floor above City Hall in Los Angeles, just as he'd always dreamed and worked toward. But then a curly-haired Cubs fan reached across his lap for the remote control and the dream, the plan, all of it went to hell. New dreams and new plans burst forth from the rocky shores of Lake Michigan. They glistened in his mind, weighing heavy on his heart.

Austin groaned and grabbed his phone from the nightstand. He yanked out the charger and cringed as the date reflected on the home screen.

July ninth.

With a glance at the time, he sat up and forced his body to move across the room to begin getting ready for the wedding. His toes met the cold tile of the bathroom, his hands gripping the nozzle in the shower. The hot water fell, filling the space with steam.

Dropping his clothes to the floor, Austin stepped inside. The water pelted his skin and roused his brain from the fog of confusion. He squirted shampoo into his palms and raked the goo through his hair. Soap bubbles dripped down his naked body, oozing along the floor toward the drain.

What the hell am I gonna do?

As he breathed out a heavy sigh, his fingers gripped the bottle of body wash—the words *Rugged Mountain Fresh* stilling the beat of his heart as the blue liquid spilled into his hands.

"I can't let you uproot your life for me, Casey girl. It's not fair."

He shook his head and slammed the bottle back onto the shelf. Austin pressed his forehead against the cold tile as the water pummeled his body. His gut twisted, churning and swirling, mimicking the turmoil in his heart.

"But I can't turn down this job either," he whispered, the truth breaking free from his lips. "I just can't. It's everything I've always worked toward."

An invisible force squeezed his heart deep within his chest, gripping and crushing the delicate strings that just yesterday had stitched back together.

It's not fucking fair.

Austin inhaled and yanked his head from the safety of the tiled wall as his phone rang on the bathroom counter. He frowned and turned the shower off, stepping from the steamy space to tap the speaker phone icon on Mitch's name.

"Yeah?"

"Hello to you too."

Austin rolled his eyes and snagged a towel from the hook. He wrapped it around his waist and leaned forward, folding the top half of his wet body over the counter. "Sorry," he muttered. "What's up?"

"You okay?"

Austin sighed. "Sure." Closing his eyes, he pressed his

fingertips into his temples, massaging the skin, bearing into the source of pain pounding in his brain. "I'm fine."

With a snort, Mitch answered. "Yeah, you sound fine."

Austin rolled his eyes again. "Kind of a tough day, Mitch. What do you need?"

"I'll pick you up in twenty, all right?"

"Why?" He wrinkled his nose, digging into his brain to recall the minute-by-minute itinerary Lauren had created, color coded, and distributed to every member of the wedding party.

"I'm supposed to pick you up." He snorted. "It's on the itinerary. That way your car isn't here, I guess." Paper shuffled on the other side of the phone, bringing a small smile to his lips.

Lauren, you don't disappoint.

"Twenty sounds good. Thanks, man." Austin moved to tap the red button, his fingers hovering over the device. "Wait… hey, Mitch?"

"Yeah?"

"Have you seen Casey? Are the girls over there?"

"The house is quiet, dude. The itinerary says something about an appointment at Curls and Cuticles." He snickered. "That sounds terrible."

Austin nodded. "Okay… yeah. It sure does. See you in twenty."

"See you in twenty."

Mitch ended the call, and Austin turned to the mirror, his reflection slowly materializing through the steam. He stared, the hazy fog circulating in the air. "All we have to decide is what to do with the time that is given us," he mumbled, dragging his hand across the mirror and smearing his reflection in the steam.

I'd rather battle a Balrog.

Austin's too-tight loafers crunched the dead grass. His elbow knocked into Josh as they walked side-by-side down the path toward the ceremony site.

"You okay?" Austin grinned, eyeing the pattern of yellow and gray bows bordering the path to the meadow.

"Nervous…" He stuffed his hands into his pockets and smiled. "Guess I shouldn't be though. I've done this before." He elbowed Austin back with wide eyes.

"Well, you've got the right girl on the other side this time." His foot squashed a yellow rose petal. "I mean, anyone is better than Tess, but Mavs…"

Josh stilled, his feet faltering on the path.

"Something I said?" Austin wrinkled his nose and turned back to face his brother. "Josh?"

His gaze lifted, catching Austin's. "I'm gonna ask you a question. And I need you to tell me the truth, okay?"

Austin swallowed. "All right."

Josh nodded and cleared his throat. "Were you with Mavis yesterday?"

The sudden ringing in his ears drilled holes in his brain. Austin blinked, working to bring his brother back into focus from the fog clouding his eyes. He coughed, dragging his hands along the back of his neck.

"I was…" Locking eyes with Josh, Austin stepped forward. "We said goodbye. Buried all our shit in the sand. For good."

Josh returned his stare, biting the inside of his cheek, his eyes inviting more.

"I swear it, Josh. Whatever the hell we—" Austin shook his head. "Closure, all right?" He shrugged.

"Closure," Josh repeated. His body straightened, the trance-like state of his dark eyes lifting. "You're sure?"

Austin nodded. "Not the best timing, I know," he muttered, stepping forward to adjust the yellow rose pinned to his brother's jacket.

Josh inhaled and nodded, stepping forward over the fallen log in the path.

"I'm sorry, Josh. I need you to know that I'll always be sorry. I never should have done… well, anything I did." He shook his head again. "I'm sorry."

Josh turned, standing in front of a burlap sign. Austin dragged his gaze across the message. *Too late to run because here she comes!* Pulling a small smile to his lips, he pointed at the sign.

"She's coming for *you*. Not me."

Josh snorted, turning to read the sign for himself. "And you're sure?"

With a nod, Austin stepped forward and guided his brother down the path. "If there is one thing I'm sure of, it's that you're about to marry the girl you always should have." He smiled, elbowing him in the gut as they stepped to the edge of the forest.

The strings of a violin met their ears, the familiar melody of wedding preludes drifting in the breeze as the brilliant afternoon sun brought the meadow to life. White wicker chairs lined the aisle in rows, each seat filled with a guest ready to celebrate.

Austin pressed a toe to the white aisle runner and turned, grinning at his brother. "Ready?"

Josh smiled, inhaling a breath before stepping forward and aiming for the beautiful white arbor Mitch had built just days before. The orange blooms of the California poppies rested intricately in the maze of wood, standing tall at the end of the aisle.

Austin followed Josh, waving politely at the guests as they followed the path of white fabric. He took his place at the front and stifled a grin as Josh got suckered into a hug by an ancient aunt in the front row. Cringing, Austin snorted as she planted a bright red kiss on his brother's cheek.

With wide eyes, Josh straightened and bolted to his side, rubbing his palm against his skin.

"Who is that again?" Austin whispered, eyeing the lipstick stain on Josh's cheek as he rubbed furiously.

"Great Aunt Millie? Mildred? Mamelda?" Josh snorted. "I don't know... but she smells."

Austin leaned forward and inhaled the reek of the old

woman's perfume clinging to Josh's jacket. He grimaced but giggled, slapping him in the arm. "Who knows, when Mavis smells you, she might just marry me instead now."

Josh rolled his eyes and snickered, the shared laughter lifting the lingering discomfort from the conversation in the forest.

Austin breathed in the ease of the moment, his best friend standing beside him. His gaze dropped to his feet as he wiggled his toes, already aching inside the fancy rental shoes—a small price to pay to feel the happiness exude from Josh, their relationship no longer cracked at the seams.

"You have the rings, right?" Josh turned, sudden panic swirling in his eyes.

Austin stuffed his hand in his right pocket and smirked, pulling out the two wedding bands. Stacking them atop each other, he brought them to his eye and peered at Josh through the center. "One ring to rule them all."

An elbow jabbed him in the gut as he doubled over, catching his mother's eye as she settled into her seat in the front row. She glowered, the look of disapproval radiating from her piercing stare.

Josh gulped and pulled Austin upright. "Almost thirty years old and that look still scares me…"

Austin stuffed the rings back into his pocket, swallowing the last bit of laughter. "Same," he muttered.

A hush fell over the meadow as the violinists pulled their bows across their strings, the familiar first chord of 'Canon in D' reverberating throughout the field. All heads turned to the entrance of the forest. In a pale-yellow dress, Lauren appeared from the trees, her heels resting on the edge of the aisle runner.

"Ready or not…" Austin whispered, squeezing his brother's shoulder as Lauren took her first step forward.

Josh's body went rigid, the nerves exuding from his soul. He turned, a wild grin appearing on his lips. "You know, I asked Mavis to marry me right here." He pointed to the ground. "We were just kids." And with a step forward, he moved closer to the minister.

A smile grew, blossoming from within as his heart accepted the truth for the final time.

She was never mine.

He lifted his gaze, smiling as his sister graced the aisle, each curl on her dark head swept back in a sophisticated bun. With each step, she matched the rhythm of the violinist until she reached the altar and wrapped her arms around Josh. She winked in Austin's direction and stepped back, standing in place on the opposite side of the minister.

Austin's gaze returned to the forest, the breath leaving his body as Casey stepped forward. Where Lauren emitted elegance, Casey emitted radiance, the sun catching in her bright blonde hair, highlighting the curls pinned to the top of her head. She smiled, her eyes focused on Josh as she made her way down the aisle, each step in her heels calculated and slow.

Josh stepped forward and wrapped her in a hug as Austin released a sigh of relief, peering over his brother's shoulders to lock eyes with Casey.

"I did it! I didn't trip!" she mouthed, falling in line beside Lauren.

Austin winked and stifled a snort. His gaze followed her, watching as she tightened her grasp on her bouquet and adjusted her dress. Laughter fell from her lips as Lauren hugged her around the middle and dropped her chin on her shoulder.

The moment froze in his mind. The music quieted, the birds calmed, and the only thing left to listen to was the soft laughter bubbling from Casey's lips. She stood, a picture of perfection, bathed in the sunlight and love filling the meadow. Austin swallowed as a chill raked his skin—the quirky girl from Wrigley Field squeezing his heart all over again.

I love you, Casey girl. I love you so goddamn much.

She winked at him, grinning ear-to-ear as she mouthed the words, "Cubs are up six to three!"

Warmth flooded through his body, her smile from across the aisle momentarily lifting the heavy choice bandaging his heart. Returning her smile, he mouthed back, "The Dodgers are a comeback team!"

She rolled her eyes and shrugged, lifting her gaze to the forest as Mitch and Mavis appeared among the trees.

The music quieted, 'Canon in D' melting away as the birds in the treetops carried their own tune. The guests rose from their seats, all eyes turning to the woman in white as the violinists raised their bows and struck the first note of 'Amazing Grace'.

Mavis seemingly floated down the aisle on Mitch's arm, her dark curly hair spiraling down her back and pinned with a single diamond barrette—the glimmer of her childhood locket catching in the sun. An elegant train followed her footsteps until her feet stilled at the base of the altar, her green gaze lifting to meet Josh's.

A swell of emotion blanketed his body as the memories of her washed over him, a tidal wave crashing into the sand as the tide pulled back and disappeared. Every secret, every kiss, every admission of love consumed his heart until he blinked and released the past into the breeze.

It's over, Princess.

Relief flooded through his bloodstream, bathing his heart with sweet release as the minister's voice boomed out over the meadow.

"Dearly beloved, we are gathered here today to join this man and this woman in holy matrimony. Who gives this woman to be married to this man?"

Mitch squeezed Mavis's fingers and held her hand out to Josh. "She gives herself, but with her family's blessing," he answered.

Austin grinned, the nerves in Mitch's voice paramount. The minister nodded and Mitch shuffled sideways, taking his place beside Austin. He sighed and bumped his elbow. "Now where's the booze?" he whispered, exhaling a breath of relief.

Austin stifled a laugh and nodded, returning his eyes to the minister.

"Joshua Michael Templeton, do you take this woman to be your wife, to live together in holy matrimony, to love her, to honor her, to comfort her, and to keep her in sickness and in health, forsaking all others, for as long as you both shall live?"

Josh trembled, but a resounding *I do* rang in the stillness of the afternoon.

"Mavis Marie Benson, do you take this man to be your husband, to live together in holy matrimony, to love him, to honor him, to comfort him, and to keep him in sickness and in health, forsaking all others, for as long as you both shall live?"

"I do," she answered, her smile touching her eyes.

The minister nodded and continued. "Joshua, repeat after me. I, Joshua, take you, Mavis, to be my wife, to have and to hold from this day forward, for better, for worse, for richer, for poorer, in sickness and in health, to love and to cherish, 'til death do us part."

Austin snuck a peek at Casey as Josh repeated the words, his vows crystalizing in the summer sun. A tear ran down her cheek, and she swiped at it with a chipped pink polished fingernail.

"Now Mavis, repeat after me," continued the minister. "I, Mavis, take you, Joshua, to be my husband, to have and to hold from this day forward, for better, for worse, for richer, for poorer, in sickness and in health, to love and to cherish, 'til death do us part."

Mavis repeated the words, her singsong voice catching in his ear as Mitch jabbed him in the back.

"The rings, please."

Austin rammed his hand into his pocket and pulled from the depths the two wedding bands. Josh turned with his hand outstretched, and Austin dropped them into his palm. "My precious," he whispered.

Josh grinned, and Mavis rolled her eyes.

"Joshua, please place the ring on Mavis's finger and repeat the following," instructed the minister. "I give you this ring as a token and pledge of our constant faith and abiding love."

Josh slid the ring on Mavis's finger and repeated the words.

"Mavis, place the ring on Joshua's finger and repeat after me," he continued. "I give you this ring as a token and pledge of our constant faith and abiding love."

She slid the ring on Josh's finger and smiled, repeating the words, their promises settling into the meadow in the exact place their love first bloomed.

Joining their hands together, the minister grinned. "By the virtue of the authority vested in me under the laws of the State of California, I now pronounce you husband and wife."

The breath caught in Austin's throat, the finality of his words to come, sealing a piece of his soul and a part of his life shut. He swallowed and prepared his heart for the final farewell.

"You may kiss the bride."

Cheers erupted from the meadow—bursts of laughter and clapping hands thundered through his body as Mitch's grip clasped on his shoulder. His brother-in-law's voice whispered in his ear, "Are you okay?"

Austin turned and smiled, nodding and releasing the breath he held in his chest. "I am. This is the way it was always supposed to be. And I know that now."

Mitch squeezed his shoulder again, his gaze following the new Dr. and Mrs. Templeton down the aisle.

Goodbye, my sweet Princess.

JULIE NAVICKAS

CHAPTER TWENTY-THREE

Casey

Her mouth hurt from smiling. Her eyes ached from the incessant flash photography. Her shoes had rubbed blisters onto the backs of her feet. And if one more person requested that she say *cheese*, "I'm walking out of this ballpark with bases loaded," she whispered to herself, shuffling her feet in the grass.

After the ten-thousandth photo of the day, the photographer released the wedding party for cocktail hour on the grounds of Templeton Manor.

"Come on, let's get a drink." Casey ripped the heels from her feet and gripped Austin's hand, pulling him toward the bar.

"Tell me how you really feel." He grinned and allowed her to yank him along.

"It's a million degrees out here. I'm thirsty. And my feet are killing me." Casey pointed to the backs of her feet, cringing at the sight of the angry pink flesh.

Austin scrunched his nose. "Ouch," he muttered and tugged her toward the house instead. "To the medic tent for you, Ms. McDaniels."

"The medic tent?" He led her up the stone patio, past the bar, and into the house—her eyes catching sight of the cold beverage dispensers wrapped in yellow ribbon.

I don't even care if that's Old Style! I just want some!

"Upstairs bathroom, Casey girl. Lauren keeps a first-aid kit there."

She trudged up the stairs, following him as he led her down the carpeted hallway and into the bathroom. Austin flipped on the lights—the meticulously furnished crisp white décor smiling back.

One fucking photo away from a feature in HGTV.

"Dr. Templeton isn't on-call tonight, so you get me instead." He tugged the top drawer open and pulled out a white plastic container with a smile.

She giggled. "Oh, I don't know if I trust your medical skills, sir. What're your credentials?"

"Hmm… good question." Austin lifted his gaze to the ceiling. "Well, I got an 'A' in freshman biology, so that means I can dissect a frog, predict our child's blood type with a Punnett square, and identify the four phases of mitosis."

Casey grinned. *What the fuck are you talking about?* "Good enough, I suppose," she shrugged and hopped up on the counter.

Austin pulled out a Band-Aid and ripped open the packaging. "Let's see that war wound, Casey girl."

She pulled her right leg upward, resting her ankle on her left knee. His warm hands collided with her skin as he examined the wound, covering the blister with the bandage and a playful squeeze. "Other foot too?"

Casey nodded and rotated her legs, watching as Austin placed another bandage on her banged-up foot.

"Glad I left my heels at home and opted for these bad boys," he joked, tapping his toes together.

"I don't know… you have nice calves. Heels would've looked good on you."

She smiled as he leaned forward and covered her mouth

with his—his kiss sensual, sweet, and soft.

More.

Casey pressed her body into him, willing him to return the desire fueling her bloodstream. Tugging his hands up, she wrapped them around the back of her neck.

He pinched her earlobes with a grin but dropped his hands and pulled away. "Always so eager," he murmured, stepping sideways to open the drawer and return the first-aid kit. "But we're missing the party."

He guided her forward until her feet returned to the tile floor, his hand reaching outward to grip the doorknob before she pulled him back.

"Hey, Austin?"

He turned.

"Are you okay?"

Wrinkling his nose, he frowned. "What makes you think I'm not?"

She tugged at his tie and lifted her gaze to his. "Because I know you."

Austin rolled his eyes, sighing until his lips found hers again, his tongue tasting her, moving in her mouth until ripples of pleasure sizzled along her spine.

"You can't distract me," she murmured. "That was a good try though." She pulled away and licked her lips.

He snorted and tilted his head, sighing as his hand gripped the doorknob behind him. "I don't know what to do about this job, Case."

She wrapped her arms around his body, resting her cheek against his chest. The scent of the yellow rose on his jacket mixed with the sandalwood clinging to his skin. The smell intoxicated her senses as his heartbeat pounded in her ear.

"Well, you have to take it."

He shook his head and pulled away. "How can you say that? You know what that means for us, right?" His eyes searched hers.

"It means you move home. I get it. Chicago was always

temporary." She smiled and reached for him, tugging his hands back around her waist. "I guess I just hoped that when you left, you'd pack me into your suitcase on the flight back." She squeezed his upper arms and smiled. "I'm pretty small. I could fit!"

His lips flattened into a thin line. "You'd really move here?"

"Well, yeah… I mean, I kind of love you and stuff." She pushed her face back into his chest as warmth flushed her cheeks.

Wait, maybe you don't want me here?

His arms tightened around her body as his lips pressed to her neck, sending a parade of tingles to march along her skin.

"Beyond any doubt, Casey McDaniels… I love you too." He cupped her chin and tilted her head upward to meet his gaze. "And that's exactly why you can't move here with me."

Her heart skipped a beat, confusion infusing with the sweet words his lips just delivered to her soul.

I don't understand.

"I, umm… so, you're saying…"

Footsteps sounded in the hallway outside, and Lauren's face appeared through the half-closed door.

"Oh! Sorry, I came for Band-Aids." A curl broke free from her elegant bun and hung in her face. She blew at it out of the corner of her mouth. "Ah, perfect," she added, snagging the white box from the still open drawer. "You guys okay?"

"Women's shoes are terrible." Austin pointed toward Casey's feet.

"Tell me about it." She lifted her right foot and showed off the smudged streak of dried blood on her big toe. "Pain is beauty and beauty is pain… or something like that."

Casey nodded and swallowed the heartbreak settling in her soul.

He doesn't want me here.

"Come on. They're getting ready to serve dinner! We

need the head table filled." Lauren grabbed Casey at the elbow, tugging her to follow.

Turning to lock eyes with Austin, Casey frowned as his gaze held firm to the floor as he shuffled behind them.

Frank Sinatra's booming voice sailed through the speakers as the dying sun dipped lower over the ocean behind Templeton Manor. Delicate white twinkle lights illuminated the dance floor as Mavis and Josh waltzed their way through their first dance as husband and wife.

From the head table, Casey eyed Mavis, swaying with perfection in her skintight lace dress as Josh dipped her body low on the dance floor. Each step demonstrated the truth of Austin's admission to junior high ballroom dance lessons for the twins.

"A perfect ten," Casey muttered as Austin dropped back in his seat beside her, two fresh rum and cokes in his hands.

"Hmm?"

"A perfect ten," she repeated, pointing to the new Dr. and Mrs. Templeton as the guests clapped at their performance.

Austin smirked. "I told you, Mrs. Pennington taught us well." He pushed one of the drinks in her direction.

Casey sipped and the alcohol slid down her throat with ease. She licked her lips and turned to watch Austin shrug out of his suit coat jacket, dropping his tie to the table.

"How about a dance, Case?"

She frowned. "Hard pass, sir."

Austin rolled his eyes. "Fine. Can we talk then?"

"Why bother? You were pretty clear upstairs." Bringing the cup back to her lips, she gulped until only the ice remained.

His eyes widened as her empty drink met the table. "Let me try to explain." He pushed his full glass over to her. "Please?"

She eyed it with a frown but tugged the glass closer. *These are really good.* "Go on then. Tell me why you don't want me here."

Austin sighed and dropped his hand to her lap as he scooted closer. He toyed with the yellow fabric of her dress, rubbing the outer layer of chiffon between his thumb and index finger.

"It's not that I don't want you here, Case. Honestly, I want *nothing* more. You were the first person I thought of after they offered me the job and selfishly, I wanted to ask you to move here seconds—"

"Selfishly?" Casey interrupted. "Austin, the day we met, you told me about this job and how much you hoped for it. Your entire career has been building toward it."

He gripped her knee and squeezed. "That's all true, but Case, I'm not all that matters here."

A shadow draped across the table, Josh's silhouette blocking the twinkle lights. "A dance with the maid of honor?" He grinned and reached his hand out.

Her stomach plummeted to the floor as her eyes widened. "Oh, God," she murmured, swatting at Austin as he barked out a laugh beside her. "Josh, umm… I don't think that's such a good idea."

Mavis giggled and dropped into the seat beside Casey, the back of her hand dragging across her brow as laughter fell from her lips.

Josh's gaze darted from Casey to Austin and from Austin to Mavis. He grinned. "What am I missing here?"

Casey shook her head and elbowed Mavis in the gut as the giggles burst from her lips in full force. "Let me level with you, Josh. I've managed to survive the entire day without tripping or falling once. But if you take me out there right now in front of all these people…" She nodded toward the dance floor. "I promise you I'll quickly become the comedic relief of your wedding day."

Josh snorted and tilted his head. "Oh, come on, you can't be that bad." He grasped her hand and tugged until her butt left the chair. "Besides, we need something to liven up this party."

Oh, shit.

"Kill me now!" she shouted over her shoulder as Josh led her to the center of the dance floor and gripped her waist with his left hand. His fingers tightened around her palm as he tugged her closer.

Squeezing her eyes shut, his voice whispered in her ear. "I won't let you fall. You know Austin would kill me if I did."

She breathed in as his body moved. Gripping him tightly, the nerves bounced around in her belly while he swayed to the tune.

"Relax," he whispered with a laugh. "You're just fine…"

"Umm, says you!" Her eyes popped open—a sea of spectators stared back as Josh pushed her away with a fancy spin. His arm yanked her back into his body. Breathless, she giggled. "Don't do that again!"

"Oh, come on! You can't tell me Austin hasn't made you do this yet." Dipping her body backward, her curls touched the dance floor. Her head dizzied as he yanked her back up, bringing her face inches from his own. "He's a showoff, you know."

Old Crow danced through her memory, the slow country song vastly contrasting with the quick steps Josh forced her into. He led her around the full floor, sureness in every step—his grip never loosening from her palm or waist.

"I'm gonna pick you up," he whispered with a mischievous smile.

"Oh, God! Josh!" A bubble of laughter spilled from her lips as he grabbed her waist and lifted her petite frame. The cool air whipped through her hair as her tired and aching feet left the ground. He spun her body in a full circle, the fancy twirl breathing exhilaration into her heart.

Her toes touched the ground as the song ended. Leaning forward, he pecked his lips on her forehead. "See. Not that bad, right?" He grinned and spun her body away until he dropped her hand into Austin's outstretched grasp.

"My turn?"

The sheepish smile on his lips paired with his pleading eyes melted her. *I can't fucking resist you, Austin Templeton.* She leaned into his embrace as Josh winked at his brother.

"It's not fair that Josh gets to dance with you, and I can't." His hands gripped her middle, pulling her body into his own as he swayed and twirled her around with the same grace and elegance to the slow rhythm of the next song.

"Well, it is *his* wedding. I couldn't exactly say no to him."

"But you said no to me." He pushed her body outward in a spin, pulling her back into the safety of his arms.

She huffed out a surprised breath as her eyes returned to his. "You said no to me upstairs, so call it even?"

Austin rolled his eyes and tightened his grip. "All right Casey girl, all my cards are out now. If you move here with me, you're giving up your internship with the mayor. I can't let you do that."

Casey snorted. "That's what this is all about? Some ridiculous internship? Austin, please."

"Don't do that. Don't shortchange the experience, or your accomplishment in getting the opportunity. You always sell yourself short, Case. It's infuriating."

"You completed the application! Not me!"

He spun her again, tugging her body back into his with more force than the last time.

"There was not one lie or embellishment in the words I submitted. Everything in there was accurate and truthful. I may have strung the words together, Casey McDaniels, but you earned that position. And I won't stand for you turning it down. Your dreams matter too."

The song ended and she turned to leave, but his arms held her tight, pinning her in place on the dance floor. "Uh-uh. We're not done here, Cinderella."

"Austin, come on," she whined as a classic country tune rattled through the speakers.

He winked. "Bet you regret not learning the Texas two-step when I offered now, don't you?"

Heat blanked her body as impending embarrassment flushed her cheeks. She shook her head and laughed. "Oh, hell no!" Pulling away from him, she attempted escape from the dance floor, but his grip tightened, tugging her backward into his arms.

"Not a chance, Casey girl." Yanking her body back into his, he started a rotation of fancy footwork she simply couldn't keep up with.

She smiled, giggling with embarrassment until inspiration struck. Hopping on his toes at the first break in his steps, he roared with laughter, his giggles setting her heart ablaze with love.

The song ended, and Austin pulled her away with a smile, leading her across the darkened yard toward the path back to the meadow, each footfall instigating lightning bugs to come alive and fly from the safety of their blades of grass.

When they reached the path, Austin sank to a fallen log and coaxed her to his lap. She sat and pressed a kiss to his forehead, the summertime crickets serenading them in the darkness once more. Laughter rang out across the lawn, the wedding celebrations in full force.

He sighed and Casey huffed out an irritated breath. "It's just an internship, Austin. I can find something—anything else."

He shook his head. "It's not *just* the internship. What about your degree? Credits don't always transfer between states. What if it puts you behind? You're on track to graduate this December."

"It's not a big deal!" She rolled her eyes. "It's taken me this long already, what's another few classes or semesters?"

I wish I never told you anything. It was better when no one knew.

Austin shook his head and rested his cheek against her chest. "How long is it going to take before you understand your education and career are just as important as anyone else's?"

"They're not, Austin. Don't pretend, and don't placate

me. A stupid associate's degree and a dumb internship? None of that measures up to a partnership at a law firm."

He exhaled as a lightning bug landed on Casey's dress. His little legs crawled across the fabric until she scooped him up with a single finger. "Make a wish," she whispered.

Austin nodded, watching as she blew the bug from her finger. He flew into the night air, buzzing away into the darkness.

"What did you wish for?"

Austin swallowed and pressed his face closer to her chest. "The strength to do something I have absolutely no desire to do, Casey girl." His eyes closed as he heaved out a breath.

Casey furrowed her brow.

I wished for cake, but I guess yours works too.

CHAPTER TWENTY-FOUR

Austin

"3909 Cedar Creek Drive. About five miles north," muttered Austin as he closed the door of the sedan, settling into the backseat beside Casey.

The driver nodded and put the car in gear, slowly rolling away from Templeton Manor in the early hours of Sunday morning.

Casey's head drooped against the window, her eyes closed. In the darkness of the car, Austin reached over and clasped his hand around her balled-up fists in her lap. At his touch, she turned and smiled.

"Some wedding, huh?" She yawned. "I swear if I ever get married, it's City Hall for sure."

Nausea stirred in his gut. The L.A. parking garage swirled in his mind, the prospect of returning to the scene of the crime rattling around in his exhausted, conflicted brain. He swallowed. "Really? No big party?"

The headlights from a passing car illuminated her face. "I mean, well maybe just a rooftop bar with Old Style or something." She squeezed his hand and grinned. "Oh! The Cubs won! Eight to four…"

Mitch owes me a hundred bucks.

"A playoff team in the making." Austin pulled his hand from hers and tucked a curl behind her ear. His fingers trailed the length of her arm, grazing the fabric of her dress along her waist. "Ouch!"

"What?"

He held up his index finger, a pinprick of deep-red blood oozing out.

Casey grinned. "To be fair, I did warn you about the pins." She pulled his finger to her mouth and dragged the tip of her tongue across the tiny wound.

A twinge gripped him low in the abdomen as she sucked gently on his finger. "That reminds me," she whispered. "The wedding's over... feel free to rip this dress off me when we get home."

A smile consumed his mouth as she leaned in and pressed her lips to his cheek. Catching the eye of the driver in the rearview mirror as the car rolled into the driveway, Austin handed a twenty-dollar bill over the front seat.

The driver winked. "Thanks, buddy. Enjoy your night."

Austin smirked and closed the door. Following Casey up the porch steps, he punched in the code and entered the house. His fingers fumbled for the light switch in the dark foyer before the chandelier brought the space to life.

"I have to pee so bad!" Casey stumbled away to the powder room.

Kicking off his shoes, Austin sank to the bottom step of the staircase and rubbed his toes. With a sigh, he propped his elbows on his knees and let his head sink to his hands, his palms meeting his forehead with a thud.

What do I do? What do I do? What do I do, Casey girl? I have to take this job! But where does that leave us?

The hours of alcohol raged through his body, still partying like his bloodstream was a slip-n'-slide in mid-summer. He squeezed his eyes closed, shutting out the slowly spinning room as his ears rang in the silence.

The tap turned on in the powder room, the water

traveling through the pipes as his heart thumped in his chest. "Casey girl," he murmured. "I don't want to lose you, but…"

The door opened and her bare feet shuffled down the hall. She sank to the stair beside him and smiled. "That's better."

Austin grabbed her knee and squeezed, pulling her closer until her head fell to his shoulder. Her breath beat against the sleeve of his shirt, the warmth inviting, comfortable.

"Can you please stop being weird now?"

Austin frowned. *You just don't get it, Case. You don't see the big picture. You don't see your future.* "I'm not being weird. I'm just thinking."

"I'm too tired to think." Her eyes closed as she rubbed her nose, smushing her face into his arm.

Austin tipped his face sideways, admiring the small grin resting on her lips. Her cheeks flushed pink, each eye smudged with makeup. "Why are you staring at me?" she asked, eyes still closed.

The pit in his stomach deepened, the alcohol spiraling downward, swirling in his gut. *Trying to picture my life without you. And I just can't.* "You're pretty." His lips pressed onto the top of her head.

She wrinkled her nose. "Oh, yeah, the picture of beauty right now." She raised her arm and pointed toward her face as a giggle tumbled from her lips.

"You have no idea, Cinderella," he whispered, shifting to wrap his arm around her.

She snuggled into him, resting her hand on his thigh. Lilacs bloomed beneath his nose, the scent of safety, comfort, and undeniable love bathed in hairspray.

"I love you, Austin Templeton," she breathed, skimming her fingernails along his pants.

"I love you too, Casey girl… more than you know."

She shifted and opened her eyes, peering into his soul.

"But maybe I'm hurting you by loving you as much as I do," he whispered, cupping her cheek in his hand.

If I move home, I'd selfishly take you with me, taking you away from your internship and…

"You could never hurt me." She pressed her lips to his, her tongue dancing along his own.

For both our sakes, maybe hurting you is exactly what I have to do. You have to stay in Chicago. It's just… how do I make you do it?

"Don't be so sure," he murmured against her mouth.

An idea thundered through his tired brain, constricting his lungs and pulling the breath from his body. Each muscle weakened, a tremor in his left-hand shooting pangs of numbness up and down his fingers with the growing thought.

"You're the one person in the world who never would," she whispered, rising from her seat as her stomach growled louder than a freight train.

"Hungry?"

Her hands dragged across her belly as a sheepish smile grew on her lips.

"Cheesy sandwich, Casey girl?"

She giggled, pulling him from his seat until he stood. "Counterproposal," she whispered, untucking his shirt from his pants. "Make love to me instead."

Austin swallowed, fighting the fear erupting in his heart at her words, the inklings of a decision tugging at the frail strings stitching his soul to Casey's.

There has to be another option here!

"Case," he murmured and stepped back.

The fuel feeding the fire behind her eyes ignited, the blue hue of her irises sparkling with excitement. A grin crept along her lips.

"Oh…" she whispered, tiptoeing forward. "Playing hard to get I see, Mr. Templeton." She fell into his arms and pressed her mouth back onto his—passion emitting from the connection she forced. "Challenge accepted then." Her palm rubbed against the length in his pants.

Austin gasped, betrayed by his body and the burning desire she ignited within him. He pushed against her, the friction magnifying in his mind as she groaned in his arms. His heart called to hers, screaming for his soulmate.

"Take me upstairs," she murmured. "I want to show you how much I love you."

What are you doing to me, Casey girl?

He scooped her small body into his arms as he climbed the stairs to his darkened bedroom. Setting Casey to her feet beside his bed, he sighed, the light from the foyer illuminating the nightstand and the note she'd penned before the wedding.

His heart faltered, each string tightening in his chest as her fingers toyed with the buttons on his shirt and stripped the material from his body. Her nails tickled his skin, trailing down his bare torso until her hands gripped the button on his pants. Warmth cascaded over his body, blanketing him in desire.

Casey sank to her knees and pulled his zipper down with her. "Let me show you," she repeated, tugging his pants and boxers to the floor. Her mouth closed over him, an instant jolt to his brain sending shivers to wrack his full body.

"Mmmm," he choked out. "Casey…"

She giggled, the light sound journeying straight to the center of his soul.

Choking on the saliva coating his mouth, he huffed out a breath and pulled himself from her grasp.

I can't do this. It's so wrong.

"Case…" He inhaled, bending over to pull her from her knees. "I can't do this." His mind raced, deprived of oxygen, dizzied from little sleep, and fueled with hours of alcohol.

"Sure you can," she whispered, wrapping her arms behind her back. She tugged at her zipper until the yellow fabric floated to the ground. Kicking the garment to the side, she lifted Austin's hands to cup her bare breasts. Pressing her lips back onto his, she moaned.

But I can't fucking resist you…

He nudged her backward onto the bed, tugging at her panties until they fell free from her body. She snickered as the weight of him crashed on top of her, his lips pressing into a freckle on her right breast and his grasp digging into the skin beneath her tattoo.

The ringing in his ears grew louder as the blood in his veins hammered through his body where his skin collided with hers.

Casey arched her back and growled in his ear as her fingers dragged through his hair.

You can't do this, Austin! Ten minutes ago, you decided to break her heart!

"Now, Austin! Please!" she begged, pressing her middle into his arousal.

Sweat coated his forehead and his body warmed, the friction of skin on skin sending a tidal wave of heat to blanket his system, roaring with confliction. He swallowed and pressed his tip to her entry. His gaze caught hers as her lids fluttered open, the impending union clouding her eyes.

He stared into the depths of her soul—her sweet and innocent soul—that desired the chance to burst free and fulfill a dream long buried in her heart, spoken to no one but himself.

I've tried to get you to see your potential, Casey girl. I've pushed you to keep dreaming. But my words haven't worked.

She arched her back again, pleading and begging for him to continue. "I want to feel you inside me…" Her mouth found his in the darkness, softly placing her love and desire on his lips, each kiss bathed in trust.

What do I fucking do?

His brain screamed as he pushed himself inside her, the instant ripples of pleasure and pressure building with intensity as she wiggled beneath him.

"I love you." Her sweet whisper bit into the darkness, her admission of love penetrating his chest and latching onto his heart in the tender, vulnerable moment.

I love you, Casey, more than you'll ever know. And it's why I have to break your heart.

In the flurry of heightened passion, the heavy decision

squashed his soul.

My words have never worked on you because I haven't found the right ones. Until now...

Austin released himself inside her as her cries of passion rang in his ear, her fingers tightening their hold on his waist. He gazed into her satiated eyes as the life fell out of his own.

"I love you too, Mavis," he whispered.

Her body stilled beneath him as immediate regret shattered his soul.

CHAPTER TWENTY-FIVE

Lauren

A drop of cheese from the casserole dripped over the pan and onto the bottom of the oven.

"Shit," muttered Lauren as the burning smell overpowered the kitchen. She yanked open the oven and wafted a dishcloth to dismiss the smoke. "Dammit," she added, pinching her nose. One-handed, she pulled out the pan and thrust it onto the cooling rack. With a slam of the oven door, the fire alarm pierced the quiet morning.

"What's burning?" Mitch hurried into the kitchen and jumped to silence the fire alarm above the doorway.

"Oh, the dumb cheese overflowed..." Lauren pulled her hair back into a low ponytail. "I'm sorry, I didn't mean to wake you."

"I was up." He rolled his eyes. "That couch sucks." Mitch yawned and turned on the coffee pot. Resting his back against the counter, he folded his arms across his bare chest.

"There's like six other beds in this house if you don't want to sleep in ours." Lauren buried her head in the refrigerator, rearranging the contents on each shelf until she found the cream.

Mitch snorted, eyeing the container as she set it down in front of him. "Since when do you want me in our bed?"

She slammed the refrigerator door closed. "Look, you only have to pretend to like me for a few more hours. As soon as brunch is over and everyone leaves, you can go back to hating me, all right?"

"I don't hate you, Lauren."

The coffee pot beeped behind him, but his eyes held firm on hers, catching her in an unexpected web of truth.

Is it the truth though?

Lauren scrunched her nose and searched his familiar face, her gaze lingering on the endearing laugh lines beneath his green eyes. *When's the last time we even laughed together? When's the last time we...* A shiver of courage snaked along her spine as her lips parted. "Well, you sure don't love me anymore, Mitch. That much is obvious."

He sighed and shook his head, scooping up a white ceramic mug from the counter. "That's not true, Peaches," he answered and poured himself a cup of piping hot coffee.

Peaches?

Her heart fluttered, the right corner of her lips pulling upward at the sweet childhood nickname as she sliced into the moderately burnt casserole with her back to him.

His soft footsteps penetrated her ear as he moved closer, his fingers grasping her waist with a small squeeze. Mitch's breath met the delicate skin at the base of her neck as his lips pressed a kiss to her.

"My feelings for you have never changed," he whispered. "And they never will." With a sigh, he disappeared through the kitchen door, the smell of fresh coffee trailing behind.

Lauren gasped, her skin tingling where his lips pressed against her. *What just happened?* The knife in her hands clanked to the countertop as she dashed after him. In her slippers, she shuffled down the hall to the base of the staircase.

"Mitch…"

His feet stilled on the second-floor landing.

"I need you to tell me right now." Tears burned behind her eyelids as she swallowed, fighting with the words threatening to rip themselves free from her heart. "Do you want a divorce?

His fingers trembled, the coffee cup shaking in his left hand as his head hung.

"Lauren…" he whispered, seemingly unwilling to turn and look at her.

The pit in her stomach deepened, the simplicity of her name driving the truth straight into her soul. Fighting back the bile clawing up her throat, she opened her mouth. "Yeah… okay, got it…"

Ripping her hand from the banister, she returned to the kitchen and picked up the knife, slicing away at the casserole with perfect, even strokes as her phone pinged beside her.

Eyeing the device, she wiped her hands on a dish towel before confirming brunch plans with her mother.

"Just get through brunch," she choked out to the silent kitchen, swiping at the tears leaking down her cheeks. "Just get through brunch and then you can fall apart." Lauren forced a smile on her face, slicing fresh fruit and baking muffins. She brewed coffee and scrubbed at the spilled cheese in the oven until the rack glistened again. "Just get through brunch…" she repeated, allowing the mantra to disguise the inner turmoil tearing her heart to shreds as she stood.

An hour later, Lauren laid the brunch buffet on the dining room table and fluffed the yellow tablecloth. A small dark stain in the center caught her eye. She cringed and dragged her finger over the blemish.

It's fucking coffee. Dammit, Mitch!

She covered the stain with a vase of flowers, bringing the illusion of perfection back to the table.

Lauren swallowed and glared at the hidden smudge, the flowers, just a Band-Aid for the larger problem, the coffee woven into the fabric with permanence. With a sudden loss of control, a cry escaped her lips as the tears cascaded down her cheeks in rivers of pain, falling from her face like a waterfall—her marriage toppling over the precipice.

It's over. Mitch is gone.

"All right kid, you first." John Templeton shoved a bite of blueberry muffin in his mouth and pointed to Mitch. "Favorite moment from the wedding yesterday?"

Mitch lifted his gaze from his father-in-law to the ceiling and grinned. "Easy… Great Aunt Millie squeezing my ass mid-way through 'The Way You Look Tonight.'"

Josh choked on his coffee, coughing into the roar of laughter filling the room.

A rare, genuine smile of amusement blossomed on Susan's lips as she reached for the coffee carafe. "I guess Aunt Millie is getting a bit frisky in her old age!" Dabbing at a tear in the corner of her eye, she nodded at Mavis. "What about you, dear? Favorite moment of the day?"

A wide grin consumed her lips as she leaned sideways into her new husband. "Saying, *I do.*"

Josh's cheeks flushed as he wrapped his arm around her and pressed his lips to hers, his fingers toying with the new wedding band on her finger. "Likewise, Mrs. Templeton."

Lauren brought a glass of water to her lips and gulped down the liquid, forcing her body to not react to the dewy-eyed love across the table. Mitch's hand gripped the back of her chair, triggering disgust to ripple through her. Her gaze dropped to her lap as she picked at the chipped nail polish on her thumb.

"And how about you, kiddo?" Her father's foot tapped against her toe beneath the table. "You know, you throw one hell of a party."

Lauren grinned, the sweet compliment turning her cheeks pink. She searched her mind, willing herself to find an acceptable answer on par with the rest of them.

Mitch picked up his coffee beside her and brought the liquid to his lips. Her eyes followed him as her stomach twisted in knots.

You didn't even dance with me.

"Kiddo?" John frowned. "You okay?"

She nodded, a grin reappearing on her lips. "Oh! I know! Watching Josh fling Casey around on the dance floor! She looked terrified!"

Josh snorted. "No one told me she had a fear of dancing!" He giggled and wrapped his arm back around Mavis.

Lifting her gaze to him, Mavis frowned. "Hey, where are they, anyway?" She wrinkled her nose and tipped his wrist to glare at his watch. "We have to leave for the airport in like fifteen minutes."

"It's that late?" Josh flipped his wrist over as the grandfather clock in the hallway chimed, announcing the eleven o'clock hour.

"Didn't you tell them ten, Lauren?" Susan sipped her coffee and eyed her daughter.

"Yeah, I did." Lauren nodded and scooted her chair back. "Let me give Austin a call real quick."

She left the dining room and retreated to the library. Sinking onto the ancient sofa in the middle of the room, its springs groaned with protest under her weight. With a quick tap on her phone, Lauren brought the device to her ear, each unanswered ring rousing unease in her stomach.

"Weird," she murmured and ended the call as his voicemail picked up. Her heart hammered in her chest as she opened a text message and tapped out the words, *Where are you guys? Is everything okay?*

She eyed her phone, willing her brother to respond, but nothing happened. "What gives, you guys?" Tapping Casey's name next, she returned the phone to her ear, listening to the same sequence of unanswered rings and subsequent voicemail.

Nerves gripped her gut. With an inhale, she pushed away

the shiver threatening her spine and returned to the dining room.

"I can't get a hold of either of them."

Mitch tipped back in his seat, balancing his body on the back two legs of the chair. "They probably just overslept. Nothing to worry about."

What if there is something to worry about though?

"Has anyone heard from them since they left last night?" Lauren circled her gaze around the table, all heads shaking back and forth.

"If we leave now, we can swing over to Austin's real quick and check on them," offered Josh, rising from his seat.

"No… no, it's okay. Let me do it. You guys have a honeymoon to get to." Lauren smiled and stepped forward to wrap her arms around the happy couple, sending them off with well wishes before dropping her butt into the driver's seat of her Lexus. The engine hummed to life as she put the car in drive and maneuvered it out of the driveway.

"Come on, Austin…" she whispered, dropping the sun visor to block the blinding rays. "What the hell?"

Her mind raced as she cruised down the empty streets, navigating each turn with a belly full of anxiety, punctuated at each turn with Mitch's voice echoing in her ear.

I'll deal with you later, Mitch.

She pulled into Austin's driveway. Snagging her bag from the passenger seat, she darted from the car and raced up the front steps. "Austin? It's Lauren! Are you guys okay?"

Nothing.

With a frown, she punched in the code and stepped inside, the eerie silence raising the hairs on the back of her neck. "Austin? Casey?" Circling through the kitchen, Lauren bit her bottom lip, the unease in her gut forcing her heartbeat to double. "Are you guys here?"

She climbed the staircase and glanced back at her phone to check for return calls or texts.

Still nothing.

As she rounded the corner on the landing, an upended suitcase met her gaze, Austin's clothing scattered across the carpet. "What the hell?" She picked up a blue shirt and eyed the half-open door to his bedroom.

"Austin?" The hinges creaked as she pushed the door open further, the sunlight from the hallway illuminating the aftermath of a tornado. Her foot tread on a shattered picture frame as she stepped inside. Dropping her gaze to the floor, her own face stared back. "What is this?" she whispered, bending down to pick up the broken glass.

Movement beneath the covers stole her attention. A muffled sob broke the silence of the room as her brother emerged. He swallowed and pulled his legs into his chest. "Lauren?" His hoarse voice gripped her heart as his bloodshot eyes zeroed in on her.

She stepped forward, her feet catching on a ball of yellow fabric in the center of the room. "Austin? What happened here? Are you okay?" Her knees bumped into the bottom of the mattress.

His gaze lifted to her face, each eye clouded from the sea of tears raining down his cheeks. He swiped at them and sucked air into his lungs as a sob escaped his lips. "She's gone, Lauren."

Her butt dropped to the edge of the bed. "Casey?" she whispered.

His head fell forward, and he buried his face in his knees. As he raked his fingers through his hair, his muffled voice gripped the stillness of the bedroom. "It's over."

Lauren shifted and slid closer until her hand rested over his blanketed foot. "What happened?" she whispered, squeezing his toes as her eyes flooded with tears.

He lifted his head. His swollen eyes emitted the deep-seated pain stirring in his soul. It reverberated outward from his body, an invisible cloud of sorrow swirling toward her in a funnel of unavoidable understanding until it landed in her lap.

"When you love someone..." he choked out.

"Sometimes you have to let them go."
Well, that… that hits home.

CHAPTER TWENTY-SIX

Casey

Five Months Later

After packing up her things for the weekend, Casey snapped her laptop closed and stood, yawning in her small cubicle.

"Heading out?"

Casey turned, one arm stuffed in her jacket as her supervisor, Brenda, poked her head around the corner.

"Oh umm, yeah. I mean, if that's okay?" Her cheeks flushed pink.

Brenda grinned and slapped the file folders in her hands against the door frame playfully. "Of course, it's okay! It's got to be…" She pulled her phone from her pocket, widening her eyes as the screen lit up. "Geez! It's almost six o'clock! What're you still doing here anyway?"

Casey shrugged and shoved her opposite arm into her jacket with a sheepish smile.

It's not like I have anything else to do. Anywhere else to be. Or anyone else to be with.

"Go home. Have a good weekend, girl." Brenda flashed

a brilliant white smile and stepped from the doorway as Casey nodded. "Oh, and umm, Casey?" She returned, poking her head back around the edge of the cubicle. "Really nice work this week. I forwarded your fundraising ideas over to the marketing team and they were really impressed. They loved everything about it. I bet we'll see it in the mayor's master campaign plan when it's released next month!"

A smirk overtook her lips, the compliment washing over her as a weight lifted from her chest.

For the first time in my life, I'm actually good at something!

"Thanks, Brenda. That means a lot."

With a wink, she stepped away and called over her shoulder. "You'll make us all look good! See you Monday!"

"See you Monday," she whispered and zipped up her coat with unexpected pride.

The wind lashed at her face as she left the building, leaving behind her internship for the weekend. Casey hopped down the giant cement staircase toward Rush Street, aiming straight for the red line. Pulling her coat tighter around her body, she rammed her hands into a pair of wool gloves as the familiar city noises of Chicago gripped her ears.

The train rattled to a stop at the platform. Forcing her way through the crowd, she jumped into the first car and stood shoulder-to-shoulder with her fellow passengers as the train jerked forward. She stared out the window, following the sights of the now familiar twenty-minute commute through the city until she pushed her way to freedom at her usual stop.

Casey rounded the corner and breezed past The Broken Shaker. She grinned, tempted to peek inside and see who Jim hired to replace her after she'd resigned six weeks ago. Brenda exceeded her bartending paycheck and offered her an extended internship that would carry her through the end of the campaign.

And I'll figure out what to do after that. All I know is that I'll never go back to pouring drinks.

Warmth greeted her as she stepped inside her building and climbed the three floors to her apartment. Casey pushed the door open, her eyes automatically averting the living room as she kicked off her shoes and ran down the hallway toward the safety of her bedroom.

Her face fell into her pillow, the soft material welcoming her wind-lashed face like an old friend. With a sigh, she shrugged off her coat as her phone vibrated with an unknown number.

"Hello?"

"Hello, yes, is this Casey McDaniels?"

Casey frowned, ready to hang up on the spam call, but her mouth opened instead. "Umm, yes, it is."

"Oh, good. Ms. McDaniels I'm calling to confirm your appointment tomorrow morning to view an open unit in the new Lakewood apartment complex. Is 10 AM still okay?"

Oh! I forgot about that!

Casey cleared her throat as her gaze darted around her room, the last nine years of her life consuming the small space. Her stomach clenched as she recalled the impulsive call she'd made three weeks ago to schedule a viewing when a unit became available. "Ten is perfect. I'll be there."

"Excellent. I'll have Jan onsite to greet you with a contract if you're ready to sign. Enjoy your evening!"

The call ended and Casey dropped her phone on the mattress. Heaving out a sigh, she swung her feet to the floor and stood, her toe catching the corner of a cardboard box.

"Ouch!" she yelled and squatted down to examine the injury.

Just a stupid stubbed toe...

She shoved the box aside in anger and frowned as the top flap fluttered open. "What is even in here?" Casey poked her nose inside, her fingers brushing against a pair of old flip-flops, an out-of-season handbag, and a mishmash of hair accessories until something hard collided with her knuckles. With a twinge in her gut, Casey shoved away *A*

Novel Approach to Political Science, the textbook a physical reminder of the previous soul-crushing summer.

Her mouth went dry as she closed the box and pushed it across the bedroom until it banged into her desk chair. "Fuck you, political science," she muttered. "No one gives a shit about a nation-state anyway." With a grimace, she stomped from her bedroom and into the kitchen.

Casey yanked down a glass and filled it to the brim with tap water, gulping down the liquid with gusto. She forced her eyes to focus on the dirty dishes in the sink, the top plate caked with dried spaghetti sauce. But the living room called, tugging and toying with her heart until she slammed the glass down on the counter and padded into the room.

Still wrapped in its plastic prison, Austin's new blue couch looked back—its cute buttons and soft fabric beckoning her, begging to be unwrapped after the last five months spent in solitude—unused, resting in the middle of the living room floor exactly where it was delivered.

Tears burned her eyes as the familiar ringing in her ears returned, the gut-wrenching pain living in her heart bubbling upward until a cry escaped her lips. Casey swiped at the first trickle of tears dripping down her cheeks and kicked at the open box on the floor housing two Cubbie blue throw pillows.

"Fucking Cubs," she whined, turning and retreating into her bedroom. "Three and out in the goddamn first round of the playoffs…"

With a groan, she flung herself onto her bed and let the floodgates open. "A fucking fitting end to the season."

"What time is your graduation ceremony?"

Casey rolled her eyes. "Mavs, do *not* fly back here. It's just a dumb community college thing!"

"Oh, my God, Casey! You're graduating. Come on. That's a huge accomplishment! I want to be there when you cross the stage." Her gaze moved off-screen. "We both do," she added.

Josh entered the frame on her tiny phone. "It's an incredible accomplishment, Case. Just look at how much you've done this last semester alone."

Well, you got the alone part right.

"You guys, please. I just don't want to make a big deal out of it, okay? Come on, please don't fly back here." Casey rubbed her eyes and slumped against the wall on the barstool. She gulped down the last half of her beer and chipped away at a dried speck of red sauce on the counter with her fingernail.

With a roll of her eyes, Mavis pulled the phone away from Josh. "Don't do this, Case. Graduation *is* a big deal. You've worked your ass off all these years, balancing work and school, and now an internship too! I'm so tired of you short-changing yourself!"

And where have I heard that before?

Casey wrinkled her nose and propped the phone up against her empty beer bottle on the counter. Picking at the hole in her jeans, she sighed. "You're sweet, Mavs. You really are. It's just… I don't know. After everything that happened, it's kinda—"

"That's just it, Case. You never told us what happened." Mavis leaned forward, her eyes boring into her own through the tiny screen. "You took off after the wedding without a word. No call, no text… no explanation."

Casey shrugged, peeking at the plastic-wrapped couch in the living room. "Look, Mavs, you said it yourself. Austin and I just weren't right for each other, okay?" She returned her eyes to the phone, ignoring the pain rebounding in her heart. "At least not after…"

"Not after what? Case, I'm not trying to pry, but it's been *months* and neither of you will talk about what happened!"

Neither of us? Well duh! How could he admit to what he did… to you of all people!

Casey shook her head, the sting of tears welling behind her lids again. Her gaze rested on the dirty pan atop the stove, the smell of cheesy sandwiches oozing from her memory.

I can't do it.

"I'm sorry, Mavs. I can't do this. I'll call you later, okay?"

"Case, please wait—"

Casey ended the call and pushed her phone across the counter. It crashed into the wall and tumbled to the floor with a resounding crack, the ache in her heart returning as the screen shattered.

Austin's voice echoed in her mind. *I love you too, Mavis. I love you too, Mavis. I love you too, Mavis.* His words pierced her soul all over again, stuck on repeat for the last five months.

"Fuck you, Austin Templeton!" she roared and dropped to her knees to examine her phone. A piece of broken glass fell into her palm. "Just... fuck you," she whispered, swiping tears from her cheeks. His face swam in her mind, his sweet grin breathing life into her tired body, his blue eyes with the white lashes piercing her soul, exuding confidence and strength, pushing her forward.

"Well, I did it, Austin. You got what you fucking wanted. I'm graduating, and I love my stupid internship..." Her body crumpled to the kitchen floor, the cool tile soothing her damp cheek as the sign that read *Boyd, Bernstein & Templeton at Law* in front of the Michigan Avenue office swam in her brain. "I hope you're just as fucking happy as I am."

A knock on the door jarred her, pulling her from the impromptu pity party on the kitchen floor. Quickly brushing away the tears, Casey yanked her body upright, blew her nose in a paper towel, and opened the door. A bright-eyed brunette and a young man in a navy-blue polo greeted her teary-eyed face.

"Hi! I'm Josie!" The pen on her clipboard whirled through the air, hanging tight to the pink string on the rusted metal ring. "I'm from K&R Realty. We have a two o'clock appointment to show your apartment. Your lease expires this month, right?" The man behind her grinned and bobbed his head.

Duh. You know I only signed a six-month extension…

Casey sighed and nodded, reaching to the dining room table to snag her bag and jacket.

"No problem," she muttered. "I'll get out of your hair." Casey stepped outside the apartment and took two steps down the staircase before inspiration struck. Turning around, she poked her head back inside. "Oh, and that couch comes with the place. Brand new. Free of charge."

Josie nodded and scratched a note onto her clipboard, nudging her polo-wearing client in the elbow.

"That's kind of perfect, actually. I don't have any furniture yet," he said.

"All yours then… the pillows too," Casey murmured before pulling the door shut and heading downstairs.

Tiny white snow flurries wafted in the cold air as she left the building, shivering beneath her jacket. Her feet trudged forward, moving her swiftly toward the parking garage and the tried-and-true Ford Fiesta.

Ramming the keys in the ignition, Casey glanced at the rearview mirror and groaned as her tear-stained cheeks and bloodshot eyes reflected back. With a sigh, her fingers lifted to tap the little mirror, a fresh wave of sadness settling in the pit of her stomach.

Why'd you have to ruin everything, Austin?

"We were so good together," she whispered into the silence. Shaking her head, she stuffed her hand into her bag and pulled out a pack of cigarettes and a lighter. With a crank of her arm, the window lowered, and she lit a cigarette with fiery rebellion in her heart—her promise to quit floating out the window in a flurry of ash.

Her lips pulled on the moistened tip, and she breathed out the smoke as her eyes caught on the angry orange fire inside the filter, roaring with the fuel her lungs controlled. Casey heaved out a breath and sank in her seat as a fresh wave of tears burned behind her eyelids.

"Do you even miss me? Was any of it real for you?"

But the quiet parking garage held no response—and her fairy godmother didn't appear.

CHAPTER TWENTY-SEVEN

Austin

Austin pulled out of the parking garage beneath City Hall and turned right, averting his gaze from the large sign that read *Boyd, Bernstein & Templeton at Law* in big, bold letters. After years of imagining that sign, the only thing it did now was squeeze sorrow from his gut.

His eyes glazed over as he navigated the familiar streets of L.A. in the daily four o'clock traffic jam, his Corvette coming to a standstill in a line of cars. "Great," he muttered and picked up his phone from the cup holder. Josh's name lit up the screen as he tapped *accept* on the message, reading, *I'm here. Usual table by Sandy's Surf. Please don't cancel on me this time.*

Austin rolled his eyes, and twenty minutes later, stepped from the concrete parking lot onto the sand, his feet shuffling to the dreaded picnic table. "I hate this *truth-inducing* table," he whispered, eyeing his brother seated alone.

Plopping his butt beside Josh, he dropped his head in his hands and massaged his temples. "Hi," he murmured.

Josh frowned. "I'd ask if you're okay, but..." He

elbowed him in the gut.

Austin snorted. *No, I'm definitely not okay.* "What's up, Josh? What am I here?"

His brother lifted the sunglasses from his face and rammed his hand in his right pocket, squinting at the phone in his hands.

"On call?"

Josh nodded and tapped out a quick reply, pocketing the device again. "Sorry, yeah, for another two hours." He sighed. "But umm, thanks for coming." Josh eyed his brother, play-punching him in the arm. "Since you finally showed up this time and I have your attention, I've got three things I need to talk to you about."

A seagull screeched overhead and landed four feet in front of the twins, squawking for the lunch scraps beneath their table.

"Fucking bird!" Austin kicked sand in its direction. "Piss off!" he yelled.

Josh furrowed his brow. "And the first one is your sour mood."

Austin shrugged and dropped his back against the tabletop with a roll of his eyes. "What're the other two, Josh?"

He shook his head. "Come on man, you've been, just not the same since… Tell me what happened. It's just you and me here."

Austin slapped his hand against the wooden seat, the gouge in the bench poking his palm with a splinter. He winced and pulled the wood from his skin. "We broke up. Nothing more to it."

With a sigh, Josh dropped back against the tabletop too, mirroring his brother's position. "You can talk to me, you know—"

"It's the new job," Austin interjected, heaving out a breath. "It's just way more than I thought it would be. That's all. Casey has nothing to do with… my mood."

That's a lie.

"Casey—"

"Isn't my girlfriend anymore." Austin swallowed, gulping down a deep breath. "Come on, Josh. Now what're the other two things?"

He frowned and blew out a breath as his gaze sank to the sand. He nodded. "Okay… then when's the last time you talked to our sister?"

Austin's stomach rolled, churning the tiny bits of salad he'd managed to choke down for lunch. Turning his head, he met his brother's dark eyes. "Couple weeks, maybe? I don't know… why?"

Josh exhaled and cracked his knuckles, lifting his gaze to the darkening sky. "Mitch told me he's moving forward… filing for a divorce."

Fucker.

"Damn it! Ugh, he's actually going through with it?" Austin closed his eyes as anger descended on his body, bathed in the cold wind from the ocean. Guilt exploded in his heart. *Lauren.* "Fuck! How is she? I should have called her."

"Yeah, you should have." Josh rammed his elbow into Austin's side again. "You've had your head lodged up your ass for too long."

Austin bit his bottom lip and peered at his brother out of the corner of his eye. "I'll call her tonight and see what she needs, find out what paperwork he's going to file—"

"I don't think it's your expertise in law she needs right now, dude. She needs her brother, her real brother. Not this weird self-loathing version."

Ouch.

Austin dropped his head to rest his chin on his chest. "You're right. I'll go over there tomorrow." He sighed. "Where's Mitch?"

"My house." Josh smirked and shrugged, widening his eyes. "I mean, he's Mavis's brother… What was I supposed to do?"

"Damn. That's not awkward at all."

Josh raised his eyebrows. "Not in the slightest."

"What's Mavis think?"

A grin spread along Josh's lips as his eyes turned to his brother. "Mavs, umm… well, she's a little distracted right now."

Huh?

Austin shuffled his feet in the sand and wrinkled his nose. "Okay, what's that supposed to mean?"

Josh dragged his hands along his cheeks and grinned. "Can you keep a secret?"

Austin snorted. "It's literally what I do best."

Josh rolled his eyes and dipped his hand into his left pocket, pulling from within a folded-up piece of glossy paper. He pressed it into Austin's outstretched hand.

"She's pregnant."

His throat went dry as his eyes scanned the images of the tiny black and white blob in his hands. *My niece. Or nephew?* With a grin, elation trickled outward from his heart, seeping into the pit of his stomach until a belly laugh burst forth from his mouth, the first bit of genuine happiness erupting in months.

"Josh!" he yelled, as a grin tugged at his lips. The image of teenage Mavis, her eyes clouded in tears before him in his dorm room, disintegrated into the past. *A second chance…* "This is fucking incredible!" Austin turned and wrapped his brother in a hug as some of the heavy weights surrounding his heart lifted. "You guys wasted no time."

Josh laughed and tapped the sonogram in his brother's hands. "Making up for lost time, maybe."

Austin smiled. "Well, congrats, dude! You're going to make one awesome dad." He squeezed his brother's shoulder and banged his knee into his.

Josh widened his eyes and blew out a breath. "God, I hope so," he answered before jamming his hand back into his pocket for his phone. Holding up one finger, he stood and stepped away from the picnic table, lifting the device to his ear.

A baby.

Austin stared at the ocean, gazing into the sinking sun in the late afternoon sky, the hazy orange glow over the water captivating his tired brain. The waves crashed onto the shore as a gentle breeze blew through his hair, tickling his skin. Leaning back into the tabletop again, he cupped his hands behind his neck and closed his eyes.

"Yep, I'll be there in ten minutes." Josh's voice drifted back through the breeze. "I've got to run to the hospital," he said, stuffing his phone back into his pocket.

Austin opened his eyes and nodded. "Do what you gotta do, Doctor Dad."

Josh smirked and kicked sand on his twin's shoes. "Before I go, I need to tell you one more thing."

"That makes four, but shoot," Austin muttered, shaking the sand from his feet.

"Casey's graduating next week. Thought you might like to know." His words caught in the wind as he jogged back across the beach to his Jeep.

A bubble of excitement grew in his chest, the swell of momentary happiness squeezing his heart. "You did it, Casey girl," he whispered. His head dropped back to his chest as his eyes closed. "I just wish…"

It didn't come at such a high price.

Austin's eyes widened as Bernice dumped another stack of folders on his desk.

"Really, Bernice?" He wrinkled his nose and dropped his forehead to his hands. "You've already given me like five new clients today."

"Sorry, boss," she muttered, backing out of his office. "Just following orders." The door snapped shut, and Austin stood, tightening the blinds closed on the windows.

I'm dying here.

Raking his hands through his hair, he blew out a breath and looked back at his desk, stacked high with folders and littered with to-do lists and multi-colored post-it notes. Austin groaned and walked to the window, gazing out at the thirteenth-story view of L.A. An outrageous lime-green Ferrari traveled down the street beneath him as Casey's voice echoed in his mind, the word *pretentious* ringing in his ear.

He dropped his forehead against the glass and allowed Casey to reappear in his brain. She tripped into his memory with a wide smile, cheering for the Chicago Cubs with a pitcher of Old Style in her hands.

His heart clenched, squeezing his soul where their two halves had been ripped in two by his words of betrayal. The scent of lilacs filled the space around him, but where once they brought him peace, the memory of the smell poured into an empty void in his heart.

"I miss you, Casey girl," he whispered as a horn honked thirteen floors beneath him. With a moan, he shut his eyes, blocking out the office, blocking out the last five months of his life without her—forcing his brain to return to the last moment in time where happiness reigned. His memory swirled, traveling back to the day of the wedding rehearsal. "Before this fucking job changed everything."

What if it was all a huge mistake?

His feet pounded against the floor as he crossed the room, an idea spawning from his heart and blossoming in his brain. Austin snagged his laptop and tapped in the words *Harold Washington Community College winter commencement*. The page loaded as December 17th flashed across the screen. He scrolled, a smile tugging at his lips as Casey's name appeared, midway through the Associate of Arts degree candidates.

Each letter in her name called to him, standing out among the hundreds of others on the page. He stared, his eyes focusing on the bold, black print. Spontaneity gripped his soul as he stood, the back of his knees sending his chair rolling across the office. "Why am I doing this to myself?" he whispered to the quiet space. His eyes scanned the room at everything he'd worked toward—his goal since childhood, culminated in the place he stood. "None of this makes any sense!"

Pressing his palms to his eyes, the memory of her erupted before him again. "Casey girl," he murmured, picturing her bright blonde curls bouncing as laughter fell from her lips. "You're all that really matters here. I'm fucking miserable without you."

All I wanted was for you to persist, to chase your dream. But in the end, you showed me what really matters, didn't you? You showed me our *dream—together.*

"I'm fucking done with this."

The realization gripped his heart as another email pinged in his inbox. Austin smiled, eyeing the latest email from Rodger as he slapped the device closed. Bolting from his office, he jogged down the hallway to conference room B, fire fueling each step.

This job tore us apart. But it's me who's going to put us back together.

"Templeton?" Steven dropped his pen to the floor as Austin's head popped into the room unannounced. He pushed his way in, gripping the back of the chair nearest to the door.

"Steven. Rodger." His heart hammered in his chest as a sheen of sweat coated his forehead, adrenaline flooding his veins.

Rodger squinted, eyeing Austin from across the room. "Is this about the Picotte file? I told Steven it wasn't—"

Austin snorted and shook his head, holding up his hand. "I don't even know what the Picotte file is. It's probably the eighteenth folder Bernice stacked on my desk just this week."

Steven wrinkled his nose and tipped his chair forward. "Well, what did you expect, kid? You're our partner now! A little increase in workload won't kill you, right?"

Austin laughed and folded his body over the top of the chair, pressing his cheek to the worn leather.

"What's wrong with you, Templeton? Are you sick?" asked Rodger.

Am I sick?

Austin giggled again, swiveling the chair back and forth. *Yeah, I'm sick. I'm sick of you. I'm sick of this place. I'm sick of living in the middle of everyone's divorce. But mostly, I'm sick of being alone! I want my Casey girl back.* The truth gripped him, sending a smile to his lips as his soul sang—the direction in his heart clear for the first time in months.

"Steven. Rodger. You've given me the career I've always wanted, and I've worked my ass off to get here. But it's not enough."

Rodger squinted. "You want *more* money, Templeton?"

A smile blossomed on his lips as he pulled his body upright, standing tall before the two seated men. "No, I don't want more money. I want *out*." Austin huffed out a breath. "I fucking quit."

Their faces froze, each pair of eyes slowly widening as Austin grinned, slapping his hands onto the leather chair. "I fucking quit!" he yelled, bringing his hands to rest at the nape of his neck, the words releasing his heart from the prison sentence he'd committed to.

"Is this some kind of joke?"

"Not even close, sir." Austin tapped the doorframe and snorted. "Consider this my resignation from Boyd & Bernstein at Law." A bubble of laughter rose from his belly at the omission of his last name, the giggles pouring forth from his lips.

Rodger stood and hammered his fist into the table. "You're out of your goddamn mind, kid! Do you even know what the fuck you're doing?" he roared.

"Actually, Rodger, for the first time in my life, I know *exactly* what I'm doing."

"You realize this is the end of your career, Templeton?" Steven's forehead squished together into a unibrow, his words a muted whisper.

Austin nodded. "It's the end of my career *here,* sir."

"Get the fuck out." Rodger pointed to the door.

And with a grin, Austin stepped back, balancing on the balls of his feet. "Gladly. I have a plane to catch."

The Windy City calls…

CHAPTER TWENTY-EIGHT

Casey

Casey dropped her butt into a hard, plastic chair in the large auditorium. The orange tassel hanging from her cardboard hat smacked her in the face with every tiny movement. With a giggle, she brushed it away and smoothed a wrinkle from the silly black gown on her body.

Why am I even doing this again?

The traditional pomp and circumstance music concluded as her last fellow graduate took their seat. Crossing her feet at the ankles, Casey tugged at her pantyhose, snagging the nylon fabric with her fingernail as she settled in for the ceremony.

The president of the college approached the podium, her well-rehearsed opening remarks melting into the boredom slowly fogging her brain. A parade of speakers followed as Casey's mind wandered, her gaze searching the smiling faces in the audience.

So many people here. So much love and support. But not one of them is here for me. Casey frowned. *Maybe I should have let Josh and Mavis come…*

Her heart jolted in her chest as the row in front of her

suddenly stood, filtering outward to the center of the aisle. She eyed each graduate, committing to memory the flow of events. *Walk up the stairs. Shake hands. Accept diploma. Smile for the camera. Walk down the stairs.*

She swallowed, peeking again at the heels on her feet. Nerves gripped her belly, pummeling the empty edges with fervor. "What if I fall?"

The girl to her right giggled. "Hang on tight to the railing, girlfriend," she whispered. "It's our turn."

Her row stood, and Casey forced her feet to move forward, following the brunette with the sound advice. Each beat of her heart slammed into her chest, fluttering with anticipation as she moved forward in line to the base of the stairs.

"Calvin Michael Madigan." A boy from her history class last year stepped onto the stage, shook hands, accepted his diploma, smiled, and stepped down the staircase with ease to a rousing round of clapping and cheering from the folks in the third row.

"Serena Ashley Matlorn." The brunette followed the same pattern of steps, shake, diploma, smile, steps—an air horn sounded in the distance.

Okay, I've got it down!

"Casey Ann McDaniels." Her legs wobbled on the lowermost stair as she climbed, blinded by the lights on the stage. Forcing a smile on her lips, her ears rang, blocking out any noise in the auditorium. She extended her hand, accepted her diploma, smiled for the camera, and reached outward for the railing, gripping the steel as if her life depended on it.

I did it! I didn't fall!

As her feet returned to the aisle, the ringing in her ears lifted, replaced with the cheering of a single mad man in the distance. His hoots and hollers echoed throughout the hall—one lone fool in the back row screaming her name with celebration.

Casey scrunched her nose. *Who the hell would be cheering for me?* Returning to her plastic chair, she turned, searching the seats at the back of the auditorium for the unknown admirer, his identity a mystery.

Fucking weirdo.

The ceremony trudged on as the parade of graduates participated in the dog and pony show across the stage until Candice Rachel Zwybar's name rang throughout the auditorium and every graduate surrounding her stood, flipping their tassels to the opposite side of their hats.

Her fingers tugged at the orange strings. *Shouldn't I feel something right now?* Silly string rained down on her as black graduation caps floated in the air. *I should be happy! I should be proud! I should be…*

The familiar slow burn behind her eyes pushed her forward, her body shuffling through the sea of black gowns until the exit sign appeared at the end of the aisle. Casey swallowed the sorrow blossoming in her broken heart as she pushed the heavy metal doors open. Her heels clicked against the title flooring, echoing through the empty space. "Where the fuck is the bathroom?" she whispered, peering down a hallway.

Turning to the left, a small staircase materialized with the sign for the women's restroom just beyond. Her vision clouded with tears as she lifted her right foot, the back of her heel catching on the second step. *Oh! Shit!* As she tumbled forward, her knee slammed into the cement step as the air left her lungs, blinding pain radiating from her kneecap.

"Dammit!" Sinking to the lowermost stair, her finger trailed over the injury, a thin layer of blood coating the now fully torn nylons. Groaning, Casey closed her eyes and ripped the cardboard hat from her head, tossing it to the floor. "I'm never wearing heels again," she murmured, resting her head against the cold wall as pain thundered through her body.

In the empty hallway, footsteps shuffled beside her as sandalwood settled in her nose. Her heart stopped, stilling in her chest, her brain unwilling to believe the source of all heartache kneeling before her.

"I don't know, Casey girl, you have nice calves. Maybe don't swear off heels completely."

His voice triggered the tears to fall, traveling down her pink cheeks as her eyes opened, his familiar icy blue gaze slicing into her soul. The breath caught in her throat as she forced her body to scoot away—her knee throbbing with pain—piercing her skin with the repeated pokes of an imaginary needle.

"Go away, Austin," she whispered, choking on the sob erupting from her heart. "I don't want to see you."

His jaw clenched as his gaze fell to her injured knee. "Case, please…" Reaching his hand out, his fingers grazed the open wound.

"Don't touch me!" Casey jerked away. "Why are you even here?" Her voice echoed down the deserted hallway.

Austin sank, his butt falling to the floor beneath the staircase. He dropped his head against the cinderblock wall and sighed, pulling a Chicago Cubs ball cap off his head. "Because Josh told me you were graduating today. I *wanted* to be here."

Her body trembled as shivers materialized along her skin, snaking up and down as a chill gripped her core. Hugging her legs into her body, Casey snorted. "Well, then, by all means, Austin, if you *want* something, you should *have* it. Where's your precious Mavis these days, huh?"

He sighed, his gaze falling to the floor. "You have every right to be angry with me."

A laugh burst forth from her belly, competing with the sobs wracking her soul. Tucking her hair behind her ears, she allowed a smile to consume her lips. "*Angry?* You think I'm *angry* with you, Austin Templeton?"

His eyes widened, cringing as her words left her lips. "Umm…"

"I'm fucking *furious!*" she roared, slapping her palms against her thighs. "You fucking destroyed me, you asshat!"

Her hands reached for the railing, and she pulled her body upright, planting her heels firmly against the tile floor. "You know what, just get the fuck out of here. I don't ever want to see you again."

"Casey!" Austin flew to his feet and stumbled up the small staircase. "Please!" he begged, reaching forward to grip her hand.

She batted him away as a fresh wave of tears released from her eyes, dripping down her cheeks. *Just leave! Walk away! He has no right to say anything!* But the ache in her heart stilled her feet, the memory of love holding her in place.

"Please, Casey. I'm begging you…" He reached out again and squeezed her palm. "Please just hear me out?"

She rolled her eyes. "Why don't you go find your princess? Maybe *she'll* want to hear whatever garbage you're about to spew." Her foot stepped forward as her knee seared with another bout of pain. She winced, bending forward to peel the nylons from the bloodied split in her skin.

"Please, let me see it," he whispered and dropped to his knees. He tugged at her gown, frowning as his gaze raked over her injury.

It's not my knee that's broken, Austin.

He swallowed and released a breath as he examined the wound. "Did you drive here?"

Casey closed her eyes and forced her brain away from the pain in her knee. "Why does that matter?"

"I put a first-aid kit in the trunk last spring." He looked up, his blue eyes finding hers as he bit his bottom lip, the corner of his eye catching in the fluorescent lighting as the white tips reflected.

She shook her head. "Of course, you did," she muttered.

"Let me walk you to the car, and if by the time we have a bandage on your knee you still don't want to talk to me, I'll go, all right?"

You've had five months to find an excuse for what you did. This should be good.

"Fine." Casey pulled away and marched down the empty hallway to the east side of the school. They trudged through the crowds, pushing and sidestepping the excited graduates and their families until the cold air of winter blasted them. "I parked over here," she murmured, limping down the stairs. Each step forward numbed her slowly bruising knee.

Casey yanked open the door to the Ford Fiesta and dropped into the driver's seat. With a groan, she pulled the latch to open the trunk. The car rocked as Austin searched, digging through the contents until he slammed the hatch closed and sat in the seat beside her with a little white plastic box on his lap.

Ramming the key in the ignition, Casey turned the engine on and unconsciously adjusted the vents in his direction. Ripping the heels from her feet, she tossed them to the floor in front of Austin.

He watched them fall to his toes and shivered. "Forgot how cold it was here," he mumbled, popping open the lid.

Oh, please. "It snowed once the entire time you lived here."

A grin tugged at his lips. "Well, it was still cold."

"You belong in L.A., California boy." Her stomach dropped as the nickname rolled so easily from her tongue.

Austin frowned and pointed at her knee. "You should take those off."

Casey tugged at her nylons, pulling the material away from her bloodied knee. "Turn around then."

Austin rolled his eyes. "Seriously?"

"Seriously. Face the window."

He turned, shifting his body to view the car parked beside them as Casey twisted in her seat to pull the destroyed nylons from her legs.

She tossed them in the back and shoved him in the shoulder. "Okay, I'm done."

Wiping his eyes with the back of his hand, he turned and rummaged in the first-aid kit.

Casey stared at the new bags beneath his watery eyes as

she pulled her bare leg up and over his lap. His palms dropped to her thigh, the warmth colliding with her skin as tingles erupted along her spine at his touch.

Fuck.

"Maybe you need stitches," he whispered and squeezed the skin.

"I don't need stitches. You're just stalling. Say whatever the fuck you came here to say and get the hell out." Casey peeked in the rearview mirror, quickly swiping at the pools of melted eyeliner beneath her eyes. "Why didn't you tell me I looked like a raccoon?"

Ripping open an alcohol wipe, he smirked. "You look beautiful. You always do."

She jerked her leg. "Shut up, Austin."

"You told me to say what I came here to say."

She rolled her eyes. "You came here to tell me I look beautiful? Okay, great, the show's over then. Get out—"

His grip tightened on her leg as he lifted his face to hers. "You know there's more, Case." He sighed. "So much more that I need to say to you." His hands dragged the wipe over the wound, cleaning away the dried blood.

She winced. "Go on then."

Austin nodded, digging his fingers back into the little container until he produced a tube of antibiotic ointment. He twisted the cap, blowing lightly on her knee until the alcohol dried.

Heat flooded through her body, warming her chilled bare skin right down to her pinky toe.

I absolutely abhor what you still do to me, Austin Templeton.

"I quit my job."

Her heart hammered in her chest, pumping her blood and working overtime. Pressing a hand over her heart, she tilted her head. "Why?"

Wait, why do I care?

"I thought it was what I wanted." He shook his head. "But I was wrong."

Casey squinted, eyeing his fingers as they squeezed the

tube—clear goo meeting her skin. With his index finger, he rubbed it into her knee.

"What is it that you want then?" she whispered, watching his fingers.

His hands stilled, his finger resting on her knee, coated in ointment. He turned, his gaze lifting to find hers. "You, Casey girl," he whispered. "I want *you*. I want *us*."

She swallowed and shook her head, his words shredding the strings around her heart, exposing the raw wound living beneath—bare flesh that would never heal. "You don't mean that."

He squeezed her knee again. "I do though, Cinderella. And I'm so sorry it took me so goddamn long to realize it." His eyes searched hers, boring into her soul and rousing the frayed strings of love that used to wrap around his own heart.

Tears stung her eyes and leaked from the corners, traveling down the tried-and-true path that never fully dried since the summer. "All right. So, you quit your job… and you say you want…" Casey gulped. "Me. Er—us."

He nodded, his eyes swimming with tears.

"Tell me again then, Austin, why you brought me home to *your* house, to *your* bed, to make love to *me*, only to spit out—" A sob erupted from the pit of her stomach, strangling the words in her throat.

The first tear in his eye rolled down his cheek, glistening in the afternoon sun reflecting off the fresh snow. He swiped at it and hung his head, squeezing his eyes shut. Pain radiated from his heart, the silent apology on his lips penetrating her soul.

"I did it to hurt you, Case." His words tumbled outward in a rush. "It was so fucking stupid." His fingers squeezed her leg again. "I just… I did it to hurt you. It was the only thing I could think of that night to…"

Casey sucked in a breath, the air catching in her throat, unwilling to travel to her lungs. "Push me away," she murmured.

"I regretted it the second I said it, Casey girl. I swear it! I never should have taken your life into my hands and made decisions for you. I was *wrong*, one hundred percent wrong."

He leaned toward her and pulled her body into his. His strong arms squeezed, encasing her small frame against his chest.

Casey exhaled and closed her eyes, allowing his words to settle in her heart. *Could this really be the truth?*

"You told me that no one had ever asked you what you want to do with your life." He choked on his own words and ran his fingers through her curls as he pressed her head against his chest. "And when you told me about your dream, I just wanted you to have it so goddamn bad. But I was too selfish and refused to give up on my own."

"Austin," she whispered and squeezed her eyes shut.

"I'm sorry, Casey. I was so blinded by my drive to make partner that I forced you into—"

She pulled away, stretching her leg as a cramp formed in her hamstring. Swiping at the tears coating her cheeks, she smiled. "I love my internship. You were right to push me."

He shook his head and ran his thumbs over her cheeks to remove the tear stains. "No, nothing I did was right."

Her heart swelled, bursting against her ribcage and threatening to jump from her chest into her lap. "So…" she choked out, "Mavis?"

"Is my past. Totally and completely my past." He nodded and tugged her back into his embrace. "I may have loved her yesterday, Casey McDaniels, but beyond any doubt, I love *you* today," he whispered.

She smiled, and her heart restarted, waking from the dormant state she'd survived in for the last five months. Lifting her gaze to Austin's, she sighed. "So, what does this mean, California boy? You quit your job. You want me back…"

From the first-aid kit, his hands pulled out a Band-Aid. Lifting her leg back to his lap, he tore the wrapping apart and pressed the bandage to her knee, covering the injury completely.

"It means I'm a Cubs fan." Grinning, he tapped the royal-blue brim of his ball cap with excitement. "You are the love of my life, Casey McDaniels. And if you'll take me back, I'd like to spend every inning of our lives trying to make up for the pain I caused you, cheering you on through every fastball thrown our way."

Her heart mended, each tear and pull and stretch stitched itself back together, and her soul reached out to his.

Casey grinned as the truth of his words settled in her heart and her stomach released a groan, begging for food. She giggled and dropped her hand to her belly as her cheeks flushed. "I'm hungry."

Austin leaned forward and picked up a high heel, placing it back on her foot with a grin. "Well, then let's get you a cheesy sandwich, Cinderella."

"Counterproposal." She giggled. "A pitcher of celebratory Old Style instead."

His smile squeezed her heart as he leaned forward and pressed his lips to hers, murmuring against her mouth. "Sweet home, Chicago, Casey girl."

Sweet home, Chicago, Austin. Welcome back.

THE END

EPILOGUE

Mitch

NOTICE OF INTENT TO FILE DIVORCE

Dear Lauren:
I am giving you this letter to formally inform you of my intent to file for divorce.

Before filing, I want to share with you the options moving forward on how this divorce case will be conducted, so that we can start off on the same page, which I think is the fairest way to proceed. Having done the research, there are two options we can proceed with:

Option 1: Traditional Divorce
Option 2: Part as Friends Divorce

Please review the differences between the two options.
Option 1: The Traditional Divorce
Both of us are likely to hire lawyers. The divorce will cost our family collectively between $5,000-$30,000 (estimate only). Both of us will wait for around 8 months-1.5 years while our divorce is pending. Eventually, we will be able to tell our story in court or to a mediator, about what we feel happened during the marriage. After hearing our

evidence:

1. The Court will divide our debts in a way it deems fair and just.

2. The Court will divide all of our personal property the way it deems fair.

3. The Court will divide our retirement/home or any other thing of value between us the way it deems fair.

Option 2. The Part as Friends Divorce

We will spend between $1,500 and $3,000 getting divorced (estimate). This divorce case will last about 61 days. One of us will have a lawyer of record and the other one of us can have a reviewing lawyer, if needed. The reviewing lawyer can help ensure that we understand the papers and the process of the divorce. We will ultimately decide and will tell the lawyer that agreement. We will work together to agree on how we should divide our property and assets. We will tell the lawyer our agreements. A reviewing lawyer or the lawyer of record can help us understand our options so that we come to a fair agreement.

I would like to ask you to please initial the divorce option that you want me to proceed with. I recognize that if we cannot come to an agreement on dividing our estate that we will not have a choice but to proceed with a contested divorce.

The purpose of this Notice of Intent is to ask you what method you want me to start the divorce with. I personally prefer the part as friends divorce, but I will respect your choice, either way.

SPOUSE'S CHOICE AS TO DIVORCE OPTIONS 1-2

I, _____ choose: Option 1: Traditional Divorce: _____ (Initial here if you choose option 1) Option 2: Part as Friends Divorce: _____ (Initial here if you choose option 2)

Date: _____

Mitch stared at the letter of intent his lawyer had drafted for him, the word *divorce* blurring.

Am I really doing this?

He dropped his pen and pushed his chair away from the kitchen table.

Mavis descended the stairs, her hands resting on the swell of her growing belly. She approached the table, her gaze digging into his soul as she glanced at the paperwork.

"You're actually going to go through with this, aren't you?" Her index finger tapped the paper.

Mitch nodded. "I don't expect you to understand."

"Try me," she challenged.

Mitch closed his eyes, hiding the letter from view, the letter that would destroy the life and marriage he'd spent the last seven years building. He shook his head.

Where do I even fucking begin?

JULIE NAVICKAS

ACKNOWLEGEMENTS

Thank you for reading *I Love You Today*, book two in the *Trading Heartbeats* trilogy! I had the most incredible support releasing book one, *I Loved You Yesterday,* and I'm forever grateful to each and every reader for continuing on the journey with me.

First and foremost, my sincere appreciation and gratitude belong to Melissa Keir and Inkspell Publishing. Melissa, without your guidance, encouragement, and willingness to take a chance on a new author, I would not be where I am today. From the bottom of my heart, thank you. You make my dream come true each and every day.

When I first started writing, I had no idea that this story would evolve into a trilogy. But thanks to the diligent work and creative minds of my beta readers, Austin and Casey's story took shape. Marcia Bufalo Juarez, Shelby Holt, Elizabeth Chupp, and Kate Boutilier, you all are my heroes!

Speaking of heroes, let me also take a moment to thank Emma O'Connell and Audrey Bobak for their incredible editing skills. Emma, without your developmental edits and guidance, this story would not look the way it does today. And Audrey, you teach me something new with every round of edits! Thank you for your patience and attention to detail.

Did you see this stunning book cover? Because I can't stop staring at it! Thank you, Shel from Fantasia Frog Designs! You bring my vision to life every time.

In addition, my gratitude and appreciation also go out to the masterminds of promotion. Claire Coffey, thank you for all your help and ideas with marketing. Daniel Almanza, you are indeed a PR wizard! And Silver Dagger Book Tours and

Itsy Bitsy Book Bits, thank you for your continuous efforts and time spent putting *I Love You Today* into the hands of romance readers everywhere.

Lastly, I'm forever grateful to my immediate support system. Mom, you are a romance novel enthusiast and like sands through the hour glass, you taught me from a young age to appreciate a good soap opera. Thank you for introducing me to this world. And my dear husband Tommy, you are a far greater writer than I'll ever be. Not only do you help me brainstorm ideas and develop witty dialogue, you also manage all the money stuff (because let's be real – you and I both know how much I suck at math).

And Lillian, Colton, and Brady, it'll probably embarrass you one day that your mom writes romance novels. But before your little cheeks flush, just know that I chased my dream of becoming a published author for *you*. Don't ever let fear hold you back. Live authentically, little ones!

Oh… and a big thank you to Google Drive for being a thousand times more reliable than a faulty external hard drive. #NeverAgain

Sneak Peek at I'LL LOVE YOU TOMORROW

CHAPTER ONE

Lauren

"I'm sorry, boss," I can't come in today." Miguel sighed. "You know I would if I could, but it's my niece's birthday dinner. I can't miss it."

Lauren closed her eyes and rested her phone against the surface of the desk. "No, no, don't apologize, Miguel. Family first. Always." With a deep breath, her fingers grasped the list of slowly dwindling bartenders on staff. Shaking her head, she frowned. *No Miguel. Angela is on vacation. Tony is out on medical leave. And Carmen requested this weekend off.* "Besides, you requested this date off weeks ago. I'm just grasping at straws here."

"Did someone call in?" he asked.

Lauren snorted. "Brandon called in sick about thirty minutes ago. His shift starts in ten." Her gaze lifted to the clock on the wall as Miguel groaned.

"I'm sorry, Lauren, you know I'd be there if I could."

A grin cracked her lips. *Miguel, you've always been my favorite for a reason.* "I know you would. And I love you for it. But don't worry. Go and enjoy the party. I've got it covered."

"What're you going to do?"

Lauren giggled. "Pray nobody orders anything I can't Google."

"Wait." He snorted. "You're not—"

She stood, the back of her legs banging into her chair as it rolled away across the office. "It's me or close the bar. And we really can't do that on a Saturday night."

Not after being in the red for three straight months.

"Boss—"

"It's okay, Miguel. Go enjoy your niece's party. Please wish her a happy birthday for me."

"Wait, I can prob—"

"Nope! I've got it!" Lauren tapped the end call button and pocketed her phone as the lights of the new restaurant across the street, Food for Thought, sparkled through the window.

The intercom on her desk phone buzzed and Lauren tapped the red light. "Yeah?"

"Lauren, there's someone named Greg Owens on the phone for you. He says he's the newest rep with a vendor for plastic goods."

Nodding, Lauren inhaled. "Yep, put him through."

The line clicked over, and Lauren forced a smile on her face. "Greg?"

"Oh, hello there!"

"Hi Greg, thanks for the call. This is Lauren Templeton, owner of Pier Ninety-Two. What can I help you with?"

"Just confirming your delivery of supplies on Thursday at four, Mrs. Templeton."

"Got it!" Lauren scratched the note onto her calendar. "And feel free to use the alleyway on the east side of the building. It's easier for deliveries."

"Will do, ma'am. See you Thursday."

"See you Thursday."

The line disconnected and Lauren frowned at the note. *How much will this shipment cost?*

Pulling the door of her office open, she marched down the back hall and entered the kitchen, the rattle and clank of the freezer gripping her ears as she paused to snag an apron from the hook. Her fingers twisted the rough material into a bow, securing the fabric around her waist.

"What're you doing?"

Lauren turned, meeting the eyes of her head chef, Louis. A bout of laughter escaped her lips. "Losing my virginity. Wish me luck." His eyes widened as she pushed through the double doors, navigated around a few tables, and hopped behind the bar.

Janine twisted, tossing a dishrag over her shoulder as a grin blossomed on her face. "Umm… where's Brandon?"

"Out sick." Propping her hands on her hips, Lauren plastered a new smile on her lips and surveyed the endless rows of liquor bottles, shooing Janine away with a head nod. "Well go on, get out of here!"

She wrinkled her nose and frowned. "Wait. Are you—"

Tugging the dishrag from her shoulder, Lauren snickered. "It's like no one has any confidence in me around here!"

Janine pressed her lips together and frowned.

With a shrug, Lauren picked up a glass. "Pour this. Pour that. I can't be that bad at it, can I?" She laughed, nudging Janine away. "Now go on, you've been here since we opened. I've got this!"

Janine held her hands up and backed out of the small space. "Whatever you say, boss!"

Her retreating figure ducked behind the double doors as Lauren returned her gaze to the mass of glass bottles. Each one sparkled in the dim lighting, their labels difficult to read. Frowning, she dug in her pocket and whipped out her phone. Tapping her best friends names, Mavis and Casey, into a new text message she typed out, *SOS girls! I need to cover the bar at Pier Ninety-Two tonight! And I have no idea what I'm doing! Experienced bartenders needed!*

JULIE NAVICKAS

Don't Miss Mavis and Josh's Love Story in
I LOVED YOU YESTERDAY

Available now at all major book retailers

Secrets always have a way of coming out.

Mavis Benson made a huge mistake. Scratch that—*colossal* mistake. *Twice.* Sleeping with her high school sweetheart's twin brother definitely wasn't part of the plan... nor was falling in love with him.

But that wasn't the only complication Mavis faced. When an unplanned pregnancy upends her life at seventeen, Mavis skips town to spare her boyfriend, Josh Templeton, from the fallout. With only a letter of apology, she disappears, but not before confiding her secret to Josh's brother, Austin.

When Austin resurfaces in her life years later, he brings the past to Mavis's doorstep. Josh wants her back, Austin isn't willing to surrender, and the path to happiness isn't clear. Caught between both men, Mavis must choose between the brother for whom she broke her own heart, and the brother who picked up the pieces.

I LOVED YOU YESTERDAY is a heart-pounding reveal of best kept secrets. The truth is never easy, and neither is putting down this page turner. Fans of Nora Roberts and K.G. Fletcher will want to get a copy of I LOVED YOU YESTERDAY.

~Winner of the ASSOCIATION FOR WOMEN IN COMMUNICATIONS CLARION AWARD.~

ABOUT THE AUTHOR

Julie Navickas is an award-winning nationally recognized contemporary romance novelist, known for her keen ability to tell heart-wrenching, second-chance love stories through relatable characters with humility, humor, and heroism. She is also an award-winning university instructor and serves as the executive director of The Writing Champions Project. Julie earned master's degrees in both organizational communication and English studies with an emphasis in book history, as well as a bachelor's degree in public relations, graduating cum laude from Illinois State University.

Website: https://authorjulienavickas.com/
Facebook:
https://www.facebook.com/AuthorJulieNavickas
Twitter: https://twitter.com/JulieNavickas
Instagram: https://www.instagram.com/julienavickas/
LinkedIn: https://www.linkedin.com/in/julienavickas/
TikTok: https://www.tiktok.com/@julienavickas
YouTube:
https://www.youtube.com/channel/UCNUW07fs9AmSR
N2o-yAjISg
Email: julienavickasauthor@gmail.com
Goodreads:
https://www.goodreads.com/user/show/134518278-julie-navickas
BookBub: https://www.bookbub.com/authors/julie-navickas

Made in United States
Orlando, FL
21 November 2022

24802723R00178